Brother Azarias

An Essay Contributing to a Philosophy of Literature

Brother Azarias

An Essay Contributing to a Philosophy of Literature

ISBN/EAN: 9783741187469

Manufactured in Europe, USA, Canada, Australia, Japa

Cover: Foto ©Andreas Hilbeck / pixelio.de

Manufactured and distributed by brebook publishing software
(www.brebook.com)

Brother Azarias

An Essay Contributing to a Philosophy of Literature

AN ESSAY

CONTRIBUTING TO A

PHILOSOPHY OF LITERATURE

BY

BROTHER AZARIAS

OF THE BROTHERS OF THE CHRISTIAN SCHOOLS

Vegliamo tu tango studio d'l grande amore

Eighth Edition, Revised and Enlarged.

PHILADELPHIA :
JOHN JOSEPH McVEY,
1906.

CONTENTS.

CHAPTER VII.

CHAPTER VIII.

CHAPTER IX.

CHAPTER X.

CHAPTER XI.

CHAPTER XII.

PREFACE

THE aim of the present Essay is to embody in a united
whole the laws and principles of literature in its most general
relations. It is now sixteen years since the Essay was first
presented to the public. In the kind reception then accorded
the book by critics of nearly every shade of opinion, the Author
has found encouragement to prepare this new edition. It
runs upon the same lines of thought as the old edition. Parts
have been revised, parts developed, and parts re-written, in
the hope that the work will be found every way less unworthy
of the subject.

There is one remark of an esteemed Reviewer upon which
the Author would dwell. The late Dr. Orestes A. Brownson
wrote, among many other complimentary things, upon the
first appearance of the book : "We have been struck with the
depth and justness of the Author's philosophical principles,
which could, as we understand them, be borrowed from no
school of philosophy generally accepted by Catholics or by
non-catholics" (*Brownson's Review*, Oct., 1874, p. 561). Every
earnest thinker must begin by breaking through the shackles
of schools and systems. Philosophy is above schools and
systems. None knew better than the great Brownson that he
who commits himself to any school of thought—any exclusive
system—thereby so narrows the horizon of his intellectual
vision, that he no longer sees things in themselves, but merely

certain imperfect aspects of things. The primary and self-
evident truths of our reason, from which start all philosophy
and all knowledge, are not of this school or that ; they simply are. Every teacher of literature, be the literature home
or foreign, will perceive the benefit of placing his pupils upon
this elevated vantage-ground from which to survey the various great authors and take their relative bearings.

NEW YORK, *May* 15, 1890.

INTRODUCTION.

PHILOSOPHY is the science of principles in their relations with things. It determines, weighs, examines, the validity of the fundamental principles upon which knowledge is based.

2. Every clearly-defined part of knowledge has elementary ideas upon which it is based, and without which it cannot exist. They are its first principles. The philosophy of the subject deals with them. It has the first word, because its province is to determine what principles are primary for that subject and in what sense they are to be taken. It lays the foundation before building the superstructure. It has also the last word; for it must see that no material enters into the construction that the fundamental principles cannot support. Thus every department of knowledge has its philosophy.

3. The Philosophy of Literature has for its object to investigate the general relations of literature, as the expression of humanity, to the epochs in which society lives and moves, to thought, to language, to industry, art, science, and religion, as each is developed and expressed; and from these relations to deduce the laws that determine its variations, the fundamental principles upon which it is based, and the elements that constitute its literature.

4. Every science has a method and a principle;

so also has every art. The principle determines the method. The method pursued in the Philosophy of Literature is this : Literature is defined in its most general aspects; its origin and functions are determined; then its general relations are dwelt upon ; after which it is considered as influenced and as an influencing agency ; and the spirit of rationalism that began to expand in the fifteenth, and became more general in the sixteenth century, is investigated in its main stem and chief branches, so far as it has affected literature. A theory of the beautiful equally applicable to art and letters is established ; in its light the conservative element of literature is expressed ; and it is shown that religion fosters and is the permanent basis of literary excellence. Some practical hints, based upon the theory and facts laid down, are given ; the problem of intelligence is touched upon, and the morality of literature is discussed.

5. Literature is not read for the mere form's sake. The product of thought, it nourishes thought, which in its turn seeks expression and adds to literature. Thus, literature is the educator of thought. But it may also be its ruin ; and it actually becomes so when regarded exclusively as a matter of memory and imitation. These views are kept in mind throughout the present Essay.

6. The following truths are postulated :

I. That there is a God and a Divine revelation.

II. That man is made in the image and likeness of his Maker.

III. That his aspirations are satisfied only on the plane of the supernatural.

A
PHILOSOPHY OF LITERATURE.

PART I.

PRINCIPLES AND FACTS.

CHAPTER I.

DEFINITION AND FUNDAMENTAL PRINCIPLE OF LITERATURE.

LITERATURE is the verbal expression of man's affections as acted upon in his relations with the material world, society, and his Creator ; that expression being as varied as the moods that pass over his soul, whether they speak of love or hatred, of joy or sorrow, of fear or hope. In a word, the language that addresses itself to the *human* in man is literature. It may be abstract, as in metaphysics ; but so long as it deals with questions that touch him as intimately as his origin and his destiny, so long will it possess a charm for all times and all peoples. Matters purely scientific do not possess this trait. Men enjoyed the light of day as well when the corpuscular theory was in vogue as they do at present, convinced of its absurdity, and of the truth of the wave theory.   But he who reads the history of society, and studies the trials and triumphs and failures of individuals like himself —who has watched the ways of a *Pendennis* and a *Copperfield*, or followed *Evangeline* in her tried and beautiful life, or imbibed the deeper and more earnest lessons taught by a Job and an Augustine—will learn to look more kindly on his fellow-man ; the light in which humanity will appear to him will be al! the brighter for his extended acquaintance. The characteristic of literature is to speak in the ordinary everyday language of humanity, as distinguished from the technical language of science.   "It is co-extensive with thought and with science, ranging as it does through every form of being, from the inmost depth of consciousness in the soul to the farthest and highest point outside of it, which is God, the Author of all being.   It differs from thought not only in form, being its outward expression, and as it were its garment, but also because to thought it adds feeling ; it differs from science, because it seeks to realize not only the true, but likewise the beautiful." *

Literature appeals to the sentiments in their widest range, from the sphere of simple delight, such as is afforded by the fable, the nursery tale, or the popular scientific treatise, through all phases of passion, to the intense strain of terror or pity inspired by tragedy. It enlists the reader's attention ; it moves him to tears;

---

* Mgr. James A. Corcoran : *American Catholic Quarterly Review*, vol. ii. p. 188.   The passage occurs in a review of the second edition of this work.

it excites him to mirth and laughter; and often, while professing only to please, it initiates him into all the secrets ot the heart.

Literature has its roots deep in the nature of man. He thinks, feels, and speaks; he has the faculty of remembering and the power of recording; and instinctively he believes his own soul to be the mirror in which he may read other men's. Hence the saying so frequently used. " He judges others by himself; " and its frequency shows how universally it is considered a criterion. " We are so constituted that each regards himself as the mirror of society; what passes in our own heart seems to us to be infallibly the history of the whole world." *   It may therefore be concluded that the fundamental principle of all literature is that a common numanity underlies our individual personalities.   What affects one, has power, as a rule, to affect all.   For each of us is it true that he is a stranger to nothing human.

"Homo sum: humani nihil a me alienum puto."†

Literature varies in its forms.   These forms are limited by the social conditions under which they are produced.   All literary ideals are determined by the environment of human association from which they issue.   The ideals of one age are not the ideals of another. Individual character has much to do in moulding both form and expression, the social conditions

* " Nous sommes ainsi faits que chacun de nous se regarde comme le miroir de la société; ce qui se passe dans notre cœur nous paraît infailliblement l'histoire de l'univers.' —.Émile Souvestre., *Le Philosophe sous les Toits,* ch. iii.

† Terence. *Heautontimorumenos,* L. i.

influencing the author are no less potent in giving color and tone to his composition. The clan-spirit underlying that sum of social conditions out of which the poem of *Beowulf* grew, is widely different from the high culture, the philosophic grasp of thought and the complex social relations out of which is evolved *In Memoriam* or *The Ring and the Book.* Hence we may infer that a law of progress and of limitations runs through the history of all literature, and that literature varies in its ends according to the degree of civilization embodied in the manners, customs and modes of thinking of the people to whom it appeals.

CHAPTER II.

THE FUNCTION OF LITERATURE.

MAN, as we now find him, is restless, ill satisfied with himself, seldom content with the sphere in which his duties lie, and always looking above and beyond, dreaming of ideal worlds and ideal situations, in which he loves to forget the smoke and dust, the thorny paths and stony roads, through which he moves in his every-day existence. Literature fosters and partially satisfies this craving of his nature. It bears him into the regions of the sublime, the beautiful, the marvellous; and his soul rejoices in the transfer. Deep in the recesses of his heart there resound vague whisperings, the exact import of which fancy seems incompetent to catch—spectres of thought to which imagination has been unable to give shape or hue ; weak impulses, whither tending he cannot tell. These it is the function of literature to interpret. It also evokes ideas ; for man is so much the creature of education, so totally helpless is he when isolated, that his intelligence cannot be developed until external influences are brought to bear upon it. The clash of thought educes new thought. Mind influences mind, even over the chasm of ages. Vergil bows before Homer, and Dante acknowledges Vergil to be his master and model. For a thousand years Aristotle is the inspiration of the philosophical world. The genius of Thackeray expands only after it has been saturated with the master-pieces of Richardson and Fielding, Thus is wrought the chain of thought that girdles the world.

We cannot perceive in either literature or science that unlimited power which modern partisans conceive the one and the other to wield as reformers of the world and restorers of man's moral excellence. Were he a being of mere intellect, such a course were well. But no ; man has a will to guide, passions to restrain, a duty to perform ; and neither literature nor science alone can avail him in these higher purposes of life. Knowledge and virtue do not always go hand in hand. The result of this misguided movement has been expressed by the poet of the day :

" Knowledge comes, but wisdom lingers, and I linger on the shore,
   And the individual withers, and the world is more and more." *

Let the people have literature and science ; let them

* TENNYSON, *Locksley Hall.*

have museums and reading-rooms and popular lectures ; but let them have more. Let them have religion. It will restrain violence ; it will be their solace when beset with difficulties, their support when all else fails them, their happiness here, and their guiding-star through life to the great hereafter that awaits them. It alone has power to reform and perfect man's moral nature. It alone gives nations their first progressive impulse. It is the basis of civilization. It has inspired the sublimest themes in all literature. It has laid down and enforced those moral laws that are the chief characteristic of our superiority. All this is beyond the sphere of literature, the legitimate function of which is to awaken sentiments and draw out parts in our nature almost smothered by the cares and duties of life.

CHAPTER III.

THE ORIGIN OF LITERATURE.

WE will begin with a survey of our position. The equilibrium of man's faculties is broken. In his consciousness, throughout his whole nature, there is disturbance. Was it always so ? All the attempted solutions of this question may be reduced to two. One school says · "Look around you, and everywhere you see a struggle for life. The weak gives place to the strong. It is the survival of the fittest.* This is true of man as well as of the rest of the brute

* Herbert Spencer.

creation ; for he is but a link in the chain of the grand whole, differing from the dog or the chimpanzee in degree of intelligence rather than in kind.* He is subject to the same impulses—ever ready to make might right—ever on the alert to show his selfishness ; for passion is simply a manifestation of self. His animal nature is the primary cause of this disturbance, and as he ascends the scale of perfectibility an equilibrium in his faculties will become more determined. See how much has been already accomplished. There is to-day greater difference between the intelligent Caucasian and the South Sea savage than between the savage and the monkey." † According to this view, language and literature are solely the result of man's progress in intelligence. But facts militate against the theory ; for the noblest monuments of literature are the earliest. Witness the Bible, the Vedas, Confucius, and Homer. We are not with this school.

The other — the conservative school — recognizes the fact that as an animal, with animal appetites, man is subject to the laws of animal life ; but that as a reasonable, responsible being, endowed with a soul possessed of a sense of right and wrong, he is bound to restrain and often suppress these appetites. It holds that the soul is of immediate origin from the Creator, however may be the process of development by which the body has come to its present shape. "For," it says, "however much races may vary, species never do. They are distinct creations. However much sophistry may confound race with species

* Darwin.   † Mr. John Fiske.

2

nature never makes the blunder. The law of cross-
ings is inviolable." Its belief in a personal God confirms this view. It sees His preservative act in life,
and defines it to be the influx of His creative act.
Therefore it sees nothing unreasonable in distinct
creations. It does not consider the soul hereditary,
though capacities, dispositions, and the like, depend-
ent on organisms, are. This school further recognizes the fact that, in certain stages of its existence,
society is progressive ; though it perceives no such
tendency in the savage state. This it regards rather
as the old age of society; and the traditions of nations are with it. They all look back to a golden
age from the ideal of which men have degenerated :
" First was founded the golden age, which, of its
own accord, without avenger, and without laws,
practiced both faith and rectitude."*

This embodiment of Roman and Grecian tradition
implies a harmony in men's consciousness to which
we are entire strangers. The history of the East
points to the same result. True, the East had its
material and intellectual growth and development,
but it is so far back, and has been so rapid, and so
distinct from anything we witness that it evidently
possessed fresher and more productive civilizing
traditions. Speaking of Egypt, Mariette says :
"Egyptian civilization manifests itself to us fully
developed from the earliest ages, and succeeding
ones, however numerous, taught it little more." †

* " Aurea prima sata est ætas, quæ vindice nullo
    Sponte sua, sine lege fidem rectumque colebat."
                              —OVID, *Metamorphoses*, i, 89, 90.
† *Aperçu de l' Histoire d' Egypte.*

The same is true of China. Historians have found
it difficult to trace her progress in literature and civilization. "At the earliest period at which Chinese
history opens upon us," says Fergusson, "we find
the same amount of civilization maintaining itself
utterly unprogressively to the present day." * And
that·book which is of more weight with this school
than all others—the Bible—confirms this universal
tradition, and points to a mysterious fact which is
the clue to all the intellectual and moral disturbance
in man's consciousness. "Original sin is a mystery,"
says Balmes, "but it explains the whole world." †
Without this faith "—in Christianity, and therefore in
original sin, says Schlegel — "the whole history of
the world would be nought else than an insoluble
enigma ; an inextricable labyrinth ; an unfinished
edifice ; and the great tragedy of humanity would
remain devoid of all proper result." ‡ The fall is
therefore to be accepted as explaining the present
disturbance in man's soul. Let us study the relations
of literature to this primary fact of all history.

Prior to the fall, there was no need of a written
literature. All man's powers — his will, his intelligence, and the affections of his soul — were so
blended together in a harmonious whole, that, in the
simple intuition of nature, his insight would have
been frequently as deep as that which to-day is the
result of discursive reasoning ; and the only approach

* *History of Architecture*, vol. L, p. 83.

† "El pecado original es un misterio, pero este misterio explica
el mundo entero."—*Filosofia Fund.*, vol. i., p. 532.

‡ *Philosophy of History*, Bohn's ed., lect. x., p. 279.

to literature would have been the endless song of praise ascending from each individual — a varied hymn, as the warblings of the feathered tribe are varied—to the Creator of all the beauty and loveliness of which he were the eloquent admirer. Tradition and history he would have remembered without the use of letters. It is a defective intelligence that calls for such aids. Discussion is more a result of our weakness than of our strength. What we comprehend thoroughly we least question. Genius, in its noblest and purest flights, approaches this condition of intelligence, though in a one-sided way. Its characteristic consists in its possessing deeper insight and a greater power of expression than other minds. In the light it throws upon the subject there is grasped a better comprehension of it than men previously possessed. The subject becomes simplified. Less words are required to explain it. From genius we can form a faint idea of how deeply unfallen man must have seen into the secrets of nature. His was no one-sided view, for all his faculties were in complete harmony.

Even immediately after the fall man possessed intellectual energy to which we are total strangers. We cannot conceive those grand old patriarchs or Rishis bent over a book or inscribing their long life experience of persons and things ; not because their language was not sufficiently developed, or that they might not have been in possession of the art of writing, for men in every stage of society found language adequate to the expression of every idea clear to their minds, and men of their years must have understood the symbolism of nature in its deepest import ; but, in truth, they had no need whatever of such artificial means. With passions subdued, and unwarped by any of the conventionalities of modern society, and ever filled with the thought of their Creator's intimate presence, with whom they spoke in prayer with simplicity and faith, the ever-changing panorama of nature and young society was a book in which these great and good men read lessons laden with significancy. It is refreshing to contemplate those intellects, fresh, calm, untrammelled, teeming with great and important thoughts, which they transmit, not to moth-eaten parchments, but by word of mouth to a posterity capable of preserving every jot and tittle of the precious legacy. Their dignified bearing and profound science sadly contrast with what we are compelled to call the little, hurried, jostling ways, with which so many of the present blindly move along, heedless whither they drift, and caring not, provided they have caught up the prevailing note of the day.

But in these antediluvian or prehistoric times there were two parties : the one, the agricultural and pastoral party, the Sethites of Scripture, of whom we have been speaking ; the other, the party that built cities and worked iron and manufactures, and made rapid strides in material civilization, but grew morally corrupt to a fearful extent. They are the Cainites. They were too busily occupied in material pursuits and in seeking personal comforts, to make use of a written language ; and their life was too vigorous, their energy too great, to require one. They were a

proud and haughty race; they were fierce and passionate, and knew no restraint; they made war on
the peaceful Sethites and among themselves. Their
deeds of prowess, their victories and their heroic
leaders—"the mighty men of old, men of renown" *
—they recounted in song and story, that breathed
deep-dyed vengeance, and extolled their own greatness and self-sufficiency to the heavens. They were
sunk deep in egotism. Nature had few charms for
them. She was their slave, which they, by their profound science and intimate knowledge of her secrets,
worked upon and made subservient to the gratification of their selfish motives. The spirits of the air
waited upon them, as the angels of God waited upon
Abraham and Lot. The elements they held under
control, for they were acquainted with the laws that
govern them. In mind and body they were giants.

A change came over the face of nature. Men
ceased to be long-lived, and no longer possessed the
energy and experience of former days. Languages
were multiplied. However the cause may be explained, it is plain to all who have given the matter
consideration, that there is sufficient connection between all the languages on the face of the earth to
show that they had a common origin, and that their
departure from this origin was not the result of a
gradual process, but rather that there are clear indications of an abrupt severing.† No matter how far

---

* Genesis vi. 4.

† Max Müller says: "We have examined all possible forms
which language can assume, and we have now to ask, can we
reconcile with these three distinct forms, the radical, the termina-
tional, and the inflectional, the admission of one common origin of
human speech? I answer decidedly, Yes." *Science of Language*,
vol. i., pp. 328, 329.

back in the history of a language w . go, we find it complete in all its essential parts, and the lapse of centuries or the most intimate intercourse with nations may add to its variety of expression, but will not change its grammar and genius, however barren the language be in grammatical forms or in flexibility and delicacy of expression. These are things, according to W. Von Humboldt, that man "could never have arrived at by the slow and progressive process of experience." * For this reason those who consider the Bible a book of myths, as well as those who regard it as of Divine origin, are agreed upon the dispersion of men, and the sundering of a common language into several tongues. Then came the dawn of a written literature. The comparative shortness of life, desire of fame, and degeneracy of intellect led men to seek means of transmitting their traditions by sign and symbol. †

The oldest form of transmitting ideas is by means of

See also CARD. WISEMAN, *Lect. on Science and Revealed Religion*, lect. ii., p. 78.

* Je ne crois pas qu'il faille supposer chez les nations auxquelles on est redevable de ces langues admirables des facultés plus qu'humaines, ou admettre qu'elles n'ont point suivi la marche progressive à laquelle les nations sont assujetties ; mais je suis pénétré de la conviction qu'il ne faut pas méconnaître cette force vraiment divine que recèlent les facultés humaines, ce génie créateur des nations, surtout dans l'état primitif, où toutes les idées, et même les facultés de l'âme, empruntent une force plus vive de la nouveauté des impressions, où l'homme peut pressentir des combinaisons auxquelles il ne serait jamais arrivé par la marche lente et progressive de l'expérience.—*Lettre à M. Abel-Remusat, Werke*, vol. vii., pp. 336-7.

† See Plato, *Phaedrus*, lviii., 274.

picture-writing. In course of time, the pictures came
to be reduced to mere outlines but faintly resembling
their originals and suggesting abstract ideas. The
Chinese have never gone beyond this form of writing.*
Afterwards, men began to make these images the
graphic symbols of sounds. At first they represented
whole words ; later on they stood for articulations or
syllables. Thus was the Japanese writing developed out
of the Chinese. From the syllabic signs were derived
the elementary sounds known as the alphabet. The
transition from one to the other of these forms was a
slow process, generally induced by intimate relations
with another people, which required a medium of
communication ; and each form represents a higher
grade of civilization. This process was evolved by
the science of Egypt.† Far back in the obscure past
was the evolution completed.‡ '' The letters of the alphabet," says the most recent authority on this subject, '' are older than the pyramids—older probably
than any other existing monument of civilization,
with the possible exception of the signs of the zodiac." §
From Egypt the Phœnicians received their alphabet ;
this primitive Semitic alphabet is the source from
which all others are derived. All the variations in
Greek and Roman and Gothic letters, in the Hebrew
and Arabic and Nagari alphabets, may be traced to

* Edkins, *Introduction to the Study of Chinese Characters ;
London*, 1876.

† De Rouge, *Memoire sur l'Origine Egyptienne de l' Alphabet
Phenicien*, Paris, 1874.

‡ The inscription of King Sent—from 4000 to 4700 B. C.—is the
first known written record. Two of our letters—*n.* and *d.*—are
derived from this inscription.-- Taylor, *An Account of the Origin
and Development of Letters.* London, 1883, vol, i, p. 61.

§ *Ibid.*, p. 62.

the genius and language of the peoples using them. Thus it is that our A B C has a history and a philosophy, and most interesting are they as throwing light upon a people's characteristic traits and a people's degree of civilization.

Diversity of races and languages caused literature to be multiplied. Different peoples would so enshrine a fact that occurred in the distant past—an idea prevalent in the old homestead prior to the dispersion—in a halo of inventions congenial to their dispositions as shaped by climate and occupation, that the fact, the idea, would assume with each a distinct appearance. Hence the diversity of mythologies based upon the same ideas among the Aryan races.* Varied as are these races, divergent as is the bent of genius of each, radically opposed as are their individual characters as separate peoples, it is wonderful to see within what a small compass might be included all that is fundamental in their literatures, and how agreed are Kelt and Teuton, Scandinavian and Hindu, in the myths and sagas that have been floating among each for thousands of years. We ask no better proof for the unity of the human family.

Tracing the first dawnings of poetry the world over,

* We designate as the Aryan races those peoples who speak the Indo-European family of languages. The parent stock is supposed to have originally inhabited the territory of ancient Persia. The Hindu and Persian of old called themselves Aryans. The examination of words common to all the languages that sprung from this Aryan source, goes to show the original people to have been peace-loving, attached to the soil, given to tillage, and passionately devoted to Nature-worship. Lassen localized the primitive home at the source of the Oxus and the Jaxartes. But in 1886, Dr. Penka (*Herkunft der Arier*) gave out the hypothesis that Southern Scandinavia was the primitive Aryan home. Prof A. H. Sayce holds the same view. (*Contemporary Review, July* 1889). The Asiatic origin still seems to us the more probable. See Burnouf *Essai sur le Veda*, chap. v. pp. 117 146.

we find that all of them have a common origin.   All
began with the celebration of religious rites and mysteries; this celebration included the choral ode accompanied by music and dance.   The ode was at first very
simple and consisted of short ejaculations and many
repetitions of the same phrase.   But what it lacked
in expression was supplemented by the music and
the dance.   In one of the ancient Chinese works the
three forms of emotional expression are thus graded :
" Poetry is the product of earnest thought.   Thought
cherished in the mind becomes earnest ; exhibited in
words it becomes poetry. . The feelings move inwardly, and are embodied in words.   When words
are insufficient for them, recourse is had to sighs and
exclamations.   When sighs and exclamations are insufficient for them, recourse is had to the prolonged
utterance of song.   When these prolonged utterances
of song are insufficient for them, unconsciously the
hands begin to move and the feet to dance." *   And
so, among the Chinese and the Hebrews ; † whilst
with Hindu and Greek and Roman, everywhere, is
the choral hymn the first literary from that poetic
thought assumed.‡   Everywhere, out of the choral
ode with its accompaniments of music and dance
was evolved the drama.§

---

* *Shih King,* Great Preface, trans. by Dr. Legge.
    † Deut. xxxi, 19 ; Exod xv. 20 . Exod. xxxii. 17-19; 1 Sam. vi.
14, 20 ; 1 Sam. xix. 22.
    ‡ Burnouf, *Essai sur le Vêda,* p. 31.
    § Bazin, *Théâtre Chinois,* intro. pp. ix. x. ; B. H. Chamberlain,
Classical Poetry of the Japanese, p. 13.   In India the drama was
called *Nataka* from *Nata,* a dancer.   Weber, *History of Indian
Literature,* p. 196.

CHAPTER IV.

LANGUAGE AND LITERATURE.

CLIMATE, in contributing to stamp the character and genius of a people, also determined several traits in its language.* And the language reacted in determining and moulding the thought. Thus, there is as clear a contrast between the soft-flowing language of the Italian and the guttural speech of the German as there is in the natural dispositions of each people, and the using of one or the other tongue begets in the speaker different states of mind and feeling. If the Greek has given in poetry and in sculpture the most complete forms of beauty—if the idea of the fair and the beautiful is elementary in his thought, assuredly the graceful construction of his language had much to do in developing that happy disposition of mind that knew not how to give even a name of ill omen to a place. In like manner, if the Sanskrit, the language of the Hindu of old, in its transparency carries the mind back to the most elementary forms of

* "Whenever any dialect, founded on human organization, has been permitted to develop itself without restraint, we clearly trace in it the operation of climate and situation. In every mountain dialect we remark a predilection for the strongly aspirated CH ; on the sea-coast the softened SCH and the nasal tone are heard ; while, on the contrary, a broad tone and sharp accent indicate a level country and an agricultural population."—F. SCHLEGEL, *Romance Literature*, Part ii., p. 232, Bohn's trans.

thought, to it in a measure may be attributed that vast system of mythology that numbers not less than millions of gods ; for the intelligence that pries into every nook and corner of nature, and has a signifi- cant name for all it perceives, and then brings an active imagination to bear on both the word and the thing, is profoundly affected by the mysteries it everywhere meets and has no solution for. Even nothingness becomes for it a thing positive, and is deified as Nirvana. Again, in the comparative in- flexibility of the Hebrew language there is imaged the persistency of character peculiar to the race. It is a solemn language, suited to a solemn subject. "In its profound significancy," says Schlegel, "and compressed brevity—in its figurative boldness and prophetical inspiration, far more than in any chrono- logical precedence of antiquity, consist the peculiar character and high prerogative of the Hebrew." * No wonder, then, that it has been the instrument of prophecy and of the Sacred Book that rules our mod- ern civilization.

But there are other elements that mould a people's language, and give color to a people's literature, and they are not to be lost sight of. Such are the occu- pations that enter into a people's daily round of life. They supply the vocabulary of words that become most familiar from constant use. Men think in the language that is made up of ever-recurring words ; even their spiritual thoughts they will translate into this language. Its metaphors and its similes will be drawn from the familiar objects and the familiar actions. Other in-

* *Philosophy of Language*, lect. iii., p. 405, Bohn's ed.

fluencing elements grow out of a people's physical and social environment. The Greek city and the Greek clan-spirit are traceable throughout Greek literature, just as Hindu village and agricultural life and the Hindu system of caste run through all Hindu literature.

And here a profound question is suggested. How comes it that Aryan intelligence and Aryan civilization, through one Book and one Teacher, have bent submissive to Semitic influence, so as to become almost Semitic in thought and action ? In cast of mind there is little common to the two races. The Aryan has great flexibility of thought, and can easily adapt himself to any conviction. He is speculative and theorizing. His language is plastic, suited both to the highest poetry and to scientific precision. The Semitic languages have no aptitude for science and speculation. They are admirably adapted to prophecy and the poetry of feeling. In proof, the Semitic mind has originated no science. It gave Aristotle to Europe, but it got him from the Greeks, or perhaps found him in the cell of some unknown hermit. In algebra, we owe it nothing but the name, and to call its numbers Arabic is a misnomer ; for both it first learned from the Hindu. And still we are under the domination of that mind through its sacred Book. There was nothing in the doctrine of that Book attractive to the Aryan. It destroyed his glowing system of mythology. It imposed upon him mysteries of a most fabulous character, but shorn of all the halo of fable, and he was bound to hush his reason and say, "I believe." It revolutionized art.

The Aryan loved the nude and the sensuous, but
under the spell of that Book he symbolized the three
persons of the Godhead as an old man, a fish, and
a dove.   He loved to contemplate nature until it
grew into his being and became part of his thinking, and the one pulse animated both ; and the
strange Semitic influence taught him to be more spiritual, to look to the Invisible One, to study his every
thought and word and deed with all the severity of
an impartial judge, and in the light of laws beyond
his imaginings.   There is nothing in the nature of
things to justify this revolution.   But the work was
beyond the power of natural influence.   It was not
a man and a book that did it.   It was God ; it was
His Holy Spirit that breathed upon the nations and
renewed the face of the earth.   It was His all-con-
vincing Mind that raised up the Aryan and the Sem-
ite so far as they would, and spiritualized the thoughts
of the one, and gave him religious convictions beyond the grasp of his theorizing mind, and broadened
the intellectual grasp of the other ; thus bettering the
natures of both.*

* It may be said that the Korân wielded an equally wide influence on the Turanian and some of the Aryan races, and thence
inferred that the change here spoken of is due to persistency of character.   To this we reply that, while Christianity raised up human
nature, Mohammedanism degraded it.   The course of the latter is
exactly the opposite of that of the former.   One opposed men's most
cherished notions ;   the other adapted its spirit to the most deeply-
rooted customs and superstitions of the Asiatic mind.   The penetrat-
ing genius of Mohammed was alive to the weaknesses of his countrymen's natures, and made use of them to further his designs.   Had
he not succeeded, the great problem would be to account for his
want of success.

Considering language psychologically, we find it to be the symbol of thought, necessary to guide and direct it through the different stages of a reasoning process. It must not be confounded with thought. Each is distinct ; and the symbol is always less than the thing symbolized. Hence the utter impossibility of putting in words the whole process of thought by which an idea comes home to the mind. Genius, in its brightest moments, may approach a rounded expression of an idea in all its relations, but it is beyond the power of inferior intellects to do so. There are under-currents of thought that seem to be independent of all language. No intellect, no matter how powerful its grasp, can give an account to itself and put in intelligible language all the reasons and motives and hidden sympathies that go to make up a conviction. " Thought is too keen and manifold ; its sources are too remote and hidden; its path too personal, delicate, and circuitous ; its subject-matter too various and intricate, to admit of the trammels of any language, of whatever subtlety and of whatever compass." * It is beyond the conditions of space and time in its activity.

There are fixed relations in which language stands to literature. When a people is in a transition state ; when old forms and old landmarks are breaking up, and a new order of things is ushered in with time ; when the horizon of men's experience is widened, and hitherto unknown wants are felt, then speech seems a confused mass ; it is neither old nor new , its elements shift their long-standing, stereotype‹

* J. H. Newman, *Grammar of Assent*, p. 273.

positions, and it seems to have outgrown its grammatical laws. A man—a genius—appears at these "plastic moments," to use a happy expression of Schlegel's, and balances himself in the chaos of language, and culls, arranges, and moulds for all future time the elements at his command, and points out the direction in which they must germinate and develop while they are a thing of life. Such a man was Cædmon. He weaned the Old English from their pagan myths and pagan traditions and by his noble songs imbedded in their hearts Scriptural language and Scriptural allusions. Such a man was Shakspeare, in the Elizabethan era of our literature. He moulded all the elements of the language for the first time into a consistent whole, and made it the modern English which we now speak and write. Such is the relation that Dante holds to Italian literature. " Dante again stood between the remnants of the old Roman civilization and the construction of a new and Christian system of arts and letters. He, too, consolidated the floating fragments of an indefinite language, and with them built and thence himself fitted and adorned that stately vessel which bears him through all the regions of life and death, of glory, of trial, and of perdition." * The author of the poem of the Cid did a like service for Spanish literature, by giving it that decisively Castilian cast that separates it forever from the Latin. Such, also, is the nature of the influence exercised by the minstrel author of the *Nibelungen-lied* on the German language. Finally, such was the chief trait

* *William Shakspeare*, by H. E. Card. Wiseman, 1865, p. 21.

of Homer's greatness. He gathered up the traditions of the heroic ages as they were passing from men's minds, and crystallized them forever in the inimitable language in which we read them to-day; and to him, more than to any other individual, is Greece indebted for that graceful expression that is the glory of her literature.

All these geniuses were masters and legislators of language—not so much because they coined words and invented phrases, as on account of the weight of their names, due to their artistic skill and great natural ability. Their views were profound, and they expressed them better than their contemporaries. Children of their age, living under its social and physical influence, they had words of wisdom for it and for all succeeding time; and they therefore became the pride and glory of their nation. Their works were revered and preserved; for they embodied the nation's spirit and symbolized the age in which they were written.

CHAPTER V.

ARCHITECTURE AND LITERATURE.

ARCHITECTURE is also symbolic of an epoch. Its relations with literature are of a most intimate character, and it will be often found a correct guide in determining the spirit of an age or people. The variety and conflict of opinion in a representative author may render it difficult to catch the prevailing tone of the society in which he moves, whereas the ex-

pression of a building is one, and therefore unmistakable.   The same national genius inspires both
the literature and the architecture, and, in consequence, both express the same spirit   Hegel says :
"Nations have deposited the most holy, rich, and
intense of their ideas in works of art, and art is the
key to the philosophy and religion of a people."

   Of the early architecture of the Hindus, and indeed
of the whole Aryan family in the first stages of its
existence, we cannot speak.   "The Aryans," says
Fergusson, "wrote books, but they built no buildings.
Their remains are to be found in the Vedas and the
Laws of Menu, and in the influence of their superior
intellectual power on the lower races ; but they
excavated no caves, and they reared no monuments
of stone or brick that were calculated to endure after
having served their original and ephemeral purpose." *
Their gods were the elements of nature ; their
temples, the woods, which were so many chapels in
the vast cathedral of earth, capped by the immense
dome of heaven, beyond which was seated their
supreme deity.   From the Turanian race they
learned how to build, but with such modifications
as the peculiar bent of their genius suggested.   Thus,
that grand monolith at Ellora, the Kailasa temple—
rich, airy, massive—is characteristic of the same
genius that inspired the *Ramayana*, of some of whose
myths it contains representations.†   By no other
people could it have been constructed.   It in-

   * *History of Architecture*, vol. ii., p. 449.

   † See Fergusson's *History of Indian and Eastern Architecture,*
p. 335.

dicates the same luxuriant imagination that breathes in their various philosophical systems. The ancient Indians were so absorbed in thought that all things else were secondary. "The Hindus were a nation of philosophers. Their struggles were the struggles of thought; their past, the problem of creation; their future, the problem of existence." * The doctrine of metempsychosis shaped their whole life. With that ever present to their minds, they worked and acted and lived with the view that their future existence might be superior to their present one. The future alone was real for them. The present was *maya*—mere illusion.

With Egypt is it particularly true that her architecture reveals her spirit, for it is the chief document she has left us; and in it we read her history, her manners, her customs, her advancement in letters, science, and civilization. Her monuments are her books. In them she wished to perpetuate herself. "People truly singular and unique in history," exclaims Rosellini, "who have employed every means to perpetuate themselves whole and entire down to the latest posterity!" † Now, through the whole range of her architecture, in the mathematical accuracy of the construction of the pyramids, in the subserviency of ornament to correctness of detail, by which there is no mistaking a head of an early period for one of a later, or one of foreign origin for a

Max Müller, *History of Ancient Sanscrit Literature*, p. 31.

† "Popolo veramente singolare ed unico nelle storie, per avere ogni opera usato a conservarsi fino nella più tarda posterità tutto intero."—*I Monumenti dell' Egitto, Mon. del Culto.*

native-born, on her monuments ; and finally, in the
astrological zodiacals that adorn her later temples,
and point to the constellations pending over their
dedication, as at Esnah and Dendara, there is evidently traceable the scientific spirit that made Egypt
from the remotest antiquity the land of insight into
the mysteries of nature—the land of Chemi *—the
land, pre-eminently, of scientific lore.   Hence it is
that while Egypt had a literature of her own—and
that varied and voluminous—it was subservient to
her art and industry ; little of it remains beyond the
fragments existing on her monuments. Her primary
conception was scientific, and that gave life and
being to all else.   Her spirit still lives in her monuments.   Through them we know her people as they
lived and acted from the remotest times—prior to
Moses, prior to Joseph, prior to Abraham.

Though Greece received her architecture from
Egypt, as she did her alphabet from Phœnicia, still
all her structures have a characteristic phase that
marks them as Grecian.   The grace and symmetry
pervading column, frieze, and architrave—

> " The whole so measured true, so lessen'd off
> By fine proportion, that the marble pile
> . . . . light as fabrics looked,
> That from the magic wand aërial rise "—†

partake of the innate beauty of her language, and
symbolize that harmony in her spiritual and physical
development, which produced a corresponding harmony in her poetry and her sculpture, and made

* Whence our chemistry.   † Thompson, *Liberty*, ii.

Greece supreme in the expression of physical beauty.

The spirit of childlike faith that inspired the en-nobling legend of the Holy Grail, and built up the *Summa,* and impelled those eight Crusadal waves to wash out with their blood the desecration to which had been subjected the places sanctified by their Saviour's presence when on earth—that same beautiful spirit breathes in the Gothic cathedral, with its graceful spires lost in their heavenward direction, its sombre aisles inspiring awe and adoration rather than melancholy or gloom—the whole diffusing through the soul a feeling of prayerfulness.

Architecture has been called "frozen music," and better still, "the poetry of repose." It were more correct, if not equally pointed, to consider it the stone embodiment of a people's genius—a grand hieroglyphic, which, when rightly deciphered, reveals the spirit in which a people thinks and works. "So true is this," says Victor Hugo, "that not only every religious symbol, but even every human thought, has its page inscribed in this immense book, which is also its monument."*

Let us test this criterion by applying it to our own age. In architecture we have nothing new, nothing essentially different from that of other times ; instead, we find a conglomeration of various styles—Grecian, Byzantine, Gothic—jumbled together with no unity of plan, and therefore without the characteristic spirit that inspired any of them ; for we lack the strong natures and simple faith of the mediæval ages ; we seem to possess but a small share of that sense of symmetry and the beautiful so common among the

* *Notre Dame de Paris,* liv. v., chap. ii.

Greeks, as we have almost totally disregarded our physical training, the great school in which they cultivated that taste ; and therefore be the style Grecian or Gothic, it has lost its meaning for us.

And in literature ? Let us see. We make strong efforts to revive the classical spirit, forgetful that as a people living under an entirely different order of things, and breathing the purer atmosphere of Christian principles, even when professing to ignore Christianity, we are out of all tune with those ideas and ways that gave life and being to paganism. In like manner we love to sing again of Arthur and the Round Table, and to restore the legends of the Middle Ages to their pristine splendor. It were well could we only recall the simple faith and earnestness of those times, and drive out that sceptical spirit that chills the noblest aims of life and gnaws at the vitals of our civilization. Not that we wish to return to those days. We enjoy blessings that they knew not ; and for them we thank the Giver of all good things. The present has its own function in the great chain of the ages. An epoch may partially mar the views of the unchanging Presence that presides over the march of society. But He knows how to wait. He patiently abides His time to set things to right, when man's perverse will turns them aside from their true path. Centuries are but as moments with Him to whom all past and future are a continual present.

But these mediæval legends never come home to the hearts of moderns with that realizing force with which they were accepted by the people whose thoughts and aspirations they represent. You admire the *Parcival* of Wolfram von Eschenbach ; you scan its construction with critic's eye ; you are in rapture over descriptions simple, beautiful as the ideal in the poet's mind ; but you smile at the spirit of credulity running through the poem ; your criterion of epic construction is shattered by such an opening as this :

> " Wo Zweifel nah dem Herzen wohnt,
> Das wird der Seele schlimm gelohnt." *

But here is the inner soul—the essential life—of the poem.   Not considering it as such, you have been dissecting a corpse.   This horror for doubt runs through all mediæval literature.   You find it in Dante. It is the "open sesame" by which he enters the world of spirits :

> " Qui si convien lasciare ogni sospetto,
> Ogni viltà convien che qui sia morta." †

You find it partially reproduced in Tennyson.   Launcelot encounters two lions at the entrance to the enchanted towers of Carbouck.   He speaks :

> " With sudden-flaring manes
> These two great beasts rose upright like a man ;
> Each gript a shoulder and I stood between ;
> And, when I would have smitten them, heard a voice,
> *Doubt not, go forward ; if thou doubt the beasts*
> *Will tear thee piecemeal."* ‡

To such language as this the critic of to-day is in-

* When doubt takes up his dwelling by the heart,
   With pain and woe he'll make it sorely smart. —*Parcival,* i, 1-2.

  † Here all suspicion needs must be abandoned,
   All cowardice must needs be here extinct.—*Inferno,* iii.
                                        —Trans.—LONGFELLOW.

  ‡ Holy Graìl.

clined to say, "Words ! words !" but had the poet omitted it, he would have raised a mere skeleton in resuscitating the legend ; for there would be no trace of the spirit that gave it life and being.

To be more than notional, to be felt and almost instinctively appreciated as a matter of course, the expression—the predominant idea of a literary work —its vivifying principle—must include directly or indirectly the expression of the spirit of the age in which it is written.

Looking to other departments of literature, we perceive that the test still holds. In history, our knowledge of oriental languages, hieroglyphics, and cuneiform inscriptions has rendered us more critical ; and we have not been altogether unsuccessful in re-habilitating certain epochs in the far past.*   Fiction is more universally read now than at any other era in literature; but fiction is only the drama in prosaic detail.   In journalism we are pre-eminent.   It is to-day, among human agencies, the greatest power on earth for good as well as for evil ; but its impressions are as fleeting as time, and, like those of time, are generally traced in ruin.   Thus we find that our age is in literature what it is in architecture—an age of comparative study, and in consequence an age of patchwork and reconstruction.

* The names of Mariette-Bey, Lenormant, Rawlinson, Sayce, Bunsen, Lepsius, Niebuhr and Mommsen here recur.

CHAPTER VI.

THE LAW OF LITERARY EPOCHS.

THE intellectual development of society is like that of the individual. It has its years of puberty, when it waxes in power and influence; then comes its period of finished manhood, when it seems at a standstill, and self-possessed and conscious of its greatness and ability, it gives mature utterance to its thoughts; then it wanes and crumbles into dissolution; its voice grows cracked; its sayings are no longer heeded, and its broken sentences and wandering words excite the pity of those who knew that voice when rich and full, that language when graceful and elegant, those words when laden with deep import.

To the period of a nation's maturity our attention is at present directed. It is preceded by one of slow preparation, when the elements and energies of a nation are combining, and it is gathering strength, and becoming a recognized power in determining the world's destiny. This time of preparation is for a people what youth is for the individual—what the formation of stem and leaf is for the plant—a necessity for its after-greatness, when it stands forth clothed in its full power and complete energies. Then the shackles of youth are thrown off. The nation's personality becomes entire. Its civilization attains its most perfect development. Its language is the mirror of its power, maturity, and self-confidence. It partakes of the external grace and polish which society affects at such periods. It is the rounded expression of its genius, and the standard of utterance for all after-times. Then we look for the graceful and finished composition, the successful development of the panorama of life, and the not ineffectual efforts to solve the world-riddle, especially in the drama. Intellectual clusters invariably appear at such times, and shed a glory on their nation, and give to the date of their appearance the name of the golden era.

In contemplating these epochs, we must say that their formation is in obedience to law. All these pinnacles of literary excellence and political and social greatness, presenting so many common traits in nations that seem in other matters to be opposite poles, cannot be without design. We look along the mountain-ranges of the earth, and we notice each capped by one peak towering higher than all others —its summit ever covered with snow—and we know that such a peak was the centre and source of vast glacial forces whose marks we read to-day long after their work has been accomplished; we know that Nature exerted her energies more abundantly at that point than at any other in the whole range; and we know that Nature is ruled by law. We search the heavens, and behold vast clusters of stars beautifying the immense dome above us, and catch faint glimpses of others in a state of formation, even as our own earth was evolved from nebulous matter and we know that the spheres of heaven move in obedience to the laws to which they were subjected at creation's dawn. We further know and believe that the same Mind that governs matter guards humanity with a care infinitely superior. We therefore consider these epochs, not as the result of any individual effort, not as a fortuitous meeting of circumstances, not as being due to chance of any kind; but solely to a law presiding over all particular facts of history—a law beyond the control of human power, and in obedience to which society moves.

The law of literary epochs is this : When a nation has grown to maturity and arrived at the pinnacle of her prosperity, she possesses a strong sense of security, and devotes herself to peaceful pursuits, especially to literature and architecture, and gives utterance to her thoughts in language strong, clear, effective, such as becomes her maturity and dignity. Wherever there has been an advanced civilization, it has been adorned by such a golden era of letters. In every nation arrived at this maturity, we can trace the growth of its literature corresponding to the various stages of its development ; at first through the clan and tribe spirit, thence into its feudal growth, thence through its town and guild life, to its final expansion into a national spirit, when under the polish of court and society influence the full-rounded expression is attained.

The enunciation of the law of literary epochs invalidates individual freedom no more than do the average tables of the statistician. But the bringing about of such periods is beyond any personal influencing power. No man can say when he chooses : " Go to ; let us create a golden era of literature." Experience proves that genius is found where it is least looked for ; and not always is the means taken to draw it out the one the most successful. The literature that lives enshrined in a people's thoughts and becomes part of a people's daily language, is a spontaneous expression of the wants and aspirations of the age.

The Elizabethan era—the age of Shakspeare and Bacon—was of this kind. The national spirit had risen high, and the fulness of life and activity found vent in fulness of noble expression. About the same time, when Spain was the greatest power in Europe, both in material resources and extent of dominion, she possessed Lope de Vega, Cervantes, and Calderon. Such another era was the age of Louis XIV., with its Corneille, its Molière, and its Racine. Such was the age of Leo X., the age of art-worship and enthusiasm for the pagan ideal. Such was the age of Augustus, when Horace and Vergil and Livy wrote their graceful productions. Such, was the age of Vikramaditya in India, when "nine pearls" adorned his court, the brightest of whom was Kalidasa.*

* "It was at the court of this monarch, that flourished nine of the celebrated sages and poets of the second era of Indian literature ; and among these was Calidas, the author of the beautiful dramatic poem of ' Sacontala,' so generally known by the English and German translations. It was in the age of Vikramaditya that the later poetry and literature of India, of which Calidas was so bright an ornament, reached its full bloom."—SCHLEGEL, Philosophy of History, lect. v. p. 180.

See Weber, History of Indian Literature, pp. 200-206.

Such, centuries before, was the golden epoch of
Pericles, which culminated in the grand works of
Æschylus, Sophocles, and Euripides.

That the two pinnacles of Roman glory did not,
like the others mentioned, excel in the drama, may
be accounted for. In the first place, the dramatic
spirit was incompatible with the patrician exclusive-
ness of social life in Rome. The family was too
sacred a thing to represent upon a stage. The lines
determining the relations of father to child and of
husband to wife were too rigidly drawn to admit of
sufficient variety for dramatic purposes. Life tragedies there were, and in abundance, among the
Roman people, but the veil of silence was dropped
over them, and they remained as family traditions or
were buried in the excitements of public affairs. "It
would have been untrue to Roman social life to have
exhibited as Roman the relations of father and son,
husband and wife, as Plautus and Terence borrowing
from Greek models exhibit them always on a thoroughly Greek stage."* In the second place, the amphi-
theatre in the Rome of old was too real ; there the people saw action intensified in the death-struggle between
the gladiators and the ferocious beasts of the forest ;
their tastes grew vitiated in the contemplation of such
spectacles, and they in consequence flouted the mere
imaginary scenes of the drama. They were not a
people of dreams. They should have reality ; and
swayed as they then were by Epicurean principles,
their realistic natures were amused only by vice and
cruelty and the pleasures of the banquet, to such a

* Posnett, *Comparative Literature*, p. 196.

degree as to well merit the strong rebuke of the satirist :

> "And those who once, with unresisted sway,
> Gave armies, empires, everything, away,
> For two poor claims have long renounced the whole,
> And only ask—the Circus and the Dole."*

The age of Leo X. was too much an age of literary dilettanteism to produce anything original in letters. Men laid too great stress on the turn of a phrase, and were too slavish in their admiration for the classical literature of Rome, to possess anything peculiarly their own.   The *Madonnas* and the *Transfiguration* of Raphael, the *Last Judgment* and *Moses* of Michael Angelo, are the real glory of this age.

The normal literature, then, of the golden era of a nation is the drama.   This we should look for, considering the origin both of a people's civilization and of its drama. Each has its roots in religion. And as a nation grows powerful, and acquires all the refinements of civilization, the ease and security in which she lives, foster views of self-sufficiency ; the religious element becomes weakened ; her ideas grow secularized, and her literature expresses her actuating principles.   Hence the drama no longer deals with the mysteries of religion ; it enters the broader and more palpable field of humanity.   But mark the result. After a nation has become completely secularized, corrupt human nature begins to play havoc,

---

* "——Nam qui dabat olim
Imperium, fasces, legiones, omnia, nunc se
Continet, atque duas tantum res anxius optat,
Panem et circenses."—JUVENAL, Sat. X., 78-81.

and she declines. Her energies soon become exhausted; her literature grows weak and sickly; she is only a shadow of her former greatness.*

———

CHAPTER VII.

INFLUENCING AGENCIES IN LITERATURE.

WHERE, in literature, shall we seek those agencies that have influenced and colored, so to speak, whatever it possesses of good and excellent? Not in criticism, for that is based upon a knowledge of the master-pieces of poetry and . eloquence. Not in poetry, for the poet, though influencing after-times, is himself the product of influence; he moulds the ideas he finds popular; he is the child of his age. Not in eloquence, for the orator simply tells the people that which they already know. To something prior to all these must we look for the influencing agencies of literature. We must look to religion. Men believed in the gods before Homer sang of them. We must look to philosophy. Men's philosophical opinions influence their actions long before they undertake to account to themselves for holding them. Balmes says, truly: "When philosophers dispute, humanity itself in a sense disputes." † And it were well to remember that religious and philosophic problems of deepest import are one. Modern sub-

* See *Velleius Paterculus*, bk. i., chaps. xvi., xvii, xviii.
† *Fundamental Philosophy*, vol. i., chap. i.

jectivism, entirely occupied as it is with the barren question of knowing, has broken up that beautiful interdependence, to the detriment of both religion and philosophy.

Let us, then, cursorily consider the sources of those doctrines and opinions that have combined to educate humanity to its present degree of intelligence.

We will begin with the East. Ever remaining at a dead level, and apparently incapable of rising beyond a certain point of material and intellectual progress, the East furnishes the whole world with the elements of a higher civilization, which grow and flourish and bear fruit in their transplanted soils with a productiveness that they know not in their native land. Its unprogressive character makes the past from the remotest time a continuous present, by which we of the more active part and greater energy can trace our origin and measure our progress.*

* "We find the Chinese just as their oldest literature describes them ; we have the wandering Monguls and Turcomans, with their wagon-houses and herds, leading the Scythian's life ; we see the Brahman performing the same ablutions in the sacred river, going through the same works of painful ceremony, as did the ancient gymnosophists, or, rather, as is prescribed in his sacred books of earlier dates. And still more, we discover the Arab drinking at the same wells, traversing the same paths, as did the Jew of old, on his pilgrim journeys ; tilling the earth with the same implements, and at the same season ; building his house on the same model, and speaking almost the same language, as the ancient possessors of the promised land." CARDINAL WISEMAN, *Lectures on Science and Revealed Religion*, lect. 1., p. 363.

I.—The East.

The cradle of humanity is also the cradle of thought, of science, of literature. Far back in the twilight of history we find the Chaldæans treating questions of astronomy and chronology with scientific accuracy, and laying the foundation of modern astronomical calculations—nay, more, constructing for us our division of time. They it was who divided our year into months, our months into days, our days into hours, and our hours into minutes and seconds; they it was who gave us the signs of the zodiac ; they divided for us the ecliptic into 360 degrees, the degree into 60 minutes, the minute into 60 seconds, and the second into 60 thirds ; * they brought numbers to a degree of perfection that has not yet been excelled. They made ten the basis of computation for whole numbers, and their fractions they reduced to sixtieths. Their expertness in the sexagesimal system was remarkable. "The people of Babylon," says Lenormant, "and of Chaldæa, constantly put this system in practice in dealing with all kinds of quantities and measurements." †

The tablet of Senkereh, in the British Museum written in cuneiform of a very ancient character, reveals numerical calculations which prove the science of numbers to have been thoroughly understood at

* " Mais le Chaldéens n'avaient pas inventé seulement la division de l'ecliptique en 360 degrés et 720 moria. Sextus Empiricus dit formellement qu'ils avaient divisé le degré en 60 minutes, et Géminus que de plus ils divisaient la minute en 60 secondes, et la seconde en 60 tierces.—Lenormant, *Essai sur un Document Mathématique Chaldéen*. Paris, 1868, p. 12.

† Ibid., p. 9.

4

least twenty centuries before our era. The tablet is a species of ready reckoner prepared for purposes of barter. Lenormant, commenting upon it in a special monograph, calls it an "heirloom of that mysterious primitive civilization which preceded the Semites in Babylon, and from which these Semites gathered their system of cuneiform writing already formed." Here is a strong light thrown upon early times. It reveals to us these primitive peoples not as living in inaction, or bewildered by the greatness of the material universe, or in awe of all things animate or inanimate, as some would picture them ; but as solid thinkers, whose speculations have already reached a practical result, entering into business transactions and commercial relations, following industrial pursuits, and learned in the arts and sciences.

"Never before the discovery of this monument," says Lenormant, in wonder at the proficiency it reveals, "would we have dared to make so bold a conjecture as to suppose that at least twenty centuries before the Christian era, at the beginning of the first Semitic empire of Chaldæa, if not still earlier, the science of numbers had made such progress in this part of the ancient world, that at that time the people of Erech, of Hur, of Larsam, of Babylon, moved with such great facility in making calculations the most delicate and complicated, knew how to form the squares and cubes of numbers, as well as to extract their roots, were acquainted with the scale of the powers of numbers, and employed a mechanism of exponents exactly like that which mathematicians of our own time make use of." [*]

[*] Essai sur un Document Mathématique Chaldéen, pp. 158, 159.

These stray rays from a remote past bring home to us the depth and truth of the remark of the Egyptian priest to Solon: "You Greeks are youths in understanding; for you hold no ancient opinions derived from remote tradition, nor any science that can boast of a hoary old age."* And the science of Greece has come out of the East. Whatever is truthful and profound—all that grand array of noble sentiment and speculation relative to the Divinity and the immortality of the soul, and those deep half-mastered allusions to the mysticism of science and numbers, and the meaning of myths, and the insight into the state of souls beyond the present life, in the writings of Plato, is of Egyptian, or Chaldæan, or Hindu origin. "Plato," says DeMaistre, "had read much and traveled much; there are in his writings a thousand proofs that he had searched the real source of sound tradition. He united in his own person the sophist and the theologian, or, if it may be rather so expressed, he was Greek and Chaldæan."† The Pythagorean school—the profoundest of the Greek schools—received nearly all its learning and its most characteristic doctrines from the East; instance the doctrine of metempsychosis and the scientific principles of numbers. So also with the teachings of Aristotle. The syllogism was formally applied in India for centuries before he initiated the western world into its use and application.

* Plato, *Timæus*, iii. 22.

† *Du Pape*, liv. iv., chap. vii. He adds this significant remark : "Plato is not understood, unless, in reading him, this idea be always present to the mind."

In the East originated every great moral truth. Let us look into the literature of China. Turning to the chief work of Lao-Tsze (604–529 B. C.)—*Tao-teh-king*, the Book of the Way of Virtue,—we are exhorted to the practice of simplicity of life, love of pastoral and patriarchal ways,[*] horror of war, humility, filial obedience, above all, self-abnegation and forgiveness of injuries, and we read this noble sentence : "The sage revenges his injuries by benefits."[†] Confucius (537–478 B. C.) considers man to be the master of his own destiny, and capable of cultivating the virtues.[‡] He recognizes as clearly as does Kant the existence of the moral sense in every human breast : "The great God," said T'ang, "has conferred even on the inferior people a moral sense, in obeying which they obey a constant nature.[§] Lao-Tsze despised learning for its own sake ; Confucius was over-fond of it, but he did not separate it from culture of the heart. He says : "The ancients, wishing to be sincere in their thoughts first extended to the utmost their knowledge. Such extension of knowledge lay in the investigation of things. Things being investigated their knowledge became complete. Their knowledge being complete their thoughts were sincere ; their thoughts being sincere their hearts were rectified ; their hearts being rectified their persons were cultivated."[‖] The Hindu child was also

[*] Chap. lxxx.

[†] Stanislaus Julien : *Le Livre de la Voie et de la Vertu*, chap lxiii.

[‡] *Chang Yang*, xxii.

[§] *Shu King*. See Douglas, Confucianism and Taoism, p 69.

[‖] *Ta-Hio*, Douglas, Confucianism and Taoism, p. 92.

indoctrinated into the great value of knowledge. He was told that "of all things knowledge is esteemed the most precious treasure"; but he was also told that "learning to the inexperienced is a poison."* So also is filial obedience inculcated as a prime virtue throughout the East. Confucius says: "Of all things which derive their nature from heaven and earth, man is the most noble; and of all the duties which are incumbent on him, there is none greater than filial obedience; nor in performing this, is there anything so essential as to reverence one's father." †

But it may be objected that these sages are comparatively modern, and their teachings are the outcome of an ethical evolution. Let us go back five hundred years earlier. We consult the fragments that have been handed down to us from the teachings of the great Iranian reformer, Zoroaster. Together with the doctrine of a Supreme Being—Ahura-Mazda ‡—Mithra, the Creator and Lord, we find conjoined the strictest principles of morality, purity of body and soul, a sense of justice, love of truth, hatred of evil—personified in Anro-Mainyas, § the spirit that kills—and responsibility for our deeds. The evil-doer makes his own hell. "This place"—the place of eternal darkness—"ye make, ye who are wicked through your own deeds and your own law,

- * *Hitopadesa.* This little book is an epitome of the *Pañcha-Tantra*, the most ancient collection of fables extant. See Weber, *Sanskrit Literature*, p. 212.

    † *Li-Ki*, Apud Douglas, loc. cit. pp. 120-1.

    ‡ Known as Ormuzd.

    § Known as Ahriman.

the worst of places, there to lead a most miserable existence."* Now it is an admitted fact that the purest and highest teachings of the *Avesta* are drawn from the older Vedic documents. Zoroaster was only bringing his Iranian brethren back to purer doctrines and practices from which they had fallen away.

We go still further back. We unearth a book that was venerable with the age of twenty centuries when Zoroaster was reforming the world. It is the oldest book on record, and dates at least back to 3500 B. C. It is now known as the *Prisse Papyrus.*† The author's name is Pita-Hotep. He is a sage old and wise : "I am become an ancient in the land ; I have passed one hundred and ten years of my life, through the bounty of the king, and with the approbation of the ancients, in fulfilling my duty towards the king in the place of favor." What says the venerable book of this venerable author? What message does it hand us down the ages ?—With the exception of allusion to some local practices, now forgotten, and an occasional plain-spokenness, now not tolerated, it differs in naught from the teachings that the more recent works have handed down. To quote Pita-Hotep is simply to repeat the later lessons of Confucius, of Zoroaster, and even of Moses. His book is a book of conduct and good advice. Here is obedience inculcated with the promise of long life : "The son who receives the word of his father will grow to be old on that account." And again : "Obedience is loved of God ; hated by Him is disobedience." We have seen

* *Vendidad :* Pargard, v. §§ 177, 178. Cf. De Harlez, *Avesta,* p. 63, and Darmesteter, *Zend-Avesta,* p. 65.

† *Fac-simile d'un Papyrus Egyptien, par M. Prisse d' Avennes, Paris,* 1847.

Confucius and Vishnu-Sarman* laud and encourage learning. Pita-Hotep is no less enthusiastic : "The learned man is satiated with his knowledge. . . Good is the place of his heart and of his tongue ; agreeable are his lips. He shall speak; his two eyes shall see; his ears shall hear." He would have his son learn from all : "With the courage given you by science, dispute with the ignorant as well as the learned." With the eloquence of Lao-Tsze he exhorts to humility and lowliness in thought and word : "If thou art become great, after thou hast been humble, and if thou hast amassed riches after poverty, being for that reason the first in thy town ; if thou art known for thy wealth and art become a great lord, let not thy heart become proud because of thy riches, for it is God who is the author of them for thee. Despise not another who is as thou wast; be towards him as towards thy equal."† This is the spirit in which Job spake. Finally, he would have all live and act with cheerfulness : " Let thy face be cheerful as long as thou livest; has any one come out of his coffin after having once entered it ?" Is this not an anticipation of the Christian joy that is the very essence of Christian living ? Verily, the circle of human thought is circumscribed.

Now, let us consider the venerable antiquity of all these writings, and then let us note the fact that their authors do not pretend to invent or discover ; they merely repeat that which they have learned from the

* Author of *Hitopadesa*.

†Brugsch-Bey : *History of Egypt under the Pharaohs*, vol. i pp. 92, 93.

ancients. Even Pita-Hotep advises that his son be taught the learning that accumulated prior to his day : "Instruct him in words of the past." When this advice was entered on the papyrus that contains it, there was already much for men to learn. The hieroglyphics were even then an ancient institution. The farther back we go the stronger and clearer flows the stream of tradition. We cannot put finger upon a single great moral truth of which we can say : With this man originated this truth. All the great authors of the ancient world simply regarded themselves as the transmitters of the wisdom and experience of past ages. Now this wisdom and this experience constitute the basis of all literature. They underlie our thinking to-day as much as they underlay the thinking of the venerable authors whom we have been quoting. Of all the beautiful and elevating thoughts found in all the great works of antiquity, there is not one that has not been crystallized into a fuller and clearer and more rounded expression in the sacred Books of the Old Testament and the New. And thus is it that Christianity, in moulding our Western modern civilization has made use of all that is ennobling and spiritualizing in the streams of human traditions. The world of grace has its foundations in the world of nature.

To the East may we also trace the errors that have disturbed the equilibrium of the world. There hung the first cloud over the distinct idea of the Godhead ; there was first lost the idea of creation ; thence flowed all the consequences resulting from the distortion of these two fundamental conceptions : idolatry, pantheism, atheism, misapprehension of the nature of evil. Zoroaster, in purifying the doctrines and reforming the morals of the Iranians, was confronted with the problem of evil, and knowing God to be all goodness and all holiness, he could not imagine Him to be the author or instigator of the misery and sin under which the world groans. So he conceived another Principle existing from the beginning, inferior to the Supreme Being, but having power over the earth, and over men's bodies, the author of all venomous creatures, and the source of all human misery. The Magian priests imported from Chaldæa materialistic doctrines and superstitions, raised the inferior spirits up to places of supremacy, and propagated Sabeism, astrology and magic.* Here are we to seek the origin of Manichæism, with all its offshoots, the Albigensian and Waldensian and Lollard heresies.

The Buddhism to which all life is simply a becoming, and to which the highest good is a merging of the individual in the general life of the race without consciousness and without a distinct personal future ; † and the Mohamedanism that fosters fatalism and fanaticism, ‡ both find their cradle and their home in the East. And if we find China so stunted in her intellectual growth, may we not attribute it in a large measure to the fact that the teacher who did most to mould her thoughts, placed before her none of the high spiritual ideals that alone are fruitful in progress ? the influence of Confu-

* Mgr. C. de Harlez : *Avesta.* intro. p. 36. Kessler, *Untersuchung sur Genesis des manich. Religionssystems.* 1876.

† Sacred Books of the East, vol. xi. *Matra-parinibtana,* translated by T. W. Rhuys-David.

‡ See Sell's *Faith of Islam,* p. 160.

cius was baneful to this extent that he ignored the supernatural life, and framed all his counsels to the bettering of men in this world alone.   He discouraged all inquiry as to the life beyond the grave.   " There is nothing spiritual," says a great synologue, who knows whereof he speaks, " in the teachings of Confucius.   He rather avoided all references to the supernatural.   In answer to a question about death, he replied : ' While you do not know life, how do you know about death ? '   Life then was his study, and life represented by man as he exists." *   He had slight concern for any but the earthly future.   His was not the lesson to seek first the kingdom of God, and so his people have never realized how all else comes therewith.   Other things being equal, the higher the ideal, the greater is the power accompanying it.   Had Confucius rested his teachings upon a more spiritual basis he would have raised Chinese civilization to a higher level.   The outcome of his teachings is a reverence for the ancestral past amounting to worship and a regard for learning that has become a superstition.

II.—GREECE.

If Egypt and India, Babylon and Chaldæa and Phœnicia, transmitted to the West the traditions of thought and progress, Greece remoulded the knowledge she received and brought it within the grasp of the Latin, the Keltic and the Germanic mind, and in

* Douglas, *Confucianism and Taouism,* p. 68.

educating Rome, became to a large extent the educator of the modern world. Her forms of expression are still our standards of excellence. The
Homeric poems are our epic models even as they
were the models of Vergil. We still attune our ears
to the notes in which Alcæus and Pindar, Sappho and
Anacreon sang, just as Horace did in his day. Plautus and Terence learned from Aristophanes and
Menander how to make us laugh. The great dramatic poets have left us compositions the appreciation of which in these days calls for high culture.
Herodotus Thucydides and Xenophon initiated us
into the great power of prose and taught us how to
write history. Demosthenes showed us how perfect
oratorical expression might be mastered, and how to
throw into a single speech scorn and pathos and ex-
hortation all fused in the glow of patriotic intensity.
Thales and Pythagoras and Euclid and Archimedes
laid for us the foundations of mathematical and
physical science. In the Greek chorus did we find
the basis of the Gregorian chant. From the symmetry and harmony of the Greek temples did we learn
to apply the sense of grace and proportion in the
building of our basilicas and cathedrals.* From
Greek sculpture did we first learn how to embody in
stone the sense of repose and correctness and physi-

* All European architecture, bad and good, old and new is derived from Greece through Rome, and colored and perfected from
the East. Understand this, once for all ; if you hold fast this great
connecting clue, you may string all the types of successive arch-
itectural invention upon it like so many beads. Ruskin, *The Stones
of Venice*, vol. i., chap. i., § 17.

cal beauty.   In the Greek language—in its prose
and poetry alike—do we find models of nicety of expression, in which the right word is always fitted
to the right thought, the right style to the proper
treatment of any subject, and the most delicate shades
of meaning are hit off with precision and accuracy.
From Greek philosophy have we borrowed the very
terms in which our own philosophic thinking is
moulded, nay, are we not still engaged upon the very
same issues ?

The philosophical problems that come up for solution at the present day are indeed very ancient.
We find many of them debated in Plato, and in the
light of modern issues his pages become instinct with
life.   Whether we sit in the agora with Socrates, and
listen to him discussing with Theætetus the limits
of science and the relativity of knowledge ; whether
we recline with him under the lofty and wide-spread-
ing plane-tree by the cool waters of the Ilissus, whilst
he talks with Phædrus of love, and art, and beauty, and
the soul in its relations to these things ; whether we
laugh at the inimitable irony with which he brings
Gorgias and his disciples to confusion, or note the
seriousness with which he discusses the rewards
and punishments of a future state of existence ; or
whether with bated breath we listen to his sublime
discourse on immortality, delivered to his devoted
followers in the prison in which he is about to drink
the poisoned cup ; be the occasion when and where
it may, we meet with the same questionings that
face us to-day.   Then as now, it is the human intellect
beating against the bars of its limitations and seek-

ing to compass the unattainable. And though Plato has not given us the solution to many of the problems that arise, still, he has opened up new vistas of speculation ; the very atmosphere of his thoughts is invigorating. Through that atmosphere was it that St. Augustine soared into such sublime heights of eloquence and philosophy.*

Turning to Aristotle we find ourselves still more dominated by his influence. He is the master of all educated men in modern Europe. He coined for us the very words in which we speak of the faculties of our soul and the virtues and vices that enter into our actions. He shaped for us the laws according to which we reason. He perfected that great dissolvent of error, the syllogism, and left it so complete that twenty-two centuries of investigation have been unable to modify or supersede it. He established the fundamental conception of being and the primary principles of thought. Plato in his own impulsive fashion, became impatient of the abuses of the drama and was for banishing all poets from the State. Aristotle coldly and calmly regarded the drama in its nature, irrespective of any abuses to which it may be brought, and investigated the laws of its existence, and laid down canons of criticism and construction that are as sound and as applicable to-day as when they were first enunciated.† In like

* *De Civ. Dei*, lib. viii. 4.

† It is to be remembered that the *Poetics* is only a fragment. On the recent controversy as to the meaning of κάθαρσις—purification—in Aristotle's definition of tragedy, see J. H. Reinkens : *Aristoteles über Kunst*, Vienna, 1870. pp. 78-167.

manner, Plato regarded rhetorical rules as so much trickery and sophism for which he could not find censure too severe. Aristotle raised the subject out of this false groove, placed it upon a philosophic footing and established the laws and principles of esthetics, clearly, distinctly, and for all time.

Nor did Aristotle confine himself to intellectual laws. All departments of science fell within his scope. They were to him parts of one grand whole. In dealing with physical science and with natural history he insisted upon fact as the basis of knowledge as clearly as any modern physicist. The principle of classification that he laid down is the principle still pursued ; namely, that the common properties of things should be considered before determining their specific differences.* Again, no modern biologist could be more earnest in impressing upon the student that he must not consider one part of an animal organism more vile or more noble than another, for they all proceed from the same source, are subject to the same laws, and have each its special functions assigned. "It were real childishness," he says, "to recoil before the meanest form of animal life; for in every work of nature there is always room for admiration, and we can apply to all without exception, the words attributed to Heraclitus, replying to strangers who had come to see and be entertained by him, when, on entering they found him warming himself at the kitchen fire, he said : Enter without fear, enter always, the gods are here as everywhere else. Even so in the study of ani

* *De Partibus Animalium*, I, 1. op., t. iii. p. 218.

mals, whatever they may be, we should never turn away from them in disdain, because in all, without exception, there is some trace of the power and beauty of nature. There is naught of chance in the works she presents us. These works have ever in view a certain end. But the end in view of which a thing subsists or is made, is precisely what constitutes for this thing its beauty and its perfection."*

We are still guided by Aristotle's rules and Aristotle's methods. Scientists who know not his name and who have never read a line of his works are daily using the implements of thought and classification which Aristotle placed within their reach.† Greece gave posterity her best. Her sophistry and fickleness of character she retained, and they were the ruin of her But her magnificent epic, her lofty ode, her profoun(philosophy, her graceful architecture, her inimitable masterpieces in the plastic arts—these we have, and by them we are still educated.

III.—Rome.

Rome was a nation of one idea, and that idea was Rome. Her ambition knew no bounds. She fought and conquered and brought the East and the West submissive to her feet. The arm of the sturdy son of the forest gave strength to her ranks. The wealth of the effeminate child of the East flowed into her coffers, and brought with it the luxury and consequent

* *De Part. Animal.* lib i. cap. v. § 5, 6.

† I have rapidly sketched the influence of Aristotle on mediæval thought, and shown how far his teachings have been supplemented by the Schoolmen in *Aristotle and the Christian Church.* Lon don, Kegan Paul & Co, 1888; New York, W. H. Sadlier, 1889.

effeminacy that afterwards weakened her. All nations feared her ; all courted her protection. They
received it ; but at the price of their liberty. Her
constant intercourse with these nations, and the com-
plexity of relations arising from home and foreign
rule, gave rise to a jurisprudence that, to all intents
and purposes, is to-day at the basis of the govern-
ment of every civilized country. In jurisprudence,
her genius expanded to the full extent of her greatness. There is its true expression, rather than in her
literature, large portions of which are of Hellenic
inspiration.

While Rome was still great, there arrived the fulfilment of time, the central fact of all history, towards
which the traditions of primitive nations point, and
from which all after-events take their march and receive their significancy—the time which Vergil was
said to have felt dawn upon the horizon of events,
and of which he is supposed to sing according to his
knowledge. The Redeemer of men came upon earth.
Henceforth Christianity becomes a visible factor in
the world's doings.

IV. CHRISTIANITY.

We cannot overestimate the influence of this great
central Fact on thought, on literature, and on civilization. No historian—no thinker worthy of the name
—be his personal opinion or personal practice what
it may, can ignore this all-important factor in the
world's history, nor Him by whom it has been introduced. Those who have ceased to believe in the
Divinity of Jesus, must still bow before His greatness.

One such places Him upon the highest summit of human grandeur. The same writer tells us that His ideal of life is the most perfect that the world has ever witnessed or shall ever witness ; that He has created a heaven of free souls in which is found what we ask in vain from earth, the perfect nobility of the children of God, absolute purity, total abstraction from the contamination of the world,—that freedom, in short, which material society shuts out as an impossibility, and which finds all its amplitude in the domain of thought. He tells us further, that whatever be the surprises of the future, Jesus will never be surpassed. His worship will grow young without ceasing ; the story of His life will call forth tears without end; His suffering will melt the noblest hearts ; all ages will proclaim that among the sons of men there is none born greater than Jesus.* No ; for Jesus is more than man. He is God incarnate ; He is the Word made flesh.

World-reformers there have been who labored within the limitations of their race and their clime and adapted their reforms thereto. They were well-meaning, with spiritual aspirations, seeking to raise up their peoples to higher and better things ; and to a certain extent they succeeded. Such a reformer was Gautama ; such an one was Zoroaster ; such was Mohammed. But they all pale before the Personality of Jesus. All the gropings of all the ages after light and life find their goal in Him. All the wisdom of all the sages is crystallized in His saving doctrines. There is not an ennobling truth the world over which

* Rénan, *Vie de Jésus*, chap. xxviii.

5

He has not announced. He touched this world, passed among men, and forthwith the face of the earth began to be renewed. He soothed misery; He sanctified sorrow ; He inspired hope; He taught men how to bear the burdens and trials and crosses of life with patience and resignation. In His own Divine Person he was meek and lowly, poor and despised by the rich and the powerful. All the material comforts that men set store by, He held at their true worth. He sought not worldly fame nor worldly goods; He sought souls, His Heart went out in yearning love for souls. Beyond all accidents of birth and environment He prized men's souls, and endeavored to establish in them the kingdom of God. His sympathy and His love knew no limits ; they embraced saints and sinners, rich and poor, the well and the sick. He loved with a love boundless as the ocean, expansive as the starry sky, and therefore he was loved, and is loved, and will ever be loved, with a constancy and an intensity that only the goodness and holiness of God can claim and could receive from men. The reign of Jesus is the reign of love. His kingdom is the kingdom of love, and therefore is its duration assured beyond all time and through all eternity. Mohammed was feared ; Zoroaster was unswervingly rigid in his teachings; Gautama, though gentle and kind and meek, saw in this world only misery and illusion, and his apostleship was that of the resignation of despair. Jesus alone is loved. His doctrines are above all others precise and clear-cut ; they alone are bearers of a message of joy and hope and love and life everlasting. "It was reserved for

Christianity," says one who does not believe in the Divine origin of Christianity, "to present to the world an ideal character, which through all the changes of eighteen centuries has inspired the hearts of men with an impassioned love, has shown itself capable of acting on all ages, nations, temperaments, and conditions, has been not only the highest pattern of virtue, but the strongest incentive to its practice, and has exercised so deep an influence that it may be truly said that the simple record of three short years of active life has done more to regenerate and soften mankind than all the disquisitions of philosophers, and all the exhortations of moralists. This has indeed been the well-spring of whatever is best and purest in the Christian life."* But that well-spring flows from the Holy Trinity ; hence its miraculous power. Hence its sway over natures the most rich and fruitful in life and activity, and intellects the most soaring and acute. We shall have occasion to note this all-penetrating influence throughout the following pages.

V. THE ALEXANDRIAN SCHOOLS.

. That was a memorable day when St. Paul spoke in the Areopagus of the unknown God to whom the Athenians had an altar erected, and converted Dionysius. From that day, Christianity has had philosophers to plead her cause, and to whom she can point as proof of her power over intelligence in its strongest condition.

Justin Martyr (A. D. 166) is a priest of the church, but he also continues to wear the philosopher's cloak.

* W. E. H. Lecky, *History of European Morals*, vol. i. p. 9.

He held that there are seeds of truth among all men.*
He proclaimed the oneness of all true knowledge,
and assured men that if philosophers had understood
this elementary truth, there would be neither Platonist,
nor Stoic, nor Peripatetic, nor Pythagorean.† He
insisted that Christians should take their full measure
of this common heritage : "Whatever things were
rightly said among all men, are the property of us
Christians."‡ Athenagoras held science in no less
esteem. He tells us that it comes from God.§ He
brought to Alexandria the rigid philosophic methods
and the best traditions of the Athenian Schools.
Pantænus, who was versed in the lore of Egypt and
India and Greece, succeeded him, and continued to
fan the sacred flame. Then, the bishop gave Clement
charge of the School, and afterwards Origen, and
both these geniuses made the Christian Schools of
Alexandria famous for all time. Behold these great
men being consumed with zeal for knowledge, going
barefooted, teaching profane learning for four oboles
a day, and gratuitously giving instruction in sacred
studies. ‖

The Eclectic School of Alexandria was Christian.
Its brightest light, Clement, gave its true principle :
"By philosophy I do not mean the Stoic, or the
Platonic, or the Epicurean, or the Aristotelian ; but
whatever has been well said in each of these sects,
teaching justice and a science pervaded by piety—

---

* *Apologia I. pro. Christianis*, cap. xliv.
† *Dial. Trypho.* cap. ii.   ‡ *Apol. ii.* cap xiii.
§ *Supplicatio pro Christianis*, 7, 9, (A. D. 170.)
‖ Matter *L'Ecole d'Alexandrie*, t. i., pp. 298–320.

this eclectic whole I call philosophy."* This is the true philosophical spirit; and while men worked in this spirit, while they separated the truth from the error in each system, and made all schools subservient to the unchangeable truth that is above all schools and all systems, they did great good, and Alexandria was the focus whence emanated all the learning that enlightened both Greek and Roman. But the Christian schools died out; Eclecticism was abandoned for Syncretism; philosophers endeavored to reconcile contradictory systems; all bonds of unity were lost; the Alexandrian schools became a chaos of disputation; the pure light of Christianity was enveloped in the mists of paganism and oriental fictions, and became the butt of open hostility on the part of the new school. It was the Neo-Platonist Maximus who inspired the Emperor Julian with that hatred for Christianity which burst forth in his cruel edicts against it, though the religion in which he had been raised. It was the Neo-Platonist school that, more than any other single cause, helped to extinguish the Christian flame that had burned so brightly in Africa. And again, it was the Neo-Platonist Porphyry who planted the seed of that long dispute concerning Realism and Nominalism in the days of Roscelin, Abelard, and St. Bernard. The dispute is as old as Plato and Aristotle, and Porphyry transmits it in all its nakedness. "Con-

---

* Φιλοσοφίαν δέ, οὐ τὴν Στωϊκὴν λέγω, οὐδὲ τὴν Πλατωνικὴν, ἢ τὴν Ἐπικούρειον τε, καὶ Ἀριστοτελικὴν· ἀλλ' ὅσα εἴρηται παρ' ἑκάστῃ τῶν αἱρέσεων τούτων καλῶς, δικαιοσύνη μετὰ εὐσεβοῦς ἐπιστήμης ἐκδιδάσκοντα, τοῦτο σύμπαν τὸ ἐκλεκτικὸν φιλοσοφίαν φημί.--*Stromatum*, Lib. I., cap. vii.

cerning genus and species," he says, "I will abstain from saying whether they are in the understanding alone, or are corporeal or incorporeal things ; and whether they are separated from sensible objects and placed in non-sensible ones, or exist in the former."*
Genera and species are realities, distinct from individual things, though inseparable from them. "Genus," says Brownson, "has relation to generation, and is as real as the individual, for it generates the individual. . . . . The genus is always causative in relation to the species, and the species in relation to the individual."†

Modern Transcendentalism has many traits of resemblance with Neo-Platonism. The latter arraigns religion and revelation before its tribunal ; so does the former. Plotinus is a pantheist ; so is Fichte. The one teaches that alone to be true knowledge in which the object known is identical with the thinking subject. This is the one point on which the modern Transcendental school is agreed. According to Schelling, nature is a manifestation of the absolute, and its pure essence is identity. According to Fichte, "the Ego and the non-Ego are both equally primitive acts of the Ego ;" that is, subject and object are identical. Emerson has also reproduced the doctrines of Plotinus. Philosophy has its cycles.

---

* "Mox de generibus et speciebus, illud quidem sive subsistant, sive in solis nudis intellectibus posita sint, sive subsistentia, corporalia sint an incorporalia, et utrum separata a sensibilibus an insensibilibus posita, et circa hæc consistentia, dicere recusabo."—*Isagoge*, cap. i. translation of Boëtius. Porphyry attempts a solution in the *Enneades* lib. v.

† Works, vol. ii , p ・ 30

VI.—Two Representative Poets.

The fourth century of the Christian era, with which we now find ourselves face to face, is in the pagan world a period of criticism. Paganism is making its last struggle; but it is a struggle in death. Still Christianity does not breathe freely enough to possess a poetry of its own. The laureate of Rome in a Christian court is Claudian, who knows Christianity, and still lives a pagan.* And though he is saturated with paganism, its poets and myths—though, like a true Roman, Rome is his idol, and he therefore has occasionally faint glimpses of genuine poetic inspiration—he is still but a panegyrist.

In contrast with the servile spirit of Claudian stands forth Prudentius (348–424). He loves Rome with a Roman's passionate love. Rome is the golden city—which he would see free from every blot and stain. He would have her rise above her former greatness by becoming thoroughly Christian: "May all the members of her empire unite in the same creed. The world has bowed; may its sovereign city bow."† After having fulfilled positions

* As the following epigram shows. Jacobus, a Christian and a military prefect, disapproves of his poetry, and he makes mocking allusions to saints of the New Testament and the Old:

> Per cineres Pauli, per cani limina Petri,
> Ne laceres versus, dux Jacobe, meos :
> Sic tua pro clypeo sustentet pectora Thomas,
> Et comes ad bellum Bartholomœus eat :
> Sic ope sanctorum, non barbarus irruat Alpes :
> Sic tibi det vires sancta Susanna suas . . . . .
> Sic nunquam hostili maculetur sanguine dextra.
> Ne laceres versus, dux Jacobe, meos.
>
> Epig. 27.

† Peristephanon, ii. 439–440.

of honor and trust in the Empire, he retires from
public life and devotes himself to the writing of
poems, the sweetness and freshness of which still
please.   He is possessed of the truly Christian spirit.
His later life is one of simplicity ; his thoughts are
all for religion ; his pen is consecrated to her praise
and her defence.   He sings the triumphs of her
martyrs. *   He defends her mysteries and her doctrines with eloquence.   Paganism is making a dying
struggle, and a movement is set on foot to restore in
Rome the altar dedicated to Victory.   Prudentius
opposes it in ringing verses from which fly sparks of
the zeal and devotedness that glow within his heart.
Therein also does he exhort Honorius to abolish the
bloody games which were then being held, as a dis-
grace to Rome. †   His whole life is a hymn of praise
and prayer to God.   The hours of the day and the
feasts of the year inspire him with fresh songs.   A
hymn consecrates each action.   When rising at
early dawn he sings ; when retiring to bed he sings ;
when about to eat, he sings ; when he has finished
his meal, he sings. ‡   He is the poet of the Christian
day and the Christian year.   His sweet accents have
been added to the chorus of praise and prayer which
the Church sends up daily§.

* See his beautiful hymn in honor of St. Agnes.   Peristephanon,
xiv.
† Contra Symmach. ii. 1114, et seq.
‡ Cathemerinon Hymn. i.–xii.
§ Seven hymns in the Roman Breviary are from the pen of Pru
dentius.

VII.—THE EARLY FATHERS.

Claudian represents the decline of the pagan world of letters ; Prudentius represents the growing vigor of the Christian world, upon which a new era was then dawning. Among the primitive fathers, the golden-mouthed John, the Gregories, Nazeanzen and Nyssa, Basil, Jerome, and Ambrose—all of whom flourished between A. D. 340 and 420—men all of them of edifying lives, of genius imbued with learning, eloquence, and zeal for religion—explained the doctrines of Christianity, fought heresy, lessened and prevented scandals, weakened paganism, spread the gospel, and profoundly impressed the people at large.* To-day the sermon is taken as a matter of course. It is considered a something to be endured, seldom enjoyed, and then simply as an intellectual treat. But in those early days it was measured by a different standard. Then it was new, and was looked upon with admiration and enthusiasm ; and its novelty and power caused it to exercise a strong influence for good. Sacred eloquence is a power unknown in pagan literature. It is the creature of Christianity. The pagan was accustomed to offer his sacrifice, say the prescribed prayer, and go his way. There are times when man is better disposed to listen to good counsel. Chris-

* Leo XII. thus speaks of "the great Basil and the two Gregories:" "From Athens, then the home of the highest culture, they went forth equipped with the panoply of philosophy. Having acquired all their riches of learning by most ardent study, they used them to refute the heretic, and to build up the faithful."—Encyclcal, *Æterni Patris*, 1879.

tianity, which has at all times a word for all classes, chose that the most opportune to speak, and impress her sublime doctrine on his heart. And, therefore, in the temple of religion, when the clash and clamor of man's worldly occupations are hushed before the Divinity, when the prayerful disposition of his soul disposes him to think on the spiritual world of which the ceremonies remind him, and he feels that there is a higher and better life after which he ought to strive— at that solemn moment the Christian minister, in the name of the God whom man worships, strengthens the feelings then possessing his heart, addresses him with a conviction that only religious zeal knows, and appeals to passions—not of national honor, not of mere personal integrity, not of self-interest—but awakens passions never before addressed in assembly; rather creates a passion in which all others are absorbed—a passion that elevates man above the natural plane of his dignity, makes him superior to himself, and equal to deeds from which human nature unassisted would shrink in fear and horror; that of loving, serving, imitating his Lord and Redeemer, the Crucified One. This is the sublime origin of sacred eloquence.

These early fathers knew and felt their indebtedness, among human agencies, to the ancient classics and the ancient philosophy for the effective language of which they were masters, and they esteemed and cherished them accordingly. Thus St. Jerome teaches them in Bethlehem, and in reply to Magnus, who accuses him of being too fond of the pagan authors, pleads their cause with eloquence. He speaks of "the sacredness of antiquity," shows that St. Paul quoted Aratus, Epimenides, and Menander, and in allusion to the Jewish law of purifying captives and admitting them as Israelites, he adds : "What wonder, then, that I, struck by the science of the age in the beauty of its features and the grace of its discourses, should wish to transform it from the slave it now is into an Israelite."* Origen (185–253) had previously made use of the same figure : "Whatever we find that is well and rationally said in the works of our enemies, if we read anything that is said wisely and according to knowledge, we ought to cleanse it, and from that knowledge which they possess to remove and cut off all that is dead and useless."† St. Basil likewise becomes the advocate of the classics against those who would be for their total destruction : "As dyers," says this doctor of broad views, "dispose by certain preparations the tissue which is destined for the dye, and then steep it in the purple, so, in order that the idea of good may be traced ineffaceably in our souls, we shall first initiate them in the outer knowledge, and then will listen to the hallowed teaching of the mysteries." ‡ Love for classic literature grew to a passion. St. Jerome blamed the clergy of his day for devoting too much time to the study of pagan authors, to the palpable and the baneful neglect of sacred learning. "They read comedies," he says," had Vergil unceasingly in their hands, recited tender verses from the

* S. Hieron. Ep. lxxxiii ad Magnum.

† In *Levit. Hom.*, vii. See Maitland's "Dark Ages," No. xi. —*Dark Age View of Profane Learning*, p. 174.

‡ Ozanam, *Civilisation in the Fifth Century*, vol. i., p. 220.

bucolics of this poet, and made a criminal pleasure of what had been a necessary occupation of their youth."* What was true among the Latin clergy at this period, was equally applicable to the Greek clergy. About A. D. 390, Heliodorus, Bishop of Tricca, wrote his *Æthiopica*, a novel of great merit, and which was very popular with the youth of that day.† The book is saturated with expressions borrowed from Homer and the dramatic poets. Theogenes and Chariclea are nominally pagans, but the heroine has all the fortitude and virtue of a Christian soul. Paganism is already so much a thing of the past, that Heliodorus finds it of interest to his readers to describe ceremonies that accompanied a sacrificial offering in a pagan temple.‡ Well and graphically has he pictured them.

Thus it was that taste for secular literature among the clergy had swung to the extreme of even reproducing exclusively secular books. Surely, in presence of these indications of excessive devotedness to the pagan classics, it were folly to accuse the Church as inimical to such studies. Religion is not opposed to literature so far as it is the expression of the true, the good, and the beautiful. It is only when it becomes the vehicle of falsehood and immorality that she condemns it. One of the greatest

---

* Ep. 146, ad Damascam.

† Nicephorus, lib. xii., cap. 34. We accept the testimony of Nicephorus as regards the popularity of the book, but we incline to the opinions of Bayle and Huet in rejecting the rest of his story.

‡ *Æthiopica*, lib. iii.—Raphael painted the first meeting of Theogenes and Chariclea at the altar, from this description. Tasso pictured the early life of Clorinda (*Jerusalem Delivered*, xii.) after Heliodorus's description of the infancy of Chariclea, and from the *Æthiopica* Guarini borrowed several scenes in his *Pastor Fido*.

intellects within the gift of humanity, and one of the most brilliant ornaments of religion, rose to saintship in the path of literary pursuits. Literature was the natural mould in which St. Augustine (354–420) was stamped.

Schooled in the philosophies of the East and the West, after an eager search through the fogs of Manichæism and the mazes of Neo-Platonism for the fountain of truth, at which alone his boundless aspirations could be slaked, he at last arrives in the broad daylight of Catholicity, and in her doctrines and sacraments satisfies his hitherto insatiable craving after truth. He is the epitome of his age. He followed all its leading phantoms until he rose above his times into the regions of holiness, whither they never followed. His *Confessions* is a sublime hymn of praise to God for having led him out of error—a profound, philosophic essay on the supremely good and beautiful, in which, in the vagaries of his own life, are the practical illustrations of the vanities of the systems through which he passed. "Neither is this done by the words of the flesh and outward sounds, but by the words of the soul, and the loud cry of the thought which is known to Thy ear."* The book proves that neither Pagan, Platonist, nor Manichæan has the clue to the enigma of life ; but that in Christianity alone is this to be found. The central idea is that God alone is true, is beautiful, is good, is great, and worthy of our love: "Thou hast wounded my heart with Thy word, and I fell in love with Thee."† In consideration of that love he would throw himself

* *Conf.*, lib. x., cap. ii.   † Ibid,. cap. vi.

away, and make choice of God ; and therefore it is that he confesses his sins : ''That so I may be ashamed of myself, and may throw away myself, and may make choice of Thee.''* And this idea is also fundamental in his great work, *The City of God ;* for he characterizes the two cities, the earthly and the heavenly, according to the nature of the loves by which they have been formed : '' Accordingly, two cities have been formed by two loves—the earthly by the love of self, even to the contempt of God ; the heavenly by the love of God, even to the contempt of self. The former, in a word, glories in itself; the latter in the Lord.''† This work is the first instalment of the philosophy of history, which was afterwards developed by Bossuet and Schlegel. Augustine witnessed the crash of the Roman empire under the blows of Alaric. The greatest power that ever ruled the world had fallen. Sophists raised a hue and cry against Christianity as the primal cause of all the evils that befell. ''No wonder,'' they said, '' that Rome should fall ; her altars were deserted, her gods despised, and Christians were plotting her ruin.'' To answer these objections, St. Augustine writes this, his master-piece, and ''the encyclopædia of the fifth century.''‡ He investigates the causes of the rise and progress of Rome, shows the secret of her strength, and points out the reason of her decline and fall, with a masterly hand, and upon principles that no historian can ignore.§ He then examines the

* *Conf.*, lih. x., cap. ii.
† *City of God*, bk. xvi. 28.
‡ Poujoulat, *Vie de S. Augustine.*
§ Bks. i., ii., iii., iv., v.   The fifth is especially noteworthy.

theological and philosophical systems of paganism, and proves that in them there is much error, and that whatever truth they possess is realized in Christianity.* The rest of the work is devoted to the consideration of the two cities, the heavenly and the earthly, and their origin and destiny. There are those who smile when they read that the two cities began with the good and the bad angels. But when we translate the idea into modern phraseology, we find in it an incontestable truth. By the two cities he means, first, the aggregate of God-loving, God-serving, and God-fearing persons on the earth—all true and faithful Christians ; secondly, the aggregate of God-despising, self-loving and self-seeking persons—the worldly minded, who look but to the present. Now, evidently, the different spirits that animated the good and bad angels are the same that live in these classes. We all are guided by one or the other. After showing where truth and stability are alone to be found, this great genius ends where all his works end, from the time he first exclaimed, "Do we love anything but the fair and beautiful ?"† to the hour he breathed his last—in God.

St. Augustine was cherished in the Middle Ages, was not forgotten at the Renaissance, and is still a favorite with the thoughtful among moderns. In endeavoring to grasp the expression of his genius, one image recurs to the mind—that of the ocean, first tossed and lashed about by storm, then calm and clear, the wreck of the previous tempest floating on its bosom. Through-

* Bks. vi., vii., viii., ix., x. Bk. viii, is especially noteworthy
† *Conf.*, lib., iv., cap. xiii.

out his writings float the wrecks of shattered systems
and fragments of dead issues, but beneath their surface are the solid gems of truth.*

About a century later (470-524) Boëtius lives, is
persecuted, suffers, and writes his beautiful work
De Consolatione Philosophiæ. It was a favorite in the
Middle Ages, and it still has admirers. Alfred the
Great translated it into Old English, and Chaucer
into Middle English. The work is not only the product of superior talent highly cultivated ; it is also
the inspiration of a noble and beautiful soul conscious
of its innate greatness. He who knows but the sunshine
of life, lives in ignorance of the world and himself.
Man's worth is tested in the crucible of persecution and
suffering. *The Consolations* would, in all probability,

---

* Let us here quote the splendid eulogy of Leo XIII. on St. Augustine : " But it is Augustine who seems to have borne away the
palm from all. With a towering intellect, and a mind full to over-
flowing of sacred and profane learning, he fought resolutely against
all the errors of his age, with the greatest faith and equal knowledge. What teaching of philosophy did he pass over? Nay,
what was there into which he did not search thoroughly ? Did he
not do this when he was explaining to believers the deepest mysteries of the faith, and defending them against the furious attacks
of the adversaries ? or when, after destroying the fictions of Aca-
demics and Manichæans, he made safe the foundations of human
knowledge and their certainty, searching out also to the furthest
point the reason and origin and causes of those evils by which man
is oppressed ? With what copiousness and with what subtlety did
he write about the angels and the soul and the human mind ;
about the will and free will ; about religion and the blessed life ;
about time and eternity ; about the nature of all changeable
bodies ! "—Encyl. *Æterni Patris*, 1879.

have remained unwritten had Boëtius ended his days while basking in the smiles of his sovereign ; but in the chill shadow of the prison his soul expanded and rose above adversity, and he wrote the thought that endeared his name to posterity,—that in self-knowledge is strength ; that the blessings of fortune are fleeting and unsatisfactory ; that in virtue alone is true happiness to be found ; and that in reality, adversity is superior to prosperity.* This thought is the burden of the work ; therefore it is that Dante speaks of the author as

> The saintly soul, that shows
> The world's deceitfulness to all who hear him."†

VIII.—CHRISTIANITY AND BARBARISM.

AND now, for centuries, the Church works continuously, works strenuously, works without once tiring or asking for a truce, at the great task of leavening the mass of barbarism that inundated and swept away the old civilization, and builds upon its ruins the new civilization, the benefits of which we enjoy to-day. Her religious orders guard in their monasteries, with the most jealous solicitude, the ancient classics from the

---

* " Etenim plus hominibus reor adversam quam prosperam prodesse fortunam."—*De Consol.*, lib. ii., prosa. viii.
> † " L'anima santa, che il mondo fallace
> Fa manifesto a chi di lei ben ode."
> *Paradiso*, canto x., 125, 126.

6

ravages of the barbarian who, not knowing their use, would have destroyed them as useless. Her clergy impose upon him the sweet yoke of the gospel ; and by means of the sacraments they dispense to him, the prayers they teach him, and the moral truths they inculcate, they tame his fierce nature, initiate him into the practice of leading a settled and peaceful life, and thus lay the foundation of prosperity and happiness. They establish schools and universities to educate him. The work of refining and enlightening him was slow. Not unfrequently would this child of nature break through all bounds ; but when the sea of passion that tore his breast would have subsided, he would return to religion repentant for the deeds of violence of which he was guilty, and religion would heal the wounds of his soul, encourage him in the path of virtue, and teach him to forgive, that he may be forgiven, and to respect his neighbor in person and property. Thus is religion the creator of our modern civilization. Ask not for books or authors while such a sublime work is going on. It is in itself an epic in action. Slavery was abolished ;* woman was elevated and respected ; the hand of vengeance was stayed by "the truce of God"; chivalry was based upon principles of honor and virtue ; and "with the virtues of chivalry was associated a new and purer spirit of love; an inspired homage for

* For a detailed account of the attitude of the Church towards slavery from the beginning, see Balmes' *European Civilization*, chaps. xv.–xix., and the decrees of Councils quoted in the Appendix, pp. 430–432.

genuine female worth, which was now revered as the acme of human excellence, and, maintained by religion itself under the image of a Virgin Mother, infused into all hearts a mysterious sense of the purity of love." *

The poetry of these ages tells of the spirit by which they were animated. That the Christian spirit was gaining ground, we learn from the popularity, as early as the ninth century, of songs based upon Scriptural subjects. † Then, also, began to grow into shape, and float among the people in fragments, those legends which, in the thirteenth century, were embodied in the *Nibelungen-lied*, in what Heine calls "a language of stone." It is a people's pagan tradition interwoven with Christian sentiments. You scarcely know that the personages are Christian until you come upon a Crimhild and a Brunhild quarrelling for precedence at the church door, or a Monk Ilsan with the incompatible appendages of cowl and sword—a fact that goes to show the necessity of the stringent decrees of the Provincial Council presided over by St. Boniface, forbidding priests and monks to take up arms even against the Mussulman : and futhermore, adds the Council, "we forbid all bishops, priests, clerics, or monks to hunt in the forests with packs of hounds, sparrow-hawks, or falcons."

* A. W. von Schlegel, *Lectures on Dramatic Literature*, p. 25.
† Those known to us are : *The Harmony of the Evangelists,* in old Saxon, published by Schmeller (Stuttgard, (1830) *Krist, or Book of the Evangeiists* (Königsberg, 1831) ; *The Song of the Sa-*
maritan Woman, and a poem on *The Last Judgment*. To this period also belongs *The Legend of St. George.*

But the *Nibelungen-lied* is a poem of more than national interest. It is another expression of the same old Aryan thought that is the vital principle of the Grecian and Hindu epics, cast in a mould different from either, and tinged with the characteristic traits of the Teuton race. It is another effort to unravel the entanglement of events that arises when generosity and valor, craft and cunning and jealousy meet, act and counteract—the golden apple of contention in this case, as well as in the *Iliad* and the *Ramayana*, being beauty.

In the thirteenth century, at the time this poem received its last touch, the poet was esteemed and patronized, and poetry wielded influence. " Believers," says Tieck, " sang of faith ; lovers, of love ; knights described knightly actions and battles, and loving, believing knights were their chief audience. The spring, beauty, gayety, were objects that could never tire ; great duels and deeds of arms carried away every hearer, the more surely and the stronger they were painted ; and as the pillars and dome of the church encircled the flock, so did religion, as the highest, encircle poetry and reality ; and every heart in equal love humbled itself before her."* Many a grim baron, by poet's song, was moved to muster his serfs and seek the Holy Land. The entreaties of Walther von der Vogelweide assisted the tardy purpose of Frederick II. to undertake a crusade. Many a feud was hushed by the song of peace. The bishop and magistrate of Assisi are in open warfare, when St. Francis passes by, singing a beautiful canticle to

* *Minnelieder aus dem Schwabischen Zeitalter*, Vorrede, x.

"his brother the sun"; his earnest, burning words pierce their hearts; their wrath subsides; the poet sings on; they can no longer resist the torrent of inspiration that gushes from his heart; they dissolve into tears and embrace.* The incident is characteristic.

IX. THE CARLOVINGIAN AND ARTHURIAN CYCLES.

Three currents of literature flowed through the popular intelligence, and were its educators in mediæval days. There were the narratives and legends of the saints. They were relished by old and young; they were recited from the pulpit; † they entered into the spiritual books that were freely circulated; they passed down into the traditions of the people. The memory of them helped to decide many a soul in some crisis of life. They bloomed into that sweet bed of violets, the *Fioretti* of St. Francis of Assisi and that garden of roses, the *Legenda Aurea*.‡ They inspired many compositions like that most charming of idyls, the legend of the dear St. Elizabeth of Hungary. How rich this field is, and how extensively it has been cultivated, we may form some conception, from the harvest of the lives and acts of the saints, which has been gathered into the great Benedictine and Bollandist storehouses.

There was, and there still is, the nursery-tale. It is of very ancient origin. It is a combination of the myths of the Keltic and Germanic races, combined

* Montalembert, *Life of Elisabeth of Hungary*, int. p. 77.

† These recitations were, in verse as well as in prose. See Ten Brink: *Early English Literature*, p. 140.

‡ By James of Voragine, Bishop of Genoa.

with the fabliaux, imported from the East by the Crusaders. It dates back to the old Aryan home-life.* It has flourished among the old-world peas-antry, and has floated down the ages freighted with a curious cargo of ghosts and fairies, hobgob-lins and nixies, cloaks of darkness and invincible armor ; the tale of national prowess is told, moulded in the national genius, and referring back to the dim twilight between the mythic period, and the clear day of fact: and the sentiment of virtue and honor is embodied in some heroic deed. These tales are still found to be refreshing, amusing, simple ; though now we possess but the scattered remains of the rich harvest of folk-lore of former times, which were pre-served says Grimm, "at the kitchen-hearth, the steps of the loft, feast-days still observed in their quietude in meadows and forests, above all, in undisturbed fancy."† As we now read them, they are a jumble of Christian reminiscences, and pagan fancies, once possessed of a meaning and a moral. They are the atmosphere in which children have inhaled a love for virtue, honor, and truth ; and in the struggle be-tween the good and evil genii, in the horrors in-spired by the transactions of wickedness, in the aspirations aroused for the noble and true, in the pity called forth at the sight of goodness in jeopardy and distress, the young soul is learning its first lessons of virtue and manhood. They awaken fancy, help memory, call forth ingenuity, and foster the racial spirit.

But the youth outgrows his nursery-tales as he does his tops and marbles. He then requires to be fed

* Weber, *Sanskrit Literature*, p. 213.   † *Märchen*, vor.

with another order of thought and fancy. And so, we find that in former days his heart was nerved and his imagination fired with the romance of chivalry. But every current of popular thought has its source in some popular institution. Such an institution was chivalry. It was the outcome of feudalism. We find it first exemplified in the exploits of the Norman adventurers who conquered a home for themselves in France, extended their conquests to Sicily and England, crossed into Russia, offered their assistance to the weak emperor of Constantinople, protected pilgrims and travellers in the Holy Land, and everywhere performed deeds of daring almost superhuman. Here were feats calculated to fire youth. Add to this romantic spirit calling forth all the sterner and fiercer energies of man, the softening and refining element of love, and fixed attachment for woman ; give direction to the whole by the influence of religion, and you have chivalry personified. God and his lady-love : such are the two ideas that occupied the knight-errant in his perilous career. He forgets one as soon as the other. Both are inseparable in his mind and in his heart. " His excited imagination transports him into a world of fancy ; his heart is on fire ; he undertakes all, he accomplishes all ; and the man who has just fought like a lion on the plains of Spain or of Palestine, melts like wax at the name of the idol of his heart ; then he turns his eyes amorously towards his country, and is intoxicated with the idea that one day, sighing under the castle of his beloved, he may obtain a pledge of her affection, or a promise of love. "*[h]

* Balmes, *European Civilisation*, chap. xxvii.

Such a spirit requires to be fed with works showing forth heroic actions and giving models of excellence to go by. To whom, among mediæval heroes, does the mind more naturally turn than to Charlemagne? Who is greater than he? Great in war by his conquests; great in peace by the schools and monasteries which he established; grèat in his únselfish relations with the Holy See; his very failings were the failings of a great nature. In song and story had his deeds been celebrated; and as time intervened between himself and after generations his name became the nucleus around which gathered many a myth. He and his paladins became demi-gods. They were considered giants in stature, even as the feats recorded of them were pictured on a gigantic scale. Such was that trumpet-blast of chivalric action, the *Chanson de Roland*. It is among the most ancient, the most beautiful, and the most artistically complete of all the cyclic poems that have been handed down. Somewhat later, about the beginning of the twelfth century, appeared in the Latin tongue a prose version of the deeds of Charlemagne—the *Karolus Magnus**—attributed to Archbishop Turpin, a contemporary and friend of the great emperor, but compiled by a monk three centuries later.† The only parts belonging to the good monks are the moralizings and allegories running through it.‡ But while its avowed object is

* Incipit prologus beati Turpini archiepiscopi quomodo Karolus Magnus Imperator subjugavit Yspaniam Christi legibus.

† Probably by a cleric of Vienne; afterwards modified by a monk of St. Denis, under Suger, who had it recorded that Charlemagne conferred on that church jurisdiction over all France.

‡ Ciampi, *Turpin*. Dissertazione, xxvii. The first five chapters

by good example to teach honor and virtue—" for," remarks one of the French versions, " to live without honor is to die—*car vivre sans honneur est mourir"*— i' wa. evidently written with a view of promoting devotion to St. James of Compostello, of calling the attention of Europe to the presence of the Mussulman in Spain, and of inciting the German emperors to imitate Charlemagne in his deference to the Holy See, and his generosity to the Church. It was copied and imitated, and helped to mould public opinion throughout Europe.[*] The Carlovingian cycle bloomed into that brilliant masterpiece, the *Orlando Furioso* of Ariosto.

Another cycle of romances allied to the Carlovingian, changes the scene of action from Spain and Palestine to France, and from the fire of resentment towards the Mussulman, to antagonism between feudal lord and feudal lord, or between vassal and king. Feudalism was the stronghold of baronial independence, and the feudal lord was the chief patron of the bard. What wonder then, that the poet should laud the boldness and prowess of the feudal lord in de·fending himself against the unjust exactions of his king, or the encroachments of his peers. Hence we meet with such songs of rude and barbaric heroism

---

were written by some one acquainted with Spain, and are probably of an earlier date. The remaining twenty-seven chapters betray a hand less cunning and are every way inferior. See Leon Gautier, *Les Epopées Françaises*, t. i., p. 194.

[*] *L' Entrée en Espagne*, MSS. Français, in St. Mark's Library. Venice, No. XXI. fo. 1, v°.

as that which recounts the feats of Guillaume Court-
Nez. *

Still another cycle is the Alexandrian.   Among the
heroes of antiquity, Alexander the Great stood out in
bold-relief.   Little was known of him personally and
historically ; but his name became the synonym of all
that was noble in knight-errantry.   At this epic-mak-
ing. period, he is transformed into a hero equal to
every emergency, capable of slaying any number of
thousands of paynims, relieving the oppressed, rid-
ling innocence of her persecutors, and under the
banner of the cross doing all that Christian knight
should do.   Alexander could not be excelled in greatness and in prowess.   In the East, and especially in
his own city of Alexandria, were gathered the myths
that converge round his name.   Simon Seth translated a Persian mythical history of him into Greek.
In this, and in the letters of the pseudo-Callisthenes,
and the writings of Julius Valerias and the arch-priest
Leo, were stored the incidents from which were
drawn the various versions that culminated in the
magnificent epic of Lambert the Crooked. †

But the cycle that excelled all the others, and that
became the great educator of the youth of Christendom in refinement and good manners, was the
Arthurian cycle.   It is a cycle of Keltic legends drawn
from Brittany and Wales and Ireland.   This Keltic
element colors the poems ; it lives in the delicacy of
sentiment—especially the sentiment of love and re-

* See Fauriel, *Histoire de la Poesié Provençale*, t. ii. p. 267 ; Léon
Gautier, *Les Epopées Françaises*, t. iv.

† Henri Martin, *Histoire de France*, t. iii. pp. 395, *et seq.*

spect for woman—which runs through the whole cycle and places it in contrast with the Carlovingian cycle, with its ruder manners and its delight in wars. In tracing the genesis of these poems, historians of literature dwell upon the contributions of Geoffrey of Monmouth, and Walter Mapes, and Robert Boron, and Chrestien of Troyes ; theirs were the hands that gave the finish to the most complete forms of the cycle. But these writers only labored upon the material as they found it. This material grew primarily out of the struggle between the Britons and the Saxons. It is a reminiscence of the long resistance made against English domination. In like manner, there runs through the Carlovingian cycle an undertone of the fierce contest for predominance between the Frank and the Gaul. Indeed, it is a law in the literature of nations, that when two races have struggled for survival, the weaker one will continue to exist in song and story, seeking to gild its present dimness by some reflex of its past glories, and covering its defeats by such excuses as save the honor and courage of the nation. Another element which these poets found to hand consisted of the lays that survived the lost annals of the Britons. A third was composed of the legends regarding the planting of Christianity in Britain. A fourth was the large remnant of pagan superstitions which survived all efforts of Christianity to uproot them, and which wrought into their Keltic natures love for the weird and the wonderful, and familiarity with scenes and incidents of sorceries and enchantments. A fifth consisted of the oriental traditions and parables spread throughout Christendom, by Jews, Spanish Moors, crusaders and pilgrims.

But in the preparation of this material there is a hand that may easily be recognized, and that did much towards the dissemination of these Keltic poems among the Teutonic peoples. It is the hand of the Irish bard. He travelled the continent, charming audiences with his sweet music. Marie of France, tells us of the Irish bard who sweetly sang the fable of Orpheus.* In the year 1078, a prince of North Wales named Gryfidd of Conan, introduced Irish bards to instruct and reform the Welsh bards.† Thus is there historical as well as internal evidence of the influence of the wandering bard of Erin upon mediæval poetry. Into the poems that he sang he wove in his own bright colors, many an incident that clustered around Queen Meibhe or the heroes of his native land.

Gradually the various poems of the Arthurian cycle were grouped around a central figure. That figure was the Holy Grail. According to the legend, the Holy Grail was the cup of which our Lord made use at the Last Supper. It came into the possession of Joseph of Arimathea, who gathered into it some drops of blood from the body of Jesus when taking Him down from the Cross, and afterwards brought it to Britain. Now, from time immemorial the chalice was employed in a symbolic sense in the performance of religious rites. It was so used in the Diony-

---

* Le lai escoutent d' Ailis
　　Que un Irois doucement note . .
　　Le lai lor sone d'Orfei.—*Lai de l' Espine.*

† Walker, *Historical Memoirs on Irish Bards :* Warton, *History of Poetry, Dissert i.,* p. xl.

sian mysteries celebrated by the Greeks.* The books attributed to the Areopagite make the chalice of the Redeemer the central point of all Christian mysteries, the chalice being the symbol of Providence which penetrates and preserves all things.† In 717, a Kymric cleric inserted in liturgical lessons the traditions of the apostolate of Joseph of Arimathea.‡ He described his vision of the book containing the account of the Holy Grail. No tongue can speak its language. It can only be read by the heart. He that opens it, and is possessed of a pure heart will rejoice with a great joy of body and soul. The author's mystical meaning is plain. The book is the book of love for God. Henceforth the Grail-saga becomes developed, and with its growth the other poems range themselves around it, and receive from it a bond of unity and a significancy far greater than that conveyed by the Round Table. The vision of the Grail is an object of expectation in the court of Arthur. There remains vacant the seat-perilous awaiting the favored knight for whom the vision is reserved. Then passes the vision through the great hall, transforming these men, cleaving them from attachment to sin, and finally leading them by the light of faith to brave all dangers in quest of the precious boon.

The Grail symbolizes the Holy Eucharist. The quest is allegorical of the soul, overcoming its passions, raising itself above the thraldom of the senses, and arriving at that state of detachment from sin and love for God,

---

* Goerres, *La Mystique*, t. i., p. 78.

† Dion. Areop. Ep. ix. *Tito Episcopo.* § iii. Patrol. Gr. t. iii. Col. 1110.

‡ Paulin Paris, *Les Romans de la Table Ronde*, t. i. 155–169.

that renders it worthy to receive the Blessed Sacrament.   He who would penetrate to the abiding-place
of the Holy Grail should pass through much tribu-
lation with great fortitude ; he should prepare himself by fasting and mortification ; he should be
humble ; he should lose himself in order to find himself ; he should guard his heart and his mind against
every affection and every thought that would in the
least sully his soul.   Even so with him who would
worthily approach the fountain of life and partake of
the Holy Eucharist ; he should conquer the powers
of darkness and overcome his evil passions ; he
should purge himself from every stain of sin in the
sacrament of penance, and then he would feel the
ineffable joy that the favored custodians of the Holy
Grail experienced when they sat at the mystical
banquet.

These romances spread throughout Christendom,
receiving local coloring in their passage from land to
land.   Episodes from the old series were worked up
into distinct poems.   Versions in prose and versions
in verse, versions abridged and versions expanded to
wearying length were made ; but every version found
willing listeners and willing readers.   The makers of
the new versions seldom improved upon the old
poems.   They made up for their insipidity of style
by the introduction of scandalous and immoral incidents.   In France they received their death-blow
from a satire which combines the grossest immorality with the most delicate sentiment, *Géant Gargantua et son fils Pantagruel.*   Rabelais not only bur-
lesques the romances of chivalry, but he throws a

lurid light upon all phases of the society of his day, lashing it pitilessly, exposing it mercilessly. In England romances received a check from Puritanism, the verdict of which may be summed up in the words of Roger Ascham, when speaking of the *Morte d' Arthur* : "The whole pleasure of which book standeth in two special points, in open manslaughter and bold bawdrie."*

Spenser in his *Faerie Queen*, attempted to reconstruct the Arthurian cycle in a Protestant sense. But he lost its Catholic and mediæval meaning, and saw in it only an agreeable manual of etiquette and good behavior. He never achieved his design. A laudation of Queen Elizabeth ; descriptions, graphic and terribly real of the suffering and persecuted Irish peasantry among whom he had lived ; a defence of the execution of Mary Queen of Scots : an idealized sketch of Protestantism in the person o. Jn such are the results ; his magnificent tragmen: stands like a broken shaft marking the grave of knight-errantry. Tennyson has in our own day selected and strung together out of the Arthurian cycle some of the most precious pearls of song in the English language. In the *Idylls of the King*, he has partially reproduced some notes and traits of the spirit of simple faith and childlike credulity in which these romances were first conceived, though the spirit itself he could not restore ; still, his exquisite art has enabled him to raise the legends up into the higher sphere of symbolism—

"New-old, and shadowing sense at war with soul —"

and to give them a many-sided meaning, whereby we may still learn from them the lesson that perfect good is to be obtained only by bearing down before

* *The Scholemaster.*

us pride and selfishness, and by conquering all-de-
stroying sin.

In Spain these romances were translated, imitated,
and adapted to the national genius. Some of them
abound in delicate sentiment, a high standard of
honor and a spirit of generosity.* For centuries
they were passionately read by the Spanish people.
They even became the guides of their lives. Their
scenes were enacted. No royal festival was complete without its tournament and its accompanying
pageant filled up with deeds of knight-errantry. "Indeed," says Ticknor, "the passion for such fictions
was so great, and seemed so dangerous, that in 1553,
they were prohibited from being printed, sold, or
read in the American colonies; and in 1555, the
Cortes earnestly asked that the same prohibition
might be extended to Spain itself, and that all the
extant copies of romances of chivalry might be pub-
licly burned."† But in another fifty years, there was
no need of an imperial decree. A greater power
gave them their death-blow. In 1605, Cervantes
published *Don Quixote.* The first and last words of
the author are that he wrote the book with the intention of demolishing the whole machinery of chev-
alresque romances, and he flattered himself that were
he to succeed his would be no small achievement.‡
He succeeded. Clemencin says that after 1605, no
new works in chivalry were published, and old ones
ceased to be printed; * and from that time to the

* Villemain, *Littérature au Moyen Age,* t. i., p. 222.
† *History of Spanish Literature,* vol. i., p. 227.
‡ *Don Quixote,* P. I. pref. P. II., ch. lxxiv.
§ Pref. p. xxi.

present day "they have been constantly disappearing until they are now among the rarest of literary curiosities." *

Cervantes is a great literary artist. The whole force of the Spanish language is embodied in his master-piece. † The book contains simple amusement for youth, and profound thought for old age. It is especially to be commended for the pleasant manner in which it brushed away an evil, without destroying with it either morality, religion, or the wholesome customs of society. It is innocent ; it is amusing ; it is serious ; it is a most accurate picture of the customs and manners of Spain in the sixteenth century ; it is with all people—and deservedly so— a standing monument of allusion and a common source of quotation. In its philosophical aspect, it represents the shock received by aspiration and daydream, when unprepared they come in contact with the prosaic realities of life. From *Don Quixote* the general mind has learned the lesson that in this work-a-day world romancing is for the imagination alone. Henceforth the Carlovingian and Arthurian cycles— the feats of Alexander and Amadis as well—cease to live, and to-day they are the literary fossils from which we are enabled to reconstruct past epochs of thought.

X.—THE SCHOOLMEN.

Side by side with these streams of song flowed other and more serious currents of thought. At th· very time that bards were embodying the traditions

* Ticknor : Hist. Sp. Lit., vol. ii., p. 140.
† Cantù : Hist. Univ. t. xv, p. 545.

of nations into poetic cycles, and jongleurs were singing them to the accompaniment of harp or viol before the people assembled in the market-place, or in baronial hall before the household of the castle near by, Anselm was anticipating the philosophic problems of Descartes in his *Proslogium ;* Bernard in honied words was singing the sweetness of the Holy Name of Jesus, and in homily and sermon building up the edifice of Christian doctrine and Christian practice, and the Hugos of St. Victor's were inditing their beautiful works on the spiritual life.

But that which occupied the mediæval mind in an especial manner was philosophy. It was particularly studied as the handmaid of the all-absorbing idea of the age—Religion. It is a mistake to consider Scholasticism as a tissue of hair-splittings. Nominalism and Realism had more than words at their foundation. They involved doctrines. The people were aware of their importance ; for we read that Roscelin, the champion of Nominalism, was compelled to retract his errors to preserve himself from their fury.* Religion was their passion, and anything bearing on religion they took interest in. Had these disputes been idle subtleties, as represented by modern philosophers, they would not have created the commotions they did. †

* "Le chanoine de Complègne, mandé au concile de Soissons (1092), y rétracta ses erreurs, pour se soustraire à la fureur du peuple."—BARBE, *Cours de Philosophie,* p. 655.

† It is a mistake to assert, as Mr. Mill does, that the Church imposed Realism "as a religious duty in the Middle Ages." When William of Champeaux asserted that humanity was the essence of each human individual, the Church did not impose it "as a religious duty in the Middle Ages." And Gilbert de la Porée, though a realist, was condemned.

But Scholasticism, from the ninth to the thirteenth centuries, was only fragmentary. There was mingled with it a strange jargon of Arabic, Judaic, and Grecian philosophy; and while it was dwindling to nothingness in the hands of the orthodox by their vain disputations, the scoffers at Christianity were weaving out of it a network of objections in which to ensnare the unwary. A master-mind was needed to sift the grain from the chaff, and gather in the whole in one grand system with a bearing and significancy that should place it beyond cavil. That master-mind appeared in the person of St. Thomas Aquinas. He brings to his task a genius labor-loving, well trained in all the learning of the age, intimate with the Scriptures, versed in the early Fathers, and complete master of the subject-matter he undertakes to arrange and systematize.* He is an independent thinker,

* "Thomas," says Leo XIII., "gathered together their doctrines like the scattered limbs of a body, and moulded them into a whole. He arranged them in so wonderful an order, and increased them with such great additions, that rightly and deservedly he is reckoned a singular safeguard and glory of the Catholic Church. His intellect was docile and subtle; his memory was ready and tenacious; his life was most holy; and he loved the truth alone. Greatly enriched as he was with the science of God and the science of man, he is likened to the sun; for he warmed the whole earth with the fire of his holiness, and filled the whole earth with the splendor of his teaching. There is no part of philosophy which he did not handle with acuteness and solidity. He wrote about the laws of reasoning; about God and incorporeal substances; about man and other things of sense; and about human acts and their principles. What is more, he wrote on these subjects in such a way, that in him not one of the following perfections is wanting: A full selection of subjects; a beautiful arrangement of their divisions; the best method of treating them; certainty of principles; strength

but he is no innovator.   He accepts what the learning
of the age provides for him, and makes the best of it.
He finds Aristotle in possession, and he builds upon
him.   How magnificently, is known only to him
who has pondered over the *Summa*, and realized the
depth of thought, clearness of arrangement, and brilliant conceptions of which it is the embodiment.*
And not the least source of amazement is the decision
with which the almost inspired author touches upon

of argument; perspicuity and propriety in language; and the
power of explaining deep mysteries.

Beside these questions and the like, the Angelic Doctor, in his
speculations, drew certain philosophical conclusions as to the
reasons and principles of created things. These conclusions have
the very widest reach, and contain, as it were, in their bosom the
seeds of truth wellnigh infinite in number. These have to be unfolded
with most abundant fruits in their own time by the teachers who
come after him. As he used his method of philosophizing not only
in teaching the truth, but also in refuting error, he has gained
this prerogative for himself,—with his own hand he vanquished all
errors of ancient times ; and still he supplies an armory of weap-
ons, which brings us certain victory in the conflict with falsehoods
ever springing up in the course of years. Moreover, carefully dis-
tinguishing reason from faith, as is right, and yet joining them together in a harmony of friendship, he so guarded the rights of each,
and so watched over the dignity of each, that, as far as man is concerned, reason can now hardly rise higher than she rose, borne up in
the flight of Thomas ; and faith can hardly gain more helps and
greater helps from reason than those which Thomas gave her.—
Encyl. *Æterni Patris*, 1879.

* "The master work of St. Thomas is the famous summation,
Summa Theologiæ, which is one of the greatest monuments of the
human mind in the Middle Ages, and comprehends, with metaphysics, an entire system of morality, and even of politics; and that kind
of politics, too, which is not at all servile."—COUSIN, *Hist. Mod.
Phil.*, tr. by O. W. Wight.

questions that are at present agitating men's minds, but which were then mere germs in the womb of thought.*

The Scholastic philosophy is said to be dead. It is dead only to those who refuse to study it and to recognize its vitality. It still lives in theology and in the dogmatic teachings of Catholicity. When we speak of the matter and form of the sacraments, and define the soul as "the form of the body," we are using language intelligible only in the light of the Aristotelian method. The two fundamental doctrines of Scholasticism are, the principle of matter and form, and the maxim, "there is nothing in the intellect which is not first in the senses." This latter principle must not be confounded with Sensism, for the Scholastics imposed a different meaning upon it. By it they wished to express the fact that sensation awakens the dormant faculties and trains the intellect, and that through the senses we have all our knowledge of external objects. They also admitted first principles or axioms—self-evident truths—independent of all external objects, and thus drew a broad line of distinction between themselves and the Sensists.

It is fashionable for a certain class of scientists to sneer at what they consider the stupidity of those who would earnestly discuss the doctrine of "matter and form," as well as at the simplicity of the Church that would impose upon modern intelligences dogmas framed on that doctrine. They call it a thing

* *e. g.* Prima Para., quaests. xlv., lxvii. art. iv. ; quaests. lxxi., lxxii., art. i. *on Creation and Genesis of the Species.* Also Prima Pars., quaest xviii., arts. ii., iii., and iv., *on Life.*

obsolete. Now, as the doctrine was originally one
of physics, let us examine it in the light of the last
word of physical science.

With Aristotle, matter is not an aggregate of atoms ;
it is by itself a mere potentiality—a principle of all
bodies—which, combined with form, gives them
actuality.* Modern science teaches, with Boscovitch
and Leibnitz, that all matter consists of indivisible
and inextended atoms, endowed with forces that are
attractive and repulsive, according to the distances at
which they act ;† that is, that matter is nothing without force. Thus, both Scholastic and modern scien-
tist are agreed that matter by itself is not a reality,
and that it is determined by something distinct. "It
is manifest," says St. Thomas, "that every actual
existence has some form, and thus its matter is
determined by its form."‡ And Faraday is with
him. He says : "We know matter only by its
forces."§ Evidently, the "force" of one is the
"form" of the other. Now, we are convinced beyond a shadow of doubt that—except as regards
purely spiritual forms, as the soul—modern science,
when it understands itself, and Scholastic philosophy
are in harmony.

The primary idea of the Scholastic "form" is ac-

* *Naturalis Auscultationis*, lib. i., cap. ix., 5; *Metaphysicorum*
lib. vii. cap. vi. 8.

† Bartlett, *Analytical Mechanics*, p. 17. Leibnitz, De primæ
philosophiæ emendatione et notione substantiæ—Opera, t. v., pp. 9,
375.

‡ "Manifestum est quod omne existens in actu habet aliquam
formam, et sic materia ejus est determinata per formam." *Summa*,
p. 1, quæst. vii., art. ii.

§ *The Conservation of Physical Force.*

tivity.   It determines the species and the kingdoms in Nature — now arranging the crystalline
structure, now appearing as the vital principle
in vegetable matter, now as the soul of brutes,
everywhere an energizing activity.   This view coincides with Grove's definition of force.   He calls
it "that active principle inseparable from matter
which is supposed to induce its various changes."[*]
To illustrate : Oxygen and hydrogen combine in cer
tain proportions and produce an entirely new substance, water.   In Scholastic phraseology there is
here a new activity, that is, the form of water.   But
modern science also recognizes a new chemical
force, acting in the combining of the elements so as
to produce water.   This force was not created; it
was simply revived, having been dormant in the
elements, and awaiting the occasion of their union.
Neither does the Scholastic philosopher conceive the
form to have been created ; it was potentially in the
matter ; "for matter," according to St. Thomas, "before receiving its form is capable of receiving many
forms ;"[†] that is, they exist in it potentially.   Even
when the form passes away, it is not said to be anni-
hilated ; it is only re-immersed in its subject, just as
it is the general opinion of advanced scientists that
no force is destroyed, that it is simply changed to
some other, as chemical force to heat force, and that
its sum is a constant quantity.[‡]   Thus we find the

[*] *Correlation of Physical Forces*, p. 19.—ED. YOUMANS.

[†] "Materia quidem per formam, inquantum materia, antequam
recipiat formam est in potentia ad multas formas." *Summa.* p. 1,
qu. 7, art. i.

[‡] This implies no sanction of the materialistic doctrine of the eternity of matter and of force.   Each is a product of the creative act.

Aristotelian "form" and the modern "force" convertible. Therefore Dr. Mayer has actually defined forces as forms. "They are," he says, "different forms under which one and the same object makes its appearance."* Here is an act of reparation, complete as it is deserving, paid to the injured genius of Scholasticism by modern science, unintentional though it be.

For centuries, the mediæval intelligence revolved upon the hinges of these two principles, and it seemed as though in them it had found its limit. It is the general history of thought. The popular mind is slow in realizing an idea. It were therefore unphilosophic to blame any one period for that which is a law of all periods. We are told of each of God's works that after it had been created, "He saw that it was good." The reptile was good as well as the bird of the air ; the blade of grass as well as the light that gave it beauty. He despised nothing that came forth at His creative words. The human intellect is also His creature. He determined its laws of operation. They are not, therefore, to be depreciated. Neither is Scholasticism, one of their most glorious products, to be despised. It is good. It has its own functions. It is a link in the evolution of thought. It built up Christian theology on a scientific basis ; it fixed the precision of terms ; it imposed this precision on the new languages that were then about to become the vehicles of national literatures. It is good, that period of syllogizing. It held the influx of materialism at bay ; it carefully watched over the sacred

* *The Mechanical Equivalent of Heat,* YOUMAN'S ED., p. 346.

fires burning at the shrine of learning, until in the march of society greater facilities were brought within the reach of men to satisfy their eagerness to know. It is good, that intellectual bridge between the ancient and the modern world. The shade of Vergil walks across it, and leaves his mantle of inspiration to Dante.

Dante is the poet of Scholasticism. In his sublime allegory—*La Divina Commedia*—he has caught up and crystallized the spirit of the Middle Ages. Their philosophy, their politics, their religion, their aspirations are immortalized in its amber pages. He is the poet of Catholicity. The elevation of his genius places him above all parties. A fierce, unyielding Ghibelline, he reproves both Guelf and Ghibelline.* An enemy of the Temporal Power, he speaks of it with respect and veneration.† Though he uses the myths of antiquity, still their subordination to the eminently Christian spirit of his poem, and especially the mystical flights of the *Paradiso*, show how Christianity was becoming more and more part and parcel of the mediæval intelligence. His lines, written with unparalleled vigor and terseness, bear profound significancy. If Shakespeare is the poet of humanity, Dante is the poet of thought.‡

* Si che'è forte a veder qual più si falli.—*Par.*, vi. 102.
So that 'tis hard to see who most offends.—*Cary.*

† Thus he says that Rome and the Roman empire

> Fur stabilite per lo loco santo
> U siede il successor del maggior Piero.
>
> Established were to be the Holy Place,
> Where sits enthroned great Peter's princely race.

Inf., ii. 23-4.

‡ In *Thought and Culture*, (chap. v.) the reader will find treated at greater length the spiritual sense and the central idea of the *Divina Commedia*.

XI.—The Mystics.

But Scholasticism is only one phase of mediæval thought. Many a learned mind, wearied with the disputes of the schools, sought refuge in Mysticism. This was especially the case in the fourteenth century, after St. Thomas had put the last hand to Scholastic philosophy. Had some of those reactionary minds been two centuries later, they would have retired into themselves and lived sceptics. But theirs was still an age of faith and religious fervor, and they were not disposed to question the foundations of all knowledge, and summarize everything said or written into a "What know I?" They rather sought in the affections of the heart directed to the supremely Good, and in the contemplation of the perfectly Beautiful, the infinitely True that their philosophy too dimly revealed.

Mysticism has had at all times attraction for the human mind. It has created the Yogi of India and the hermit of the Thebaid. Both seek "vision by means of a higher light, and action under higher freedom."* But outside of Christianity, Mysticism generally ends in pantheism, immorality, and inaction. Christianity, by presenting for contemplation the sacred Humanity of the Redeemer, places the only safe barrier to its abuse. The soul leaves reason and imagination behind, forgets itself, and all its faculties become entirely absorbed in the contemplation of the Divinity. In such a state it is only the greatest purity of life, a total detachment from things earthly, that can save

* This is Görres' definition of Mysticism.

it from illusion. **Imagine an age with aspirations**
for a more intimate acquaintance with the infinite
truth than books could impart. Such was the fourteenth century. The Mysticism of Italy at this
period was Platonic, and therefore ideal. It was a
learned mysticism. But in Germany, along the banks
of the Rhine, it became the passion of the people.
They flocked by thousands to hear Henry Suso and
the celebrated Tauler. They received, remembered,
and reported the words of these two great men with
respect and veneration. They practised their counsels. Religious confraternities were formed, headed
no longer by clergy, but by pious laymen. Tauler
himself, in his mystical life, was the disciple of such
a layman—the one that organized the society of the
Friends of God. From this society emanated that
flower of mystical life—the book of the *Imitation of
Christ*—the unadulterated product of the spirit of
Christianity, written with that characteristic simplicity
and dignity that belong only to the sacred Scriptures.
Its fundamental doctrine is that God alone is worthy
of the intelligence, life, and aspirations of man.*
" O Truth, my God," exclaims the simple-hearted
author, " make me one with Thee in everlasting love.
I am wearied with often reading and hearing many
things ; in Thee is all that I will or desire. Let
all teachers hold their peace ; let all creatures be silent
in Thy sight : speak Thou alone to me!"† Such is
the spirit in which this book is written. Faith before
reason, love before understanding, good life before
fine words : these are the mottoes in which it every-

---

* Bk. i., ch. i.   † Bk. i., ch. iii.

where abounds, and on which it not unfrequently is profound, mystical, and eloquent.*

XII.—MIRACLE-PLAYS AND MORALITIES.

Somewhat earlier than the time of appearance of this work, the influence of the Holy Scriptures became manifest in the mysteries or miracle-plays and moralities that were popular throughout Christendom. They consisted of some mystery or parable of Scripture dramatized for the purpose of instructing the people in a pleasing manner, and initiating them into the spirit of the festivals which the Church celebrated. Few among them could read and study the explanations of the festivals, but all could take in and appreciate what was placed before their eyes. Hence the popularity of these plays. They are the originals of the modern drama. It is the common history of all dramatic poetry. "A tragedy was a religious festival,"† says Villemain, speaking of Grecian literature. "The English drama," says Richard Grant White, "like the Greek, has a purely religious origin." ‡ And Lorinzer says : "Dramatic poetry, in its source, was above all, religious poetry." § The Crusades

* The author has made a fuller analysis of *The Imitation of Christ* in his *Culture of the Spiritual Sense.* This analysis has been quoted at length by Dr. F. R. Cruise, in his admirable book, *Thomas à Kempis.* London, Kegan, Paul & Co., 1887, pp. 13-31. See *Thought and Culture,* chaps. iii, iv.

† Une tragédie était une fête religieuse."—*Littérature Française,* leçon xc.

‡ *The Genius of Shakspeare.*

§ "Die dramatische Poesie in ihrem Ursprung überall eine religiöse war."—*Geistliche Festspiele,* b. i., Vor. s., 43, *et seq.*

helped to render these plays popular. "Those who returned from the Holy Land," says Disraeli, "or other consecrated places, composed canticles of their travels, and amused their religious fancies by inter-weaving scenes of which Christ, the Apostles, and other objects of devotion, served as the themes."*

The great heart of the people yearned to witness them. Confraternities were formed for their com-position and representation, and in the latter the scenic accompaniments were grand and imposing. The student just returned from the university would consider himself honored in seeing his maiden pro-duction placed before the public, as in the case of the unfortunate Chrysostom mentioned in *Don Quixote*— that faithful mirror of the age in which it was written : "I had forgotten to tell you," says the shepherd, "how this Chrysostom deceased was a great hand at composing verses, so much so that he made Christ-mas carols and *Autos* for Corpus Christi, which our young people play ; and everybody says that they could not be beaten." † And Pellicer says that these sacred dramas were in such general favor "that they were not only enacted in the theatres, but separately before the royal court, and even before the head of the Holy Inquisition."

The mediæval bards who wrote these pieces often "builded better than they knew." There is art in their construction ; point, variety, and sentiment are to be found in their language ; even graceful diction is not wanting in their expression. The authors' motives in writing were elevated ; their sub-jects were in themselves grand and inspiring ; the

Curiosities of Literature, ii., p 15.   † Part i., ch. xii.

occasions for which they wrote were worthy of both ; and not unfrequently did they rise to the dignity of both subject and occasion.   With the universal popularity of these plays came their abuse, and they were finally discouraged by the Church.   They are said to be immoral.   Vulgar expressions are to be found in them, especially in the English plays ; but their spirit and scope are invariably moral.   Vulgarity is not immorality, and our standard of propriety is not that of our forefathers.   This is an age of books, and reading has made us so artificial that we are shocked at expressions that passed harmlessly among them. Warton does not find them degrading in tone.   He says : "Rude, and even ridiculous as they were, they softened the manners of the people, by diverting the public attention to spectacles in which the mind was concerned, and by creating a regard for other arts than those of bodily strength and savage valor." They even left their impress on architecture.   All those grotesque figures, now of buffoonery, now of tragedy, in the Gothic cathedrals are drawn from these religious plays.

Not only were the miracle-plays not immoral, but they never did thrive in an immoral atmosphere ; and therefore it is that we find comparatively few in the sunny land of Provence—the land of chivalry, and love, and song, and also the hot-bed of doctrinal novelties and heresies—the stronghold of the Albigenses, Waldenses, and Huguenots.   Not in the soft-flowing verses of the love-sick troubadour, are the great truths of religion sung ; but rather in the more hardy tones of the *langue d'Oil* does the sturdy trouyere, from the fulness of his pious Catholic heart, send forth a flow of well-attuned verses and cleverly adjusted dramas, illustrative of the lives of the saints, the spirit of their religion, the ways of their Saviour, and the perfections of their God. These plays are truly, as Onesime LeRoy remarks, "the religious philosophy of our fathers." *   Their spirit is discernible in the *Divina Commedia*, and they are the inspiration and foundation of the *Paradise Lost.†*

But if these religious plays had produced no other result than to bloom into the *Autos Sacramentales* of Calderon de la Barca (1600–1683), they would deserve well of posterity. These *Autos* are the handiwork of one of the great world-authors. They are stamped with the impress of all time. They are the highest effort of human genius in their artistic presentation of the truths of religion. Under the magic hand of Calderon the whole universe is transfigured. Men and things, history and philosophy, myths and

---

* "La religieuse philosophie de nos pères."—*Études sur les Mystères*, int. vii.

† It is well known that Milton began his *Paradise Lost* as a miracle-play. When the author first approached the subject of miracle-plays, he found every avenue in English literature pronouncing them "rude scenic performances," with Hallam ; or "rude, gross, and childish," with Richard Grant White ; or "rude, and even ridiculous," with Warton. But *à priori* reasons led him to infer that the religion so successful in every other department of art —capable of scoring the Gregorian Chant, of erecting the Gothic cathedral, of dictating the *Divina Commedia*, of inspiring *Paradise Lost*, and of tracing the *Transfiguration* on the canvas—could not, after working for centuries, have produced such barbarous things as these critics represent. Deeper research has proved his inference to be correct.

facts are all transformed and clothed with a spiritual
sense ; the spectator soars above space and time into
the sphere of eternal truth. The very mysteries of
religion are made palpable with consummate art.
Visible form and plastic roundness are given to the
most abstract conceptions. They belong to the same
world of allegory with the great pictures of Titian
and Raphael and Orcagna. In order to appreciate
them we must abandon the present routine of thought
and transport ourselves to the ages of faith in which
their every word bore significancy. Through them
all there runs a central thought ; they have one object, that of paying homage to the Blessed Eucharist.
They were represented before a Catholic people believing in the Real Presence.

Calderon is both poet and priest. All his *Autos* are
built upon that magnificent poem, the beautiful
office in the Roman Breviary for Corpus Christi, composed by St. Thomas. This is the foundation on
which those aërial temples of poesy have been constructed, and therefore it is that they remain such
noble monuments of the philosophic thought, the
theological lore and the plastic genius of the author
who built them up, and of the intense faith of the
people who witnessed them. These plays were accompanied by music and scenes the most gorgeous.
Remembering these things, and noting the ease and
skill with which the poet projects his inmost thought
into outward representation, we must needs marvel
at the power of his genius. It is customary to judge
Calderon by his secular plays. They are the least
part of him. His best work, his most perfect art, he

put into his religious plays. This is evident to any-body who takes the pains to discern their real worth. They stand alone in the whole range of literature. They are the most beautiful wreaths of dramatic art ever woven by human genius to be placed upon the altar before that central fact of Catholicity, the Real Presence. The incidents of the play are not given for their literal worth ; they are so many symbols of higher truths. The long monologues which weary him who has not insight into their bearing, are sublime presentations of the profoundest doctrines and dog-mas of the Church. Indeed, the poet makes use of the symbolism and allegory of the whole universe and its history in order to bring home these great truths to his audience. " We feel," says Baron Von Eichendorff, "that under the terrestrial veil lies silent and asleep the unfathomable song which is the voice of all things, lost as it were, in dreams of unutterable longing; but Calderon speaks the magic word, and the world begins to sing." *

XIII.—THE RENAISSANCE.

IT is customary with a certain class of writers to identify the revival of letters with the downfall of Constantinople. This is a mistake. " It dates at least from the eleventh century, "says Dr. Nevin, "and there is abundance of evidence that the pro-gress made between that and the age of the Refor-mation was quite as real and important as any that has taken place since." † The Church at all times

* *Zur Geschichte des Dramas.* Leipsig, 1854, s. 57.
† *Mercersburg Review*, March, 1857.

encouraged letters, and we can trace the literary tradition in an unbroken line from Boëtius and Cassio-
dorus to Isidore of Seville, from Isidore to Beda,
thence to Alcuin, thence to Scotus Erigena, thence to
Lanfranc and Anselm.   Down the ages it flows clear
and strong. Columbanus, with twelve religious men,
arrives about 590 at the Court of Gontran, and recommends the reading of the ancient poets as well as of the
Early Fathers.* About the same time Virgilius Maro
teaches grammar in Toulouse, and organizes a school
of esoteric Latinity which exercises a baneful influence on style for centuries after.†

Women vie with men in the pursuit of learning.
St. Lioba, a kinswoman of St. Boniface, instructs her
nuns in the convent of Bischofsheim.   Their reputa-
tion extends far and wide. They are in great demand,
and there are few religious houses in their day that
did not have some of them as teachers.   St. Melanie
transcribes manuscripts with ease, grace and correctness.   The nuns of the convent of St. Cesar's become no less famous for their excellent penman-
ship. ‡ Adelaide of Luxembourg, leaving the chapel
after matins, goes to warm the feet of the children
who are cold, and caresses those who answer her
questions in grammar correctly. §   The incident
speaks volumes. In the tenth century St. Hrosvitha, ab-

* Columbanus ad Hunoldum. Usher: Epist. Hibern. Sylloge.
† The works of Virgilius were published by Cardinal Mai :
Classicorum auctorum e Vaticanis codicibus editorum. t. v., Roma,
1833. For an account of his school see Ozanam : *Etudes ger-
maniques*, pp. 480, sqq.
‡ Mabillon : *Etudes Monastiques*, Paris, 1691, p. 39.
§ Acta SS. O. S. B., t. viii., p. 128.

bess of the convent of Gandesheim, composes plays full of bold thought and striking scenes, and not altogether lacking in literary polish. We find in them wit and humor and pathos. The innocent mirth and laughter lurking in her pages still resound in our ears. Hers are no dead pages ; they are instinct with life ; love's throbbings still palpitate beneath her lines, and in more respects than one has she anticipated the modern drama.* The theme into which she has especially poured her soul is the triumph of chastity. Bruno, Archbishop of Cologne, brought artists and professors from Constantinople. To some of these learned men did St. Hrotsvitha submit her compositions, and from them she received encouragement to give them to the public. She believed herself imitating Terence, but she was anticipating Racine.†

In this century Irish monks flock to the continent, build monasteries, reclaim whole tracts of wilderness, found towns and cities, open schools and become the schoolmasters of the West. "Shall I speak of Ireland," says an eye-witness, "which, despising the perils of the sea, has almost wholly emigrated upon our shores with its herd of philosophers ?" ‡ And of the latter part of this same century, which is usually designated as the iron age, Meiners says : "In no age, perhaps, did Germany possess more

* Compare the tomb scene in *Callimachus* of Hrotsvitha with the tomb scene in *Romeo and Juliet* of Shakespeare.

† Charles Magnin, *Théâtre de Hrotsvitha.* Paris, 1845 ; Chasles *Revue des Deux Mondes,* 1845, p. 708.

‡ Heiric of Auxerre, Epist. dedicat. ad Carolum. Vita S. Germani. Patrologia, vol. cxxiv., col. 1133.

learned and virtuous churchmen of the episcopal order than in the latter half of the tenth and beginning of the eleventh century." * The name of Gerbert is enough to redeem the age from the imputation of midnight darkness. As Pope Sylvester II., he was the patron of learning and science, and established chairs of mathematics, astronomy, and geography. † "The eleventh century," says Renan, "had witnessed in philosophy, in poetry, in architecture, a renaissance such as humanity has seldom remembered."‡ With the advance of time, a thirst for learning increased. The lecture rooms could not contain the throngs that assembled to hear great teachers. Abelard counted his audience by thousands. Albertus Magnus was compelled to lecture in the public square that still bears his name.§ Students sat in the streets on litters of hay and straw discussing their themes or listening to their masters. ‖ They travelled from afar, gave up all the luxuries of home, and turned valets, that they might acquire an education.¶ Schools for the poor were especially attended to. The poor scholar was held in honor. Masters gave him their cast-off clothing. Sometimes,

---

* Quoted in Hallam, *Literature of Europe*, vol. i., p. 31.

† It is erroneously stated that Gerbert studied with the Arabs at Cordova; he studied with Hatton, Bishop of Vich, in Catalonia. Richer, *Hist.* lib iii. cap. 43.

‡ *Revue des Deux Mondes*, t. xl. p. 203.

§ The *Place Maubert*, i. e. *Maitre Albert*.

‖ This is the tradition that accounts for the name of the *Rue du Fouarre* in Paris.

¶ The custom was still prevalent at Salamanca in the 18th century.

in order to make a living and to study, he swept rooms, or copied books, or if he was possessed of a good voice, he sang in the streets for the common amusement.* The Councils of the Church—those landmarks of civilization—from the beginning, decree that every church that has the means, provide a master for the gratuitous instruction of the poor "according to the ancient customs." That of Lateran, in 1180, says that the Church of God, "like a dutiful mother," being bound to provide for the indigent in soul as well as in body, to every church shall be attached a master to instruct the poor gratuitously.† Innocent III., in 1215, reiterates the same decree.‡ The study of languages was encouraged. The Council of Vienne, in 1311, decreed that the Hebrew, Arabic and Chaldaic tongues be taught wherever the Roman Court was held,§ as well as in the universities of Paris, Oxford, Salamanca and Bologna ; and that two professor-

* De Disciplina Scholarum, cap. iv. p. 980. This book was attributed to Boëtius. Roger Bacon quotes it ; but it does not date earlier than 1200.

† "Quoniam Ecclesía Dei et in iis quæ spectant ad subsidium corporis, et in iis quæ ad profectum veniunt animarum, indigentibus sicut pia mater providere tenetur : ne pauperibus, qui parentum opibus juvare non possunt, legendi, et proficiendi opportunitas subtrahetur, per unamquamque Ecclesiam cathedralem magistro, qui Clericus ejusdem Ecclesiæ et scholares pauperes gratis doceat, competens aliquod beneficium assignetur, quo docentis necessitas sublevetur, et discentibus via pateat ad doctrinam."—*Concil. Lateran.*, sub. Alex. III., cap. xviii.

‡ *Concil. Lateran.*, sub. Innocent. III., cap. ii., *De Magistris Scholasticis.*

§ It was then held at Avignon ; Clement V. was the reigning Pope.

ships of each language be established and maintained at the expense of the bishops and the Pope in each of these universities, except that of Paris, the expenses of which the King was to defray. Though such wholesome decrees were not always responded to as cordially as could be wished, they still prove that the Church fostered learning in all classes, noble as well as peasant.*

The Renaissance, then, is not one of letters. It is of another stamp. The spirit that animated Roscelin and Abelard, that flowed down the ages in undercurrents, and appeared in the Cathari and Paterini, in the Lollards and the Hussites, and perpetuated itself through the channels of secret societies, now rose to the surface, and became the predominant spirit of the age. It is the spirit of rationalism. In 1326 Massiglio of Padua caught up the whole spirit, and embodied it in his book *Defensor Pacis.* Therein he advocates the supremacy of State over Church and family, regards Holy Writ as the sole foundation of faith, considers all priests equal, and the primacy a matter of convenience that might be changed. In the fifteenth century, this spirit assumed the shape of enthusiasm for the pagan ideal. Petrarch (1304-1374) had thrown the whole vigor of his poetic soul into the study and diffusion of Latin and Greek let-

* That expression said to be found on mediæval documents— " This one being a nobleman, attests his inability to sign his name," —is a piece of exaggeration and historical formalism. See Maitland's *Dark Ages,* p. 9, *et seq.*

The reader will find a more detailed account of mediæval learning and mediæval schools in Kenelm Digby's grea* work : *Mores Catholici ; or Ages of Faith,* bk. iii. chaps. v., vi.

ters. Men without his genius imbibed his enthusiasm
for literature, and grew blind in their admiration not
only for the authors of Greece and Rome, but even
for every non-Christian writer. Petrarch tells us
that they did not think that they had done anything
for philosophy, unless they had barked at Christ and
the supernaturalness of His doctrine. Averroës they
placed above the Fathers and Apostles. Thus one
of Petrarch's friends says to him on occasion of his
having quoted St. Paul: "You still hold to your
Christian religion; I don't believe a word of it. Your
Paul, your Augustine, and all those you so extol,
were great babblers; and could you only bear the
reading of Averroës, you would soon perceive how
much superior he is to those jesters of yours."*

Later the Humanists are intoxicated with Plato.
Marsilius Ficino keeps a lamp before his bust,† and
is said to have addressed the people: "Beloved in
Plato." His name sounded sweeter to the ear than
that of the Saviour. His writings were cherished

* "Egli [Petrarca] se ne duole spesso nelle sue opere, e fra
l'altre cose racconta ciò che gli avenne in Venizia (*Senil.*, L. 5, ep.
3) quando venuto a trovarlo nella sua biblioteca un di colori i quali,
com' egli dice, *secondo il costume de' moderni filosofi pensano di non
aver fatto nulla, se non abbaiano contro di Cristo e della sovrumana
di lui dottrina,* costui prese a deriderlo e ad insultarlo, perche nel
parlare avea usato di qualche detto dell' Apostolo Paolo; *Tien tu
pure,* disse egli al Petrarca, *la tua Religione cristiana : nulla di
tutto ciò io credo. Il tuo Paolo, il tuo Agostino e tutti coloro che
tanto esalti, furone uomini loquacissimi. Cosi potessi tu sostenere
la lettura di Averroe, tu ben vedresti quanto egli sia maggiore di
cotesti tuoi gioccoliere.*"— TIRABOSCHI, *Storia della Letteratura
Italiana,* lib. secondo, vol. v., p. 282-3.

† Cesar Cantù, vol. xv., p. 8.

more than the Gospel.   Men imagined that they had found the whole scheme of Christianity in his pages. The simplicity of the sacred writings grew distasteful to them.   Cardinal Bembo writes to Sadoleto not to read the epistles of St. Paul, lest their style corrupt his taste. *   Upon the fall of Constantinople (1453), the presence of Greek scholars among them added more fuel to their enthusiasm.   Their academies fostered an anti-Christian spirit, and yearned for pagan freedom ; and some of them were known to have revived the worship of Madre Natura.   Their language was considered elegant only in proportion as it was enveloped in mythological allusion.   The epoch was a partial reversion to the nature-worship and love of the sensuous, always characteristic of the Aryan race. All this effort to revive a bygone spirit caused literary men to lose the real spirit of their own times, and the cold literalness of their imitation was destructive of native genius.   The religious influence that for ten centuries had been gradually gaining ground began to be weakened, reason began to revolt against faith, though both, proceeding from the same Divine Author, are not, and cannot be contradictory ; and the harmony that was being consummated between the secular and clerical elements of society was changed to discord.

That is the more perfect society which is best in accordance with the nature of things.   In the Mind of their Divine Author, faith is intrinsically-superior to reason, grace to nature, the supernatural to the

* And he adds : Omitte has nugas ; non enim decent gravem virum tales ineptiae. See Cantù, vol. xiv., p. 442.

natural. The society in which this order obtains is the one best in accordance with the nature of things, and is therefore the most perfect. Now this is what society was coming to in the Middle Ages, and the checking of this tendency, the estrangement of the two orders, the natural and the supernatural, and the initiation of a revolt of one against the other, are among the most baneful effects of the Renaissance. It turned the destiny of society from its natural course. It induced universal indifferentism—indifferentism influenced by a spirit of rapacity in England, by a spirit of cupidity and immorality in Germany, and by a spirit of philosophical speculation in Italy. In their hearts' core, the literary men of Italy were Catholic ; their indifferentism was affected, because it was the fashion ; but it blinded them to the real dangers of the age. They trifled when they should have been serious. But the people were still sincere in their faith and piety.

Such was the state of affairs among the literary circles of Italy, when there came among them a young monk from Germany, simple and unsophisticated, and though lacking discrimination, still possessed of quick perception. He enters Rome, and is astonished at the enthusiasm with which fragments of an antique statue are triumphantly paraded through the streets ; he is horrified at the pæans that are sung upon their discovery. He comes in contact with some of the literary men ; he hears them converse : their language is almost unintelligible to him—it is the language of pagan Rome. He is shocked at the familiarity with which holy things are treated ; he finally wonders if he is not in dreamland, carried far back on the stream of time to the days of Augustus, surrounded by just enough of Christianity to give his dream still more the appearance of reality. Young Luther returns to his native land, and broods over the words he heard and the scenes he witnessed, until a chain of circumstances places him in position to make use of his recollections ; and, entrenching himself in faith alone as the key to salvation, by the fire of his eloquence he sets aglow the mass of corruption and dissatisfaction he found in Germany. Luther was the most remarkable man of his age. He had all the versatility of character to be the chief instrument of circumstances in the religious movement then afoot. He knew at the same time how to flatter the people and to pay court to the great. He made a deep impression upon letters. His translation of the Scriptures did as much for the formation of style in German literature, as did King James's version for English letters. But what influence did the Reformation have upon letters ?

CHAPTER VIII.

LITERATURE AND THE REFORMATION.

THE sixteenth century was a transition period. Men's minds were in fermentation on all subjects. The aspects of society were changing. The Crusades were past, and the Crusaders had brought with them from the East many an intellectual novelty. The press had been invented, and reading-matter was disseminated more freely among the peo-

ple. The New World had been discovered, and every day accounts were coming from it that exceeded the brightest dreams of wonderland. Monks, not a few, had lost the primitive spirit of their institution, and lay an incubus on society. "Monasteries," says Cæsar Cantù, "formerly active centres of thought and of the fine arts, were plunged into the torpor of old age and the remissness of opulence." *
The clergy loved their own ease too well ; they were too great pleasure-seekers and gold-coveters to attend to their flocks with that pastoral spirit of simplicity and good faith that is to be witnessed in the Church to-day. The bishops were no better. They looked for emoluments and court favor. Even the better class of ecclesiastics gave themselves up to the intellectual luxury of admiring Plato and imitating Cicero.

While a general laxity of morals in all orders of religious life—among priest and monk, pope and cardinal—was bringing odium on the Church, and weakening her hold upon the people—especially upon the Teutonic races—the seeds of regeneration were germinating in her own body. She was even then the mother of sanctity. A host of great saints, both men and women, arose— Loyola (1491-1556), Peter of Alcantara (1499-1562), Teresa of Jesus (1515-

* *Histoire Universelle*, t. xv., l. xv., ch. xvi., p. 11. In which chapter the reader will find this outline more fully and masterly traced. See also ch. xix., pp. 89, 90. See also Janssen's great work, *Geschichte des Deutschen Volkes seit dem Ausgang des Mittelalters*. Freiburg, 1887, Bände i, vi. This historical monument of vast erudition, patient research, and impartial judgment, supersedes all other works on the period of the Reformation in Germany. In studying the Reformation in England, consult Father Bridgett's *Life of the Blessed John Fisher*, 1888; *Queen Elizabeth and the Catholic Hierarchy*, by Bridgett and Knox, 1889. Father Gasquet, *Henry VIII. and the English Monasteries*, 2 vols., London, 1889, and S. Hubert Burke's *Historical Portraits*. 4 vols.

1582), Philip Neri (1513-1595), Charles Boromeo
(1538-1584)—all representatives of large classes of
equally holy persons,—and all of them sincerely
and energetically put their hands to the work of reform.   New religious orders were founded, and old
ones reformed.   The spirit of primitive Christianity
became once more the animating principle of religious congregations ; and the bright flame of charity
and zeal with which they were enkindled spread
among the people and ascended to the high places in
the Church.   The Council of Trent sealed the good
work.   The Catholic hierarchy at last realized that
with themselves should begin the reformation they
would see established ; they therefore pronounced
the most withering denunciations upon the clerical
and religious abuses of the day.

In the meantime, all this laxity had fostered the spirit
of rationalism ; and Luther, when most vehemently
throwing himself behind the ramparts of faith alone
and the Bible, was a rationalist so long as he undertook to take revelation apart, to examine it piece-
meal, and to accept and reject at will whatever suited
him.   Revelation must be taken in its entirety, or rejected altogether.   Human reason cannot logically
constitute itself judge of the supernatural, for the
supernatural is beyond its sphere of reckoning. In at-
tempting to do so, it is no longer calm reason ; it is
blind rationalism ; it is reason intoxicated.   And such
in its effect is the principle of private judgment
that was at the foundation of the new religion.
Blacksmiths left their anvils, and shoemakers their
lasts, to preach the new inspiration they had re-

ceived. For the first time in the world's history was the spectacle presented of a religion without an altar, a self-constituted priesthood, and a faith in mystery subjected to reason. This is the philosophy of the Reformation. It is the religious current of rationalism.

Now, the spirit of rationalism invariably tends to break away from the moorings of tradition, from all that goes to make up the past glory of a people, and dwell alone in the self-sufficiency of its own cold reasonings. It can destroy, but it never builds up; it can teach man his rights, but it forgets his duties; it can dethrone one ruler, only to set up a thousand despotisms in his stead. It feeds principally on dreams and abstractions, and is the sport of imagination, even when loudest in its appeal to reason; it is crossed in the world of reality, and frustrated in its designs; for man, being a creature of education, cannot forget in a day what he has spent centuries in learning. It contemns, ignores, desecrates the old, and pays homage to the new. A spirit possessed of these characteristics is unable to inspire a literary master-piece. Recall the eighteenth century. It is the embodiment of philosophical and political rationalism. It has given us the materialism of Locke and Abbé Condillac, and the giant efforts of the cyclopædists; but in all that the century has of its own, we perceive few influences favorable to literature.† The

---

* Les influences qui dominent la littérature du XVIIIe siècle sont, au contraire, la philosophie sceptique, l'imitation des littératures modernes, et la réforme politique.—VILLEMAIN, *Littérature au XVIIIe Siècle*, t. i., p. 2.

master genius of the age writes tragedy ; but it is noteworthy that he forgets his hostility to Christianity, and once more resumes the chain of traditions ; it is no longer Voltaire the sophist ; it is the docile child of humanity, repeating in his own way the language that humanity has known from the beginning.

Thus considering the historical significancy of the Reformation as the religious current of rationalism, we would be led to conclude summarily that it is composed of elements better suited to the retarding of society than to its advancement. But thought has been developed since the sixteenth century. Let us not commit ourselves to the sophism, *post hoc, ergo propter hoc.* Let us examine the Reformation in its nature, in its relations, and in its results, and see if it possesses any new element capable of fostering letters and intellectual development.

1. The Reformation in its nature was not favorable to literature. It added no new idea to thought. It asserted no positive doctrine that had not been previously professed. It simply denied certain parts that had as much authority for their belief as those it retained. But negation is not productive. It ends in nihilism.

2. The Reformation in its relations is unfavorable to letters. By the illogical habits of mind it begets, it is ruinous to thought. For example, it bases belief on the Scriptures alone, and professes to throw tradition overboard ; still it knows only by tradition that the Book it reveres is genuine. Again, it is cut up into a vast number of sects, each of which chips off from revelation whatever suits its purpose.

One believes in the Trinity, another rejects it as an absurdity. Yet both call themselves a part of Christianity, and each believes it is the same Christianity, that both denies the Trinity and accepts it at the same time. Each individual member may not assert as much to himself; but practically his intelligence lives in this contradiction. He accepts and rejects with the same breath.*

The numerous controversies to which the Reformation gave rise were not favorable to letters. They absorbed the intellectual energies of the sixteenth and of the greater part of the seventeenth centuries. Controversial works are one-sided; and a one-sided book, no matter with what ability it is written, does ..ot appeal to our common humanity. It is wanting in the essential conditions of general classic. Its life, with rare exceptions, is ephemeral. It passes away with the occasion that gave it birth.

3. The Reformation in its results has been unfavorable to literature. Its immediate effect was to destroy the literary spirit. Erasmus said that wherever it prevailed, letters went to ruin.† Hallam remarks

We occasionally see the various sects of Protestantism likened to the primitive colors of white light after it has passed through the prism. It is a pretty figure, but a splendid sophism. There is no contradiction in the colors of the rainbow. Their relations are expressed by the different degrees of intensity with which waves of light reach the eye. They are of the same kind, whereas contradictories are different in nature, and can never agree. Their reconciliation would involve their annihilation.

† Ubicunque regnat Lutherianismus, ibi literarum est interitus. (*Ep.* 1162, 1528.)

that "the first effects of the great religious schism in Germany were not favorable to classical literature."[*] Minds of intelligence were too busy in getting up the arguments in favor of the religious tenets they adopted, to think of cultivating poetry, or philosophy, or history, or the dignified eloquence that becomes a classic standard. But it is said that Protestantism did good afterwards ; especially that it caused the Elizabethan era of letters, and emancipated the human intellect. Let us consider each of these statements.

In name and to all appearance the Elizabethan era was Protestant. But the new religion sat on the people's consciences an ill-fitting garment, and the old religion they still cherished in their hearts. Indeed, they scarcely knew that they had changed their religious belief. Ignorant as they then were—they must have been nearly as ignorant as they are to-day, and there is no more benighted people in Christendom than the lower class in England [†]— they could have scarcely been able to realize the difference. They knew not the full meaning of the changes made in the external ceremonies ; they said the same prayers that they had been saying from their childhood ; their *Book of Common Prayer* was merely a modified translation of the Roman Missal. The only fact they realized was that they had to pay no more "Peter's pence" to support a power about which they knew little and cared less ; and that they considered a gain. Whatever training the learned

[*] *Literature of Europe*, vol. i., p. 339.
[†] See *London Labor and London Poor*, by Mr. Henry Mayhew ; also, Father Thébaud's *Irish Race*, pp. 470-474.

and great of those times had, it was the same that their ancestors had been receiving. And though the new spirit of rationalism had pervaded nearly every branch of letters, still the tone of poetry remained intact, and the Shakespearean drama is preëminently Catholic in its grandest and purest passages. Compare the Elizabethan poets with those of the golden era of Spain. They are contemporaries ; they are also identical in spirit, though one lives within sight of the *auto-da-fé*, and the other basks in the smiles of a queen who hates and persecutes Catholics. Their peculiarities may all be accounted for by difference of country and individual idiosyncrasy.*

It is further alleged that the Reformation created an enlightened Christianity, and emancipated the human intellect. It has been seen in what the nature of that enlightenment consists, and how a medley of contradictions has in consequence been saddled on the mind. The word "emancipation" is a misnomer for that undue preponderance given to reason, and that love of speculation characteristic of the whole Aryan race, but especially persistent in the Teutonic and Scandinavian families, developed to the extreme under rationalistic influence. The preponderance is undue, because man in acquiring knowledge has need of more than reason alone ; the instinct of faith is equally strong within him, and he

---

* See A. W. von Schlegel's *Lectures on Dramatic Poetry ;* the Lectures treating of Shakespeare and Calderon. In philosophy, erudition, and eloquence there was at this period in Spain but mediocrity. *L'inquisition arrêtait l'essor de la pensée.* (Caesar Cantù. *Hist. Un.,* t. xv. p. 563.)

who lays most stress on the supremacy of reason, when he comes to analyze his opinions, will find that he too is only repeating—that he is an uncon· scious disciple. Now, taking emancipation of the intellect for what it is worth in its literal sense, it is apparent that the throwing off of all restraint is not good for the intelligence. It impedes the develop-ment of thought. Without wholesome restraint, the mind wanders ; it has no starting-point, no goal ; it gropes about like a blind man, and takes hold of the first idea it meets ; it rejoices in what it considers a grand discovery, and puts out as new what every passer-by has already perceived and taken as a matter of course. Its normal condition is scepticism. Is not this in a nutshell the history of liberal thought since the Reformation ? Look at the world-authors since then, and examine what is fundamental in their writings. We will begin with those who have come into more immediate contact with the spirit afloat.

There is Montaigne. He is professedly a Catholic. But so great is the confusion of ideas in the sixteenth century, a man's outward profession may be one thing, and the life-giving principle of his writings may be entirely the opposite. For that reason no stress is to be laid on the religious profession of an author. It proves nothing. He is the child and spokesman of his age ; when not of its predominant spirit, of the reactionary spirit it necessarily induces. What then is the spirit that pervades the *Essais* ? On every page of this sincere book—*ce livre de bonne foy* —there is clearly stamped a total absence of convic-

tion.   One of his most characteristic essays is that in
which he goes to show that everybody ought to be
familiar with the thought of death.   He rightly considers it the supreme act of life.   The day of our
death he calls "the master-day ; it is the day that
judges all others." *   He calls that a beastly indifference—*cette nonchalance bestiale*—that refuses to think
of it.   Now, the outcome of all this solicitude is that
he would like death to find him in a mood indifferent
to his coming, and while planting cabbage. †   It is
thus he trifles with subjects of the greatest moment.
He is a complete sceptic.   "The essence of his
opinion," says Pascal, "consists of that doubt that
doubts of itself, and of that ignorance that ignores
itself." ‡   In all this there is no progress.   No idea
is made to germinate and bring forth fruit that might
be considered a boon to humanity.   All that fund of
knowledge, that power of expression, and that richness of illustration that abound in the *Essais*, are
stricken with barrenness under the chilling influence
of scepticism.

There is Rabelais.   The Curé of Meudon is also a
child of the rationalistic spirit that gave birth to the
Reformation.   His works breathe the same atmos-

* "C'est le maistre iour ; c'est le iour iuge de tous les aultres ;
c'est le iour, dict un ancien, qui doibt iuger de toutes mes annees
passees."—*Livre* i., ch. xviii.

† Ie veux . . . . que la mort me trouve plantant mes choulx,
mais nonchalant d'elle, et encores plus de mon iardin imparfaict.—
L. i., ch. xix.

‡ "C'est dans ce doute qui doute de soi, et dans cette ignorance
qui s'ignore, que consiste l'essence de son opinion."—*Pensées*, tome
i., p. 278.

phere of scepticism.   He ridicules everything sacred.
All authority—be it king or cardinal, priest or magistrate — is torn to tatters in his inimitable romance.
The only law it inculcates is : Do what you like —
*Fay ce que vouldras.** If Montaigne trifled with grave
subjects, Rabelais jested at them.   He laughed away
seriousness ; he laughed away responsibility ; he
laughed away thought ; he laughed away all man's
better emotions ; he even for a while laughed Protestantism out of France.   Jest is sometimes wholesome ; but not such jest. Its licentiousness too often
shocks.   It is too frequently out of place.   It is grim
as the laugh of a death-head.   Rabelais supplied a
powerful lever with which to move the foundations
of society.   He should have procured the wherewith
to clear away the rubbish that had been accumulat-
ing for centuries.   He did shake down the cobwebs,
but it was by making the whole edifice totter.

There is Descartes, the Luther of philosophy.   He
declared war upon Aristotle and the scholastics ; he
divorced theology from philosophy, and thus opened
the door to many of the philosophic vagaries now
agitating the world of thought.   He took a part of
philosophy for the whole ; for the supernatural order
is a living fact, and in every sound philosophy must

* "Toute leur vie estoit employée, non par loix, statutz ou
reigles, mais selon leur vouloir et franc arbitre. Se leuoyent du lict
quand bon leur sembloit ; beuvoyent, mangeoyent, traualloyent,
dormoyent, quand le desir leur venoit. Nul ne les esueilloit, nul ne
les parforceoit ny à boyre, ny à manger, ny à faire chose aultre quel-
concque. Ainsi l'avoit estably Gargantua. En leur reigle n'estoit
que ceste clause : FAY CE QUE VOULDRAS."—*Gargantua*, liv. i.,
ch. 57.

be taken into consideration as an essential factor in the production of thought, the progress of life, and the march of society. His fundamental principle, *Cogito, ergo sum*, gives him his own identity, and nothing more. Hence, his proof of the existence of God is defective. He knows that God is, from the idea of perfection in his mind ; but how knows he that the idea conforms to the object ? His methodical doubt excludes all knowing of it. Thus, the spirit of rationalism would lead him one way, while his faith directed him to an opposite result. Fichte is Descartes reduced to logical consistency.*

These men were rationalistic, and yet they were not children of the Reformation. It is because the rationalistic spirit of their day pervades all classes of intelligence and checks thought. Great minds beneath its influence feel the ground of certainty move from under their feet ; and whether they abandon themselves to the current, as did Montaigne and Rabelais, or with Descartes attempt to direct its course, they are borne along with it, and their writings give testimony to its universal sway. Let us take, as representative authors of each of the three succeeding centuries, men who all of them lived and died in a Protestant atmosphere : Leibnitz, the philosopher, of the seventeenth ; Burke, the statesman, of the eighteenth,

---

* Our strictures on Descartes may sound ill on the ears of his numerous admirers. We have yet to get as impatient of him as did Pascal : "Je ne puis pardonner à Descartes : il avoit bien voulu, dans toute sa philosophie, pouvoir se passer de Dieu ; mais il n'a pu s'empêcher de lui faire donner une chiquenaude p_ur mettre le monde en mouvement ; après cela il n'a plus que faire de Dieu."— *Pensées, Ire Partie,* art. x., 41.

and Goethe, the poet, of the nineteenth century—intellectual giants of their times, who wielded in their respective departments vast and permanent influence. Is not the secret of their strength due to the religious influence of the spirit they were inhaling in every breath, and which pervaded their thoughts and gave color to their views? It is perceptible in their manner of writing ; it crops out in many a phrase ; it is inwoven in their thoughts ; but of all that is permanent and influencing in their works, not a jot or tittle is traceable to the rationalistic spirit that they inhaled.

In Leibnitz there are two men—Leibnitz the courtier and diplomatist and Leibnitz the philosopher. It was as a courtier and diplomatist that he labored to bring about a reconciliation between the two great religious parties. Catholic France was in the ascendant, and what more efficient means of keeping on good terms with this great power? He sought to establish the reconciliation upon a basis of compromise. But his primary idea was that of a civil and political union ; later on, he attempted the religious union only to abandon it as a hopeless task. "I worked hard," he writes to Fabricius in 1697, "to settle religious controversies, but I soon learned that the reconciling of doctrines was labor in vain. Then I imagined a species of truce of God." * Though a Protestant seeking the best terms for his own creed, he went back to a mediæval and Catholic custom for

* *Œuvres*, vol. ii, intro. XLV., Ed. A. Foucher de Careil.

his model. Hè sought to establish an intellectual truce of God, a suspension of judgment upon disputed points till they should have been arbitrated upon by a competent court of appeal. But he soon learned the futility of such an attempt, be it ever so well-intentioned. He ceased to hope for more than civil toleration. In 1698, he wrote : " I have labored for civil toleration ; as regards ecclesiastical toleration, the day will never come when the two parties will not mutually condemn each other." * Such was the spirit in which he corresponded with Pellisson and Bossuet. During ten years, letters were exchanged at varying intervals. At times the subject would be dropped, and again renewed ; but it ended in no practical results either for the individuals or for the parties they represented. The hopes of the Hanoverian House to succeed to the throne of England extinguished the already cooling ardor of Leibnitz. It is the man of policy who, in order to set himself right with Burnet, spoke of his controversy with Bossuet and the hopes Catholics had entertained of his entering the Church, as a thing of the past.† It is the man of policy who penned these lines : "Our whole right to the throne of Great Britain is based on our hatred of the Roman religion. This is why we should avoid all show of indifference towards that church."‡ Let us leave the courtier seeking above all things the good pleasure and temporal

* To Fabricius, ibid.
† Letter, Dec. 14, 1705.
‡ To Fabricius, Oct. 15, 1708. *Œuvres,* vol. ii., intro, xcix.

well-being of his master, and turn to the philosopher.

As a philosopher truly encyclopædic in the extent of his knowledge, Leibnitz had no peer among his contemporaries.   His fertile genius touched upon no subject that it did not advance.   In mathematics, in jurisprudence, in philology, in metaphysics, in history, he made discoveries and originated ideas that, even at the present day, are instructive, profound and suggestive. He seemed to possess special insight into the world of matter and the world of mind. Throughout his letters are sentences of great wisdom ; his very conjectures have frequently become commonplace truths.   Now this truly philosophical mind left, as the outcome of his controversy with Bossuet, a remarkable book with a remarkable history.   He planned an innocent ruse, by which a Catholic divine was to write an explanation of Christian doctrine on so broad a basis that it could be approved by the Protestant Universities, while he would write an explanation which could receive Catholic approval. Both works being published, the two parties would be enabled to see more clearly what little difference there really was in the essentials of their Christianity and how easily they might unite upon these essentials. Actuated by these motives, he wrote a system of theology that no Protestant could reasonably reject. Therein he leaves aside all prejudice as far as it is possible for man to do so ; and having invoked the Divine assistance, he listens to the teachings of the sacred Scriptures, venerable antiquity, sound reason and well-authenticated facts, and draws his conclusions independently of any received system.   Now, what is the outcome of this impartial investigation, carried on as though he were a neophyte coming from another world and addicted to none of the prevailing creeds ?* Leibnitz, in his *Systema Theologicum,* produced the *Summa* of St. Thomas in epitome. His acute philosophical mind deduced the whole essential body of the Catholic faith as the one rational form of religious doctrine that follows from the premises of the knowledge of God and a Divine revelation. For a whole century this book lay unknown. Its discovery was a surprise to the literary world. Catholics seized upon it with avidity and published editions and translations of it in several modern tongues.† They knew not then the web of diplomacy in which the book was shrouded. The additional light that has been thrown on the circumstances under which Leibnitz wrote it, by his own letters,‡ shows that he was not giving the inner convictions of his soul, but rather that he was putting forth "an ultimatum of Protestantism." § And though he may not have had the faith to accept all that he therein demonstrated— for one's faith comes not according to the degree of

* See the opening sentence of the *Systema Theologicum.*

†Abbé Emory in 1819 gave the first edition ; the Prince de Broglie made a French translation of it; in 1825, Lorenz Doller published a German-Latin edition. Later, Dr. Russell of Maynooth published an English translation.

‡ Published for the first time in 1860 by A. Foucher de Careil.

§ Foucher de Careil, *Œuvres de Leibnits,* t. ii., intro. p. xcvii. But when this painstaking editor adds that the *Systema* was "nothing less than the religious testament of Leibnitz," we cannot agree with him. The after-conduct of Leibnitz is sufficient refutation of the assertion.

one's knowledge—still, the fact remains that his acute philosophical mind deduced the whole essential body of Catholic dogma as the one rational form of religious truth that flows from the premises of the knowledge of God and a Divine revelation.   He was granted a glimpse of the unity and consistency, the grandeur and holiness of the Catholic Church, and it caused him to grow lukewarm towards the creed in which he was educated.   " He does not attend the Lutheran communion, but he is otherwise a good man :" this was the testimony of the Landgrave of Hesse, who knew him intimately.   He himself would at one time insist that he belonged to the body of the Catholic Church.   In 1691, he wrote to Madame de Brinon : " You are right in believing me to be a Catholic at heart.   I am so even openly ; for it is only obstinacy that makes the heretic, and of that, thank God, my conscience does not accuse me."*

Again, the spirit that animates the philosophy of Leibnitz is the same that inspired the genius of St. Thomas and dictated the Scholastic philosophy of which he frequently wrote in terms of praise.†   With the Schoolmen he held that " philosophy and theology are two truths which agree one with the other."   " It is very remarkable," says Balmes, speaking of the coincidence between his views and those of St. Thomas on pantheism, "that under an historical as well as a meta-

---

*Œuvres, t. i., p. 163, Lettre xliii.

†He was wont to say : " Aurum latere in stercore illo scholastico barbariei." Lettre 3ème à Remond de Montmort, Opera, t.v., p. 13.

‡ Œuvres, t. ii, intro., xcvii.

physical aspect, Leibnitz agrees with St. Thomas ;
both express the same idea in very similar words."*
Nowhere in his writings do we find a profound truth
evoked, even by his genius, from the cold negations
of rationalism, religious or philosophic. On the
contrary, their historical significancy is that they are
reactionary against that spirit ; and therefore is Leibnitz in truth a child of Scholasticism.

The genius of the great modern statesman kept
equally intact from the political rationalism of his
age. It is a matter of historical evidence that the
great conservative statesmen of Europe since the days
of Edmund Burke—De Maistre, De Bonald, Goerres,
Schlegel—have made the deep philosophical vein of
thought underlying his luxuriant eloquence their
careful study. And that school is pre-eminently Catholic. Take Burke's master-piece, *Reflections on the Revolution in France.* The principles running through
it—those principles that are the secret of his political
far-sightedness, in consequence of which he saw a
measure in all its bearings, and grasped its ultimate
result long before his contemporary statesmen had
mastered its first elements—are the very opposite of
those dictated by the spirit of rationalism. That
spirit cried liberty. Edmund Burke asks : " Is it
because liberty in the abstract may be classed among
the blessings of mankind, that I am seriously to
felicitate a madman, who has escaped from the pro-
tecting restraint and wholesome darkness of his

* *Fund. Phil.*, bk. I., Note to ch. x.

cell, on his restoration to the enjoyment of light
and liberty ? " That spirit would destroy religion.
Edmund Burke says : " We know, and what is
better, we feel inwardly that religion is the basis
of civil society, and the source of all good and
of all comfort." That spirit tore away the con-
stitution of France. He calls it not a noble effort
of genius, a triumph of humanity, and the like;
he rather considers it the result of sloth, inability to wrestle with difficulties, and a degenerate
fondness for tricking short-cuts. " It is this inability to wrestle with difficulty which has obliged the
arbitrary assembly of France to commence their
schemes of reform with abolition and total destruction. . . . Your mob can do this as well as your
assemblies. The shallowest understanding, the rudest
hand, is more than enough to the task."* He
stemmed the current manfully, and broke its powerful waves on the shores of England. His life was ?
warfare against it. If Leibnitz reacted against the
religious and philosophical rationalism of the seventeenth century, Burke reacted against the political
rationalism of the eighteenth.

The poet of the century—of its partial return to
naturalism, of its scepticism, of its sentimentalism—
owes nothing to the Reformation. He held aloof
from all creeds.† Whatever religious sentiment he

* Works, vol. i., p. 531.

† " Was mich nämlich von der Brüdergemeine so wie von andern
werthen Christenseelen absonderte, war dasselbige, worüber die
Kirche schon mehr als einmal in Spaltung gerathen war."—*Aus
Meinem Leben*, 3r Th., 15es Buch.

possessed, he imbibed from the pantheistic teachings of his favorite Spinoza. But that was not deep.
He was a modern pagan. His life was a splendid
bubble ; it lacked seriousness, and was the real-
ization of nothing more than self. But all that is
positive in his poetry is drawn from the same
source from which poets have drunk from the beginning. The relations of the real and the ideal, the
warring of intellect and heart, human aspirations
and natural love—such are the themes of this magnificent, many-sided dreamer. Calmly and coldly,
like his own Mephistopheles, does he stand apart
from men and human concerns and weave his magnificent time-verities into that expression most
interpretive of the aspirations of the age. Wherever he
is powerful the Reformation has no say. He fathoms
human nature in all its varied depths and soundings,
from the idyllic simplicity of *Hermann and Dorothea*
to the complex, world-embracing character-study of
Faust, which sums up man's oscillations between
the finites and the infinite. It is an old theme.

There is an element of modern thought which the
Reformation has been instrumental in producing.
It is a spirit of Biblical criticism—that irreverent,
self-destructive criticism which animated the Neo-
Platonists, and which, in our own day, has inspired
Rénan and Strauss. Revelation requires a divinely
appointed authority to be its custodian and expoun-
der. The Reformation, in making reason sole judge
of revealed truth, ignored this authority, and sowed
the seed that has germinated into the *Vie de Jésus*
and the *Alte und der Neue Glaube*, the fruits of which

are a cosmic sentiment that would substitute music and poetry for prayer and the sacred Scriptures.

There now remains for us but to draw the inevitable conclusion. It is that the Reformation has not only been unfavorable to intellectual development in its nature and relations, but that results go to show that this intellectual development has gone on, that world-authors have written and impressed succeeding times, in spite of its principles, which are rationalistic, negative—no principles at all—the destruction of thought and logic where they obtain ; and finally, that all that is genuine and lasting in literature since then, is either reversionary or reactionary.*

* We deem it necessary to apologize for having dwelt so long on the Reformation. It is now a dead issue. But so many writers on general literature have fallen into the sophism, *post hoc, ergo propter hoc*, and attributed to the Reformation results that belong not to it in the remotest degree, we thought it well to lay stress on its character and place in the history of thought. We have said nothing stronger of it than have its greatest champions. Guizot says ; "The religious revolution of the sixteenth century did not understand the true principles of intellectual liberty." "The first reformers," says Madame de Staël, "thought themselves able to place the pillars of Hercules of the mind according to their own lights ; but they were mistaken to hoping to make those who had rejected all authority of this kind in the Catholic religion submit to their decisions as infallible."—*De l'Allemagne*, p. 523.

CHAPTER IX.

LORD BACON AND MODERN THOUGHT.

RATIONALISM took its legitimate course when it applied itself to the development and application of the material energies of nature ; for it must be borne in mind that reason is good, the conveniences of life are good, and the physical sciences are good, and between them and religion there is no contradiction. It is only when scientific men leave their proper sphere, and begin to speculate on things they have no mental aptitude for, that in their ignorance they clash with truth and religion.   When Lalande sweeps the heavens with his telescope, and catalogues the stars, he is doing a service to science ; but when he tells us that he has not found God at the end of his telescope, he is introducing an idea foreign to his subject, and answering a question it is not within the province of astronomy to put him.

Scholasticism was so mingled up with the old religion, that the nations that drifted from the one, despised the other, yearned after a change in intellectual pursuits, and hailed every philosophical innovator.   Wearied with verbal strife, and disgusted at seeing the same questions still open after centuries of dispute, men sought repose in the more fruitful work of mechanical pursuits and scientific investigation.   Francis Bacon became the exponent and representative of this phase of thought.   His unques-

tionable genius and his elevated social position gave
weight to his words, and he was hailed as the apostle
of the inductive method. That method he made the
one idea of his genius.

Bacon is misunderstood by two classes of men.
One regards him as the creator of a new and previously unknown method, to which modern science
is indebted for all its triumphs. This is an impossibility. He could not change the intellect. He could
not give man another faculty distinct from the faculties he already possessed. Intelligence works now exactly as it worked prior to my Lord Bacon. The sum
and substance of his philosophy is this : "Leave
scholastic disputations. You have talked enough over
words. Turn to things. Interpret nature. Experiment. Be careful of the biases of your mind. Be not
over-hasty in your inferences. Look to facts. Wait.
Read the lessons of nature as it is, and not as you
think it ought to be." This simple piece of advice
constitutes his title to immortality and our gratitude.
And though it is a good one, there is nothing in it
that had not at all times occurred to the careful man
in the experiences of his every-day life. Bacon added
no real truth to any of the sciences. He enforced his
views generally by the crudest facts and by childish
illustrations. He invented no new method. He
only called attention to that which men should follow in investigating the laws of nature.

The other class denounces him as the ruin of all
genuine thought, the bitter enemy of metaphysics,
and the father of modern materialism. This view of
him is equally incorrect. He was an innovator ; and

all innovators are so absorbed in the idea they would enforce, that they are invariably led to exaggerate its importance, and to belittle that which they would have it supplant. So it was with Aristotle; so it was with Descartes; so it was with Lord Bacon. He claimed for his method that it was intrinsically different from the syllogism. Here, in his eagerness to assert its superiority, he took a part for the whole. The observation and grouping of facts do not constitute a syllogism; but neither do they give anything more general than facts; and with these alone the mind can never attain to the knowledge of a general law. It is impossible to set aside the rule of logic that the terms of the conclusion ought never be taken with greater extension than in the premises. No number of particulars makes up a universal. Induction, then, only gives the material for one premise; and when, from a certain number of particular facts, a general law is inferred, there is implied in the background a universal truth that is a necessary factor, not in making the induction, but in deducing the law. In this manner alone is the inductive method legitimate.*

In discussing the philosophy of Bacon, it is well to bear in mind that we possess only a fragment of it, and that this fragment has reference principally to physical science. It is therefore one-sided in its development, which, exclusively considered, is materialistic. But Bacon has not abused the metaphysics, nor is he their bitter enemy. On the contrary, he

* " At si rite perpenditur, inductio a syllogismo essentialiter non discrepat, sed forma tantum."—*Liberatore, Inst. Phil.,* p. 94.

thinks them good in their place.   He thinks that they give unity to the other sciences.   He even censures them for accepting, unchallenged, scientific principles on the testimony of each individual science.   He considers it within the province of metaphysics to test the foundations of all knowledge in the light of the principles they establish. *   And he is right.   He censures the syllogism, but it is with his eye on the physical sciences.   Thus, when he tells us that "the syllogism is not applied to the principles of the sciences, and is of no avail in intermediate axioms as being far from equal to the subtilty of nature," and adds, that "it forces assent, therefore, and not things,"† he says what is at least in part true ; for first principles are not deduced, and no amount of exclusive syllogizing can discover a law of nature.   Here his favorite method of observation and experiment is required. It has been as well as truly said of logic, that "its chain of conclusion hangs loose at both ends ; both the point from which the proof should start, and the points at which it should arrive. are beyond its reach ; it comes short both of first principles and of concrete issues."‡

The inductive method, as elaborated by Bacon, is impracticable.   "Hitherto," he says, "the proceeding has been to fly at once from the sense and par-

* De Augmentis, lib. iii.

† Syllogismus ad principia scientiarum non adhibetur, ad media axiomata frustra adhibetur, cum sit subtilitate naturæ longe impar. Assensum itaque constringit, non res."—Novum Organum, Aph. xiii.

‡ John Henry Newman, Grammar of Assent, p. 272.   See also pp. 255, et seq.

ticulars up to the most general propositions, as certain fixed poles for the argument to turn upon, and from these to derive the rest by middle terms."* He is correct in censuring too hasty a transition from facts to principles. It misleads the mind, and becomes the source of numerous errors. Men are to-day as incautious as ever. It is not uncommon to see them on a single fact build up a whole theory—men, too, who plume themselves on being disciples of the inductive philosopher. Now, what is the method Bacon would substitute? To set out also with sense and the particular facts, but without skipping any chain, and, by multiplying observations and experiences, to arrive but at the last place at the most general propositions.† But there is no last place in the observation of facts. They multiply with the discerning power of the observer, Nature is a book so extensive, so difficult to read, and, withal, so precisely written, that the little compass of a man's life—the combined efforts of an age—can accurately decipher but few of her phenomena. Accordingly, the true Baconian is the Positivist who looks only to facts, and studies "the laws of phenomenon, and never the mode of production." ‡ The greatest triumphs of intelligence have been, and will continue to be, made by anticipation. Still, Bacon could not insist too strongly on patient investigation—on the mind's carrying lead rather than wings.

* " Adhuc enim res ita geri consuevit ; ut a sensu et particularibus primo loco ad maxima generalia advoletur, tanquam ad polos fixos circa quos disputationes vertantur ; ab illis cætera per media deriventur."—*Distributio Operis*, vol. i., E. & S. ed.,London, p. 136.

† *Nov. Org.*, 19-22-26. ‡ Comte.

It is often asserted that Bacon flouted final causes
altogether from the domain of knowledge as of athe-
istical tendency.* He is far from any such act. He
has even taken the pains to state expressly of their
consideration : "Neither does this call in question or
derogate from Divine Providence, but rather highly
confirms and exalts it."† He would relegate final
causes from physics to metaphysics ; for to the latter
they more properly belong. He is correct. Design
alone is a most fallacious guide in studying the laws
of nature. He explains himself in the same place:
"For the handling of final causes in physics, has
driven away and overthrown the diligent inquiry
of physical causes, and made man acquiesce in those
specious and shadowy causes, without actively
pressing the inquiry of those which are really and
truly physical, to the great arrest and prejudice of
science."‡ He is not to be blamed for this treatment
of final causes. It is the merit of his genius that he
thus assigned to them their proper sphere ; and in
doing so he removed the greatest obstacle in the
way of the advancement of the physical sciences.

Bacon's views were those of his age. The neces-

* See Liberatore, *Institutions*, p. 348 ; also F. Hill, *Elements*,
p. 227.

† " Neque vero ista res in dubium vocat Providentiam Divinam,
aut ei quicquam derogat, set potius eandem miris modis confirmat
et evehit."—*De Aug.*, lib. iii., cap. iv.

‡ Tractatio enim *Causarum Finalium* in *Physicis* inquisitionem
Causarum *Physicarum* expulit et dejecit ; effecitque ut homines in
istiusmodi speciosis et umbratilibus causis acquiescerunt, nec
inquisitionem causarum realium, et vere Physicarum strenue
urgerent ; ingenti scientiarum detrimento."—*De Aug.*, lib. III.

sity of scientific reform was felt throughout the learned world. Descartes felt it, and endeavored to bring about in mathematics and metaphysics the reform Bacon sought to achieve in the domain of physics. They both gave direction to the movement. But they did not create it; they could not have impelled it a step, if if did not march of its own accord. Had they attempted to stop its progress, great as were their geniuses, it would have crushed them into oblivion.

Three centuries and a half before Francis Bacon wrote, there lived a monk who attempted to achieve in science exactly what was achieved in the sixteenth century, but who failed because the mental soil of his age was not prepared for his opinions. He was an innovator, but an untimely one, and public opinion scarcely noticed him at first, for it understood not his language. He would abuse its lack of comprehension, and loudly assert his views as the only correct ones, and public opinion thereupon turned on the outspoken Franciscan, and persecuted him as a babbler that knew not whereof he spoke. Therefore it is that, though deeply learned in the sciences,* Roger Bacon made little or no impress on his age. In nearly every point of his method, the monk has anticipated the chancellor.

---

* L'admirable moine, Roger Bacon, dont la plupart des savants actuels, si dédaigneux du moyen âge, seraient assurément incapables, je ne dis point d'écririe, mais seulement de lire la grande composition à cause de l'immense variété des vues qui s'y trouvent sur tous les divers ordres de phénomènes.—COMTE, Phil. Pos., tome, vi., p. 206.

I.

Both approach their subject in the same spirit. Both get impatient with the disputes of the schoolmen. Francis Bacon complains of their barrenness. He says it is no longer subject developed after · subject; it is school pitted against school.* Roger Bacon is equally loud in his complaints. He finds the books of the ancients full of doubts, obscurities, and perplexities. He finds his contemporaries, with few exceptions, not a whit better. Few of them really understand the Aristotle they laud so highly.†

II.

They are both equally penetrated with a sense of humility before the grandeur of nature and the little they really know of her mysteries. .

FRANCIS BACON.

It is most certain, and proved by experience, that a little philosophy can lead to atheism; but much knowledge brings back to religion.

ROGER BACON.

He is mad who thinks highly of his wisdom; he most mad who exhibits it as something to be wondered at.

TEXT.

Certissimum est, atque experientia comprobatum, leves gustus in philosophia movere fortasse ad atheismum, sed pleniores haustus ad religionem reducere.—*Nov. Org.*, lib. i.

Insanus est qui de sapientia se extollit, et maxime insanit qui ostentat et tanquam portentum suam scientiam nititur divulgare. —*Op. Maj.*, lib. i., p. 15. Ed Jebb.

* Dist. Op.   † *Opus Majus*, Ed. Jebb, p. 10, *et seq*.

III

Both of them mention the same number of obstacles in the way of acquiring true knowledge.

FRANCIS BACON.

Four species of idols beset the human mind. The first kind we call idols of the tribe; the second, idols of the cave; the third idols of the market-place; and the fourth idols of the theatre.

ROGER BACON.

There are four great stumbling-blocks in the way of comprehending truth, which impede all wisdom whatever; and with difficulty do they permit anybody to arrive at the true title of being wise. They are: the force of weak and unworthy authority, prolonged custom, popular opinion, and the hiding of one's ignorance with a semblance of wisdom.

TEXT.

Quatuor sunt genera Idolorum quæ mentes humanas obsident. Iis (docendi gratia) nomina imposuimus; ut primum genus, Idola Tribus; secundum, Idola Specus; tertium, Idola Fori; quartum, Idola Theatri vocentur. —*Nov. Org.*, lib. i., 39.

Quatuor vero sunt maxima comprehendendæ veritatis offendicula, quæ omnem quemcunque sapientem impediunt, et vix aliquem permittunt ad verum titulum sapientiæ pervenire; viz., fragilis et indignæ auctoritatis exemplum, consuetudinis diuturnitas, vulgi sensus imperiti, et propriæ ignorantiæ occultatio cum ostentatione sapientiæ apparentis.—*Opus Majus*, lib. i., p. 2.

IV.

Their agreement here is more than fanciful. Both have the same ideas in view, and their reconciliation

will not take many words. Take the first illusion
mentioned by the chancellor : "The idols of the
tribe," he tells us, "are inherent in human nature, and
the very tribe or race of man ; for it is a false assertion that the sense of man is the measure of things."
That is, things may be otherwise than as man conceives them. This, by the way, was the error of
Vico, who identified the true and the made*—a theory
that does not hold good outside of mathematics.† We
are not, therefore, to submit in scientific matters to a
view of the thing simply because other men—perhaps
the great majority—accept that view of it. Witness
the belief that color resides in objects. It is among
the worst of arguments to say : This was maintained
by the ancients, and must therefore be held as true.
We are quoting from the friar. His idea coincides
with that of the chancellor.

FRANCIS BACON.

Idola Tribus sunt fundata in
ipsa natura humana, atque in
ipsa tribu seu gente hominum.
Falso enim asseritur, sensum
humanum esse mensuram rerum.
—*Nov. Org.*, L 41.

ROGER BACON.

Fragilis et indignæ auctoritatis
exemplum . . . . . Nam quilibet in
singulis artibus vitæ et studii et
omnis negotii tribus pessimis ad
eandem conclusionem utitur ar-
gumentis, scil. hoc exemplifica-
tum est per majores . . . .
ergo tenendum.—*Opus Majus*,
p. 2.

V.

Again, the idols of the cave, that is, the illusions of
the individual man, are based upon the bias the mind
receives in education.‡ It becomes accustomed to

* "The criterion of truth, and the rule by which to recognize it,
is to have made it." *De Antiquissima Italorum Sapientia*, lib. i.
cap. i. § 1.
† See Balmes' *Fundamental Philosophy*, bk. i. chaps. xxx., xxxi.
‡ "Idola Specus sunt idola hominis individui. Habet enim

a certain way of thinking, and sees things only in that direction. Here is the "prolonged custom" or traditionary habit of Roger Bacon.

VI.

The third illusion, the idols of the market-place, consists of a wrong and silly imposition of words, resulting from the intercourse of man with man. But the sense of the ignorant many is not the one scientific accuracy requires. This is the "popular opinion" of the friar:

FRANCIS BACON.	ROGER BACON.
Homines enim per sermones sociantur; at verba ex captu vulgi imponuntur.—*Nov. Org.*, i., 43.	Vulgi sensus imperiti.—*Opus Majus.*

VII.

The fourth illusion, the idols of the theatre, is identical with the pride of imaginary knowledge of Roger Bacon; for such a pride, in order to hide its ignorance, grows disputatious, and assumes to play a part that is as unreal to it as is the rôle of king to him who impersonates him on the stage.

FRANCIS BACON.	ROGER BACON.
Lastly, there are idols which have immigrated into men's minds from the various dogmas of philosophies, and also from wrong laws of demonstration.	Authors write, and the common people hold many things which are utterly false, by arguments feigned without experiment.

unusquisque (præter aberrationes naturæ humanæ in genere) specum sive cavernam quandam individuam, quæ lumen naturæ frangit et corrumpit; vel propter naturam cujusque propriam et singularem; vel propter educationem et conversationem cum aliis."—*Nov. Org.*, i. 42.

FRANCIS BACON.

These we call idols of the theatre, because all the received systems are, in our judgment, but so many stage-plays, representing worlds of their own creation after an unreal and scenic fashion.

ROGER BACON.

What is worse, men blinded by these four hindrances do not perceive their ignorance, but with the utmost assurance, wrangle and defend their opinion, seeing that they can find no remedy; and worse still, when in the thickest darkness of error, they consider themselves in the full light of truth.

TEXT.

Sunt denique Idola quæ immigrarunt in animos hominum ex diversis dogmatibus philosophiarum, ac etiam ex perversis legibus demonstrationum ; quæ Idola Theatri nominamus ; quia quot philosophiæ receptæ aut inventæ sunt, tot fabulas productas et actas censemus, quæ mundos effecerunt fictitios et scenicos.— *Nov. Org.*, i., 44.

Nam multa scribunt auctores et vulgus tenet per argumenta quæ fingit sine experientia quæ sunt omnino falsa.—*Opus Majus,* pars vi.

Sed pejus est quod homines horum quatuor caligine excæcati non percepiunt suam ignorantiam, sed cum omni cautela palliant et defendunt, quatenus remedium non inveniant ; et quod pessimum est cum sint in tenebris errorum densissimis. æstimant se esse in plena luce veritatis.—pars i., p. 2.

VIII.

It has been seen that Francis Bacon asserted the superiority of the experimental over the syllogistic method ; so does the friar, but without destroying the latter.

FRANCIS BACON.	ROGER BACON.
We reject demonstration by syllogism . . . . for the syllogism is made up of proposi- tions, propositions of words ; but words are only marks and signs of notions.	There are two methods or knowing—argument and experi- ment. Argument concludes a question, but does not give cer- tainty nor remove doubt, so that the soul rests in the perception of
Consequently it enforces as- sent, not things.	a truth, unless that truth is aided by experience.

TEXT.

At nos demonstrationem per syllogismum rejicimus . . . quod syllogismus ex proposi- tionibus constet, propositiones ex verbis, verba autem notionum tesseræ ac signa sunt.—*Inst. Mag. Intro.*	Duo sunt modi cognoscendi ; scilicet per argumentum et per experimentum. Argumentum concludit et facit nos concludere questionem ; sed non certificat neque removet dubitationem, ut quiescat animus in intuitu veri-
Assensum itaque constringit non res,—*Nov. Org.*, i., 13.	tatis, nisi eam inveniat viâ expe- rientiæ.—*Opus Majus*, pars vi., p. 445.

"It is indeed an extraordinary circumstance," Whewell remarks, "to find a writer of the thirteenth century not only recognizing experiment as one source of knowledge, but urging its claims as some-thing far more important than men had yet been aware of, exemplifying its value by striking and just examples, and speaking of its authority with a dignity of diction which sounds like a foremurmur of the Baconian sentences uttered nearly four hundred years later." *

The spirit and scope of the great chancellor's method are the same with those of his greater name

* *History of the Inductive Sciences*, vol. i., p. 579.

sake ; while in scientific attainments the latter was by far superior to the former. "In this respect," says Whewell, "he was far more fortunate than Francis Bacon."*

Enough has been laid down to show that the seed of the Baconian method was deeply implanted in the soil of thought, and was there germinating and patiently abiding its time ; and as a premature day in spring brings forth an occasional blossom or fresh blade, to be nipped away by the next frost, so did the times and a short sunshine of papal favor draw out that blossom of the inductive method, to show its head for a moment, and then to rest in oblivion for nigh four hundred years, until the intellectual atmosphere became more favorable to its growth and development.

CHAPTER X.

THE LAW OF THOUGHT.

THE history of literature is the history of ideas and their influence. They appear and disappear ; but in obedience to law. What Montesquieu says of political changes is equally applicable to intellectual ones. "As men have always the same passions," says this only too pagan philosopher, "the occasions that produce great changes differ, but their causes are always the same."† There is Phœnicia of old. She was mistress of the sea, the queen of commerce,

* *History of the Inductive Sciences*, vol. i., p. 521.
† Comme les hommes ont eu dans tous les temps les mêmes pas-

the synonym of all that was precious in silks, dyes,*
and the like. Her people were wealthy, enterpris-
ing, and nursed in luxury. They were also material-
ists in their views. The philosophy that can be considered theirs is based on the doctrine of atoms ; it is
materialistic. So it is with that nation in modern
times which is the mistress of commerce. With her,
too, originated that modern materialism that infected
Europe during the eighteenth century, Her philosophy—the philosophy of Locke, and Hume, and
Bacon, and Herbert Spencer, the only philosophy
that is characteristically hers—is materialistic in
its principles and in its application. It pervades
much that has been since written in English literature. Materialistic criteria run through the poetry,
the fiction, the philosophy of England in the estimate of the age, its progress and civilization, as
well as in the ideal of perfect happiness drawn in
these subjects. It is so, under like circumstances, at
all times and in all places. The laws of thought are
as constant as the movements of the spheres of the
heavens. Christianity has not changed them. It
does not alter man's nature ; it ennobles, purifies,
directs it ; but it is still the same human nature, in
which are inherent the same passions, and possessed
of the same fundamental tendency of thought.

We hit upon an idea ; we consider it our own, and
publish it to the world as such. Some one more
deeply versed in letters, takes a dusty tome from the
shelf of his library, and reads the same thought dif-

sions, les occasions qui produisent les grands changements sont
différentes, mais les causes sont toujours les mêmes.—*Grand. et Dec·
de Rome*, chap. L.   * *e.g. point*, and all its derivatives.

ferently expressed. Bacon the worldly chancellor, and Bacon the studious Franciscan, are both depositaries of the same idea. Two centuries before Luther struck the note of a religious revolt, Wyckliffe hoisted the same banner. So the same seed produces in different countries the same fruit, but modified in each case by variety of soil, climate, and cultivation. But to produce anything, the seed must be there ; it must have been planted. And these germs of thought that spring up and thrive so diversely in various intellectual soils, whence are they, and by whom planted ? We have watched them pass from the East to the West ; we have seen Grecian and Roman cultivate them ; we have observed that the child of the forest receives them, and combines them with his primitive notions, even as did before him those he received them from, and, fostered by him, they produce a fruit alike and different—alike in kind, different in color and flavor. In China, in Hindostan, in Greece, in Germany, let us but go deep enough, and we will find the same primitive germs. One side of a truth is presented at one time ; at another, we are given another side. Yesterday, an idea was popular ; to-day, it dies out of men's minds ; a thousand years hence, when called to light by the vivifying influences that first acted upon it, it springs into favor once more, and becomes the actuating thought of an age.

Truth, then, is independent of man. The power is his to discover, develop, and apply it ; but he cannot create it. That belongs to the Infinite Intelligence alone. He it is who creates it, and who creates the light of our reason by which to perceive it. He is the

Word, by virtue of which we have power of speech and understanding—"He who from the beginning—from the foundation of the world—sowed nutritious seeds ; He who in each age rained down the Lord, the Word ; " * that Word from which are all things, and which all things speak ; † that Word whose splendor is reflected in the beauties of language and literature, though brokenly and dim!y so, on account of man's darkness of understanding and the presence of the human spirit which absorbs the Divine radiance. Now, truth being independent of man, man might be forever on this globe and never know truth unless his intellect were predisposed to recognize it when presented, and to apprehend it as such. Truth, then, has been communicated to man, perhaps directly, probably indirectly, through the medium of the laws to which the Creator both of man and of truth subjected the human intellect.‡ Thus is man from the beginning a creature of education. Therefore it is that no people has ever by itself been able to rise from barbarism to civilization. No nation, of its own accord, and without external influence, has ever developed a literature. And the universal history of literature goes to show that the sum of natural truth is a constant quantity. This is the most general law of thought. Reason further confirms it ; for at all times, and in all places, the material world, humanity, the general relations of life, the social problems arising therefrom, and their solutions, the questionings

* Clement of Alexandria, *Strom.*, lib. i., cap., vii.
† *Imitation*, bk. i., ch. iii.
‡ *Summa*, 1 a. 1 ae. Quæst. 87, ad. 1.

of the soul, are all the same ; the same truths are
evolved, and the same thoughts appear in different
garbs.   "Nothing under the sun is new ; neither is
any man able to say : Behold, this is new, for it hath
already gone before in the ages that were before
us." §

§ *Ecclesiastes*, chap. i., 10.

CHAPTER XL

CHARACTERISTICS OF ANCIENT AND MODERN LITERATURE.

THERE is a marked difference between ancient and modern literature. The words Pagan and Christian do not express this difference with sufficient discrimination ; for Pagan authors have always had some gleams of primitive revelation and the common fund of natural truths to draw from, while Christians are under Pagan influence in letters on account of a nameless something—a harmonious development—that pervades Pagan writings, and which no amount of elaboration seems capable of attaining. Idiomatic differences will, in part, account for this difference of style. The ancient classics were living languages when written by Cæsar and Cicero, Plato and Homer. These men wrote in the idioms they thought in. Hence that grace and naturalness that seem ever absent from a modern production in the same tongues. There is always something lost in translation ; and that is a rapid process of translation by which we think in one language and write in another. Now, there is a compactness in ancient dialects which modern ones possess not, and seem to have lost in parting with the method of inflections in their grammatical structure. But though the ancients of Greece and Rome said their say well, moderns have equal facility in expressing themselves, and need leave nothing un-

II

said for want of a medium. Especially is our English speech equal to all shades of thought, from the tenderness of love to the highest abstractions of philosophy. Perhaps moderns ought to look higher, for a more spiritual and spiritualizing standard of excellence in literature, than that physical and natural beauty which characterizes Pagan masterpieces.

Another cause of this difference is to be found in the antagonistic natures of the Pagan and Christian religions. Christianity addresses itself to all classes, be they Aryan, Turanian, or Semitic; Paganism is national, and varies with the genius of each people. Christianity imposes a law that is opposed to, and curbs the inclinations of, corrupt human nature; whereas Paganism drifted in harmony with men's passions—consecrated them in their most enormous excesses—and clashed not with the spirit of the times, whi 1, as Tacitus profoundly remarks, "is to corrupt and be corrupted "*—an expression by the way, tinged with Christianity. Therefore it is that Christian thinkers are out of harmony with their age, while the great men of antiquity are thoroughly imbued with the spirit of theirs. But there is an exception ; and it is noteworthy, for it is the rule of modern times. When Socrates rose above the level of Pagan greatness and Pagan thought, and attempted to teach his countrymen the great truths of which he was the depositary—attempted, so to speak, to made headway against the stream of corruption in which Greece was drifti g—he was scouted as a fool and a perverter of

* " Corrumpere et corrumpi seculum vocatur." *De Germ.*, xix.

youth. Modern times have had benefactors of humanity, who also endeavored to stem the tide of corruption—men of God, saintly characters—and they like Socrates, have been the butt of calumny and misrepresentation, but by men who would have been foremost in presenting the cup of hemlock to Socrates.

Thus Christianity introduced a social problem which was of easy solution for the Pagan world—which the Middle Ages were approximating to—but which, since the sixteenth century, seems almost impracticable. It is the reconciling of the secular and religious elements of society. There is at present an antagonism between these two spirits that is gathering into a death-struggle for predominancy. All the earnest thinkers of the world have this problem at heart, often without their knowing it, and each endeavors to solve it in his own way—the Positivist for instance, by substituting the worship of humanity for that of God ; the Illuminati, by replacing religion by learning and enlightenment of the understanding. The school-room is the battle-ground to-day. Let the child have a religious moulding, and, as a rule, religion will have a hold on him through life ; bring him up indifferent to creeds, and, in all probability, he will turn out a disciple of naturalism.

While this struggle lasts, we cannot hope for a literature completely developed in all its relations. For that, there must be an all-absorbing idea—as Rome was for the Roman, as the beautiful was for the Greek, as Jehovah was for the Hebrew, or as the illusory nature of the present life was for the ancient Hindu.

Men's minds must live content in that idea, feed on it, feel secure in its truth and uncontrovertibility ; and with the ease and calm thus induced—an ease and calm unknown in this age of antagonism between conflicting doctrines—they would produce a literary era to which, so far as regards harmony of parts and completeness of finish, the other golden eras of modern times only approximated. As has been seen, they were possessed of this sense of security, and hence their pre-eminence. Not till the millennium will all these conditions obtain.

In the master-pieces of the day a void is clearly perceived. They abound in strikingly beautiful passages, but, as a whole, they fall short of expectation. They are, in a manner, failures. They only reflect the discord of the age, its party spirit and its partial truths. Hence the subjectivism so prevalent in modern literature. Nearly all the poetry and fiction, and history even, of our days, is written, not to give the reader objective reality, but rather with an aim to promote some view or speculation of the author. Such is the spirit of *Childe Harold*, of the *Excursion*, of *Sartor Resartus*, of *The Revolt of Islam*, all of which are inspired by the desire of imparting personal impressions. Only in lyric poetry is it legitimate ; for lyric poetry at all times, as Niebuhr remarks, is eminently subjective.* It is based on the false principle that things are necessarily as they are conceived to be ; and accordingly, whatever the author touches upon, he colors with his individual moods. The spirit is an outgrowth of the rationalism of the sixteenth century.

* *Ancient History*, vol. i. p. 356.

But Christianity has imparted to modern literature, over that of antiquity, a pre-eminence that makes up for its other deficiencies. It has turned man's attention upon himself as man, and taught him to know himself. The light of its truth thrown upon his heart has revealed the innermost folds thereof, and drawn out its most secret aspirations. Hence that intimate knowledge of character—that development of soul-study in the drama, and still more in the novel. Take, for instance, the two supreme efforts of ancient and modern tragedy—the *Hamlet* of Shakespeare and the *Œdipus Rex* of Sophocles. They point the distinction exactly; for one is a soul-study, and the chief interest of the other lies in its intricacy of plot. One runs on the line of personal motive and personal responsibility; the other is based on the ethical doctrine of inherited guilt and its punishment in the clan or tribe—a doctrine largely influencing nations at an early stage of their development. Indeed, it is a law of Christian influence upon literature, that with its growth it develops a more intense personality.

Another effect of Christianity, favorable to the diffusion of thought, is the breaking down of all distinction between Jew and Gentile, Greek and Barbarian, and the uniting of peoples of all climes in a common bond of brotherhood; in consequence of which, ideas that in former times were confined within the limits of a very narrow circle, now gird the globe with the speed of the lightning flash, and interest the whole civilized world. They act, move, revolutionize; they even have their martyrs. The average intelligence of the majority is elevated; but what is gained in extension is lost in comprehension ; for ideas so crowd upon us, that we take time to pursue very few to their ultimate conclusions. We have grown fast. And America is pre-eminent in this particular ; for, if there be no people more credulous, and more easily imposed upon for a time, there is no people on earth who sooner perceive a sham. Thus, twenty years or more ago, when Coleridge and Carlyle were talking the English into the doctrines of German transcendental-ism, America was fully initiated into its tenets, and has since outgrown them, having found them to be insubstantial nothing—mere day-dreams—while the same theories are still gaining ground in England and France.

In consequence of the advantages possessed by moderns, the many fare better. Society no longer consists of the opulent minority entrenched behind their civic rights, and the slave-bound majority who cater to their comfort and subsistence with fear and hatred, on account of the power of life and death that is held over them. In these days the poorest individual possesses inviolable rights, open disre-gard for which would bring the most powerful into odium. The distribution of industries renders the adept in every mechanic art necessary, enables him to treat with the rich on terms of equality, and pro-cures for him conveniences of life that in antiquity the wealth of Croesus could not have purchased.[*]

Let us now examine the most important attempts of the day to reconcile the secular and religious ele-ments of society, absorb them all into a united whole,

[*] See Cæsar Cantù, *Histoire Universelle*, t. xiv., pp. 10-15.

and set upon them the seal of harmony. Four systems especially present themselves for our consideration, viz : Positivism, Evolutionism, Hegelism, and Pessimism. A few remarks on each in its relations with literature and intellectual development.

CHAPTER XII.

POSITIVISM AND LITERATURE.

AUGUSTE COMTE is the founder of Positivism. He thought that we had arrived at a period when men's minds were so agitated that they required a resting-place, and therefore a doctrine adequate to bind them in unison and harmony. He saw the inconsistencies we have pointed out in Protestantism, and found there no refuge for the troubled mind. The Catholic Church he stopped longer at, and recognized the noble work it did in the past ; but considered it insufficient for the intellectual classes. The demands of its faith were, in his opinion, too trying upon reason. He therefore established a religious system to meet the moral anarchy, and a philosophical system to meet the intellectual anarchy, into which society in his view had fallen. The religion he proposed was the worship of humanity ; the philosophy, Positivism. Is the remedy adequate to the evil ?

The worship of humanity is not a new thing. Ever since the coming of the Redeemer, humanity, regenerated and deified in His Divine Person, has been the object of Christian worship. But Comte would do away with the supernatural, and consider humanity by itself as "the continuous whole of convergent beings." *   Now humanity cannot give more than it has.   Humanity is only society ; and according to Comte's own statement, society is out of joint, and suffers from intellectual and moral anarchy.   This is what society is equal to.   It has never, in any stage of its existence, been able to regenerate itself.   It has always required extraneous assistance.   It bears in its womb the seeds of corruption, dissolution, and distraction, rather than the germs of its own regeneration.   When, in pre-historic times, the whole world becomes corrupt, the Supreme Being destroys it, saving only one family with which to repeople it.   When, again, it merges into idolatry, it does not rise from the shadows of death in which it finds itself ; the Redeemer comes, and teaches a purifying and supernatural doctrine, and raises man into that higher plane of life that has become the basis of our modern civilization.   These illustrations are for the Christian reader, not for the Positivist.   For him we are content to lay statement against statement, for he proves not, and we are in possession.

M. Comte states that there is no absolute truth, and therefore no God ; that the idea of God is a metaphysical hypothesis, and, like every hypothesis, a fiction of the mind, though good for a time, inasmuch as it led to the system of rationalism that does away with it, being able to work better without it.   He arrives at this conclusion by an hypothesis—a fiction

* *Cours de Politique Positive*, tome i., p. 30.

of the mind also—in which he states that the progress of religion has been, first fetichism, then polytheism, afterwards monotheism, and finally the present religion, of which he is high-priest, the worship
of humanity.* Now, reason conceives this order to
be impossible; for as right is before wrong, or health
prior to sickness, so must truth have been before
error.   Therefore fetichism or polytheism could not
have been previous to the true religion, whether it be
the humanity-worship of Comte, or monotheism, as
we hold it.   Nor does the history of religion point to
this order of development.—We turn over the pages
of the sacred Scriptures, and we everywhere meet
with one living God—existing from the beginning
—"the ancient of days; † whose "years are unto
generation and generation." ‡ We consult the Vedas
of India, and we read of a supreme deity, Indra—
"him whom harvests do not age, nor moons ; Indra,
whose days do not wither." § In the poetry of Greece
there is also greater than all others "the great Zeus
in heaven, who watches over all things and rules."††
. In the poetry of the Latins we meet with the same

* Cette loi consiste en ce que chacune de nos conceptions princi-
pales, chaque branche de nos connaissances, passe successivement
par trois états théoriques différents : l'état théologique, ou fictif ;
l'état métaphysique, ou abstrait ; l'état scientifique, ou positif. *Phi-*
losophie Positive, tome i. leçon 1. p. 14.

† Dan. vii. 9.

‡ Ps. ci. 25.

§ Nà yàm jàranti s'aràdah nà ma'sah nà dyà'vah l'ndram s'àkars
àyanti. *Rig Veda*, vi. 24, 7.

†† ἔστι μέγας ἐν οὐρανῷ
Ζεὺς, ὃς ἐφορᾷ πάντα, καὶ κρατύνει.—SOPHOCLES, *Electra*, 174, 175.

distinction.   They also have their Jupiter—their
father Zeus—who rules and overawes the affairs of
both gods and men.*

Whichever way we look, we find an acknowledg-
ment of one Supreme Deity, whether it be to the
dusky child of the West, to whom He is known as
the Great Spirit, or to the son of the Celestial Empire,
in whose philosophy, as in that of Lao-Tsze, we
read of Tao, the primordial reason, "a being immense, silent, immutable, but always active; who
is the creator of all things—'the mother of the
world.'" †   And the earlier the document, the more
clearly is the existence of one Supreme Being asserted.   Thus, in the most ancient code of rites in
China—*I-li*—we read : "In time of calamity we offer
the supreme sacrifice to Shang-ti;" and the commen-
tator adds : "All things draw their substance from
heaven; they receive their existence and particular
form from Shang-ti. ‡   Monotheism is prior to polytheism or fetichism, as the thing symbolized exists
before the symbol.

Error is invariably based upon truth, and its only

* O qui res hominumque Deûmque
Æternis regis imperiis, et fulmine terres."
Vergil : *Eneid*. I.

† M. Abel-Remusat, *Mélanges Asiatiques*.

‡ *I-li*, l. XXI, f° 16 R°, and 17 v°, 1-5. For the full text of this
remarkable passage, which has only been recently brought to light
by Mgr. de Harlez, in his refutation of M. Reville's work, *La Religion en Chine*, see *La Revue Generale*, Bruxelles, Avril 1889. See
also *Religion des premiers Chinois*, by Mgr. de Harlez.

effective refutation is to strip the truth of its false covering, and show it up as it really is. This deifica-tion of humanity in the sacred person of the Re-deemer we have seen to be a fact. But inasmuch as the Positivist believes not in the supernatural, this is not the fact he has in view. It is another, also due to Christianity. Only since its introduction can it be rightly said of man, "The truth will make you free." Christianity taught true liberty. It abolished slavery, placed all men upon an equal footing, and gave the individual, for the first time in the world's history, his true place in society. In Pagan times he was not his own master; he was a child of the State, devoted to the State, living for the State, claimed by the State, absorbed in the State. Christianity inspired him with a sense of his dignity, and taught him that there was something higher than the State to live for. In this feeling he has grown up and waxed strong, and it is a misapprehension of this feeling and its true cause that dictates the religion of Comte, and leads another philosopher of atheism to say : " The historical progress of religion consists in this, that what was regarded by an earlier religion as objective, is now regarded as subjective; what was formerly worshipped and contemplated as God, is now per-ceived to be something human." * But to exaggerate humanity as a whole is to belittle the individual, de-prive him again of his personal rights, and absorb him into the masses. Indeed, the Positivist says that the

* Feuerbach, *Das Wesen der Religion*, §§ 2, 8, 10. Werke, pp. 411, et seq.

individual man has no rights, no free will, that he is
a creature of law, and that he imagines himself free,
because of his ignorance of the complex laws of
sociology.

In the philosophy of Positivism, the only legitimate aim of man is industry, the industry that benefits humanity. In this is to consist the sum of his
happiness; in this is his whole being absorbed. The
Positivist lays stress upon this theory of disinterest-
edness as an improvement upon what he calls the
selfish doctrine of a future reward promulgated by
the gospel. This is a sophism. It ignores the fundamental principle of Christianity, which is the principle of love. And love is unselfish. The reward
that follows the fulfilment of the law of love is a
necessity of the end of our creation, and due solely
to the goodness of the Creator. He might have
created us to fulfil a temporary purpose in life, such
as the horse and the dog fulfil—and this is the theory
of the Positivist ; but since, in His infinite love, He
has, in creating us man, bestowed upon us an immortal soul, with infinite yearnings, that are never
satisfied until they find rest in their Creator, we ought
to be doubly thankful, and bless him for it the more.

The Positivist says, with Herbert Spencer and Sir
William Hamilton, that as we cannot have absolute
and infinite notions, we cannot have notions of the
absolute and infinite. But if we had no notions of
absolute and infinite being, how could we think it as
such, how have words to express it, how use these
words so accurately in all our reasonings? Evi-

dently, then, we have such notions, and our knowledge is more than relative.

But the spirit that actuates the Positivists is the same that inspired the Encyclopædists of the eighteenth century. It is a matter of pride to them to think that they are continuing and perfecting the work of D'Alembert and Diderot. They are children of the same spirit of rationalism. They might accumulate scientific facts and develop scientific theories; but in their hands the higher species of literature would be cramped and considered a thing of silly amusement. "Such a mere mathematical people," says Schlegel, "with minds thus sharpened and pointed by mathematical discipline, would and could never possess a rich and various intellectual existence, nor even probably ever attain to a living science, or a true science of life." * The influence of a people so narrowed in their mental training is calculated rather to blight than foster poetic genius; and when a rationalist wishes to touch humanity, he must become a child of faith—a believer in tradition and in the supernatural—even as humanity is. The immediate effect of such doctrines is to ignore the position and importance of the human soul, to belittle personality by merging persons into things, and to recognize in genius and virtue but a combination of external circumstances with internal temperament.

Not in Positivism, then, do we find a bond of reconciliation, in which all the elements of society may become a unit. It is contradictory in its phil-

* *Philosophy of History*, p. 238.

osophy, absurd in its religion, and in its tendency destructive of the higher literary spirit. How is it with Evolutionism ?

CHAPTER XIII.

EVOLUTIONISM AND LITERATURE.

HERBERT SPENCER is the philosopher of Evolutionism. Now, Evolutionism holds many tenets in common with Positivism. But it has also its lines of divergence. Comte, in making humanity self-sufficient, instead of raising it up and deifying it, as was his intention, would have been the death of humanity. Exaggeration invariably induces reaction. Therefore, Herbert Spencer conceived humanity as only one element of the Cosmos, evolved in the slow process of time from the primary forms of life, but entirely subject to the same laws which all matter, organic and inorganic, obeys. He is more logical than Comte. For while, with the latter, he believes that there is no absolute truth, he does not assert as an absolute truth that there is no God ; but holding to the relativity of all knowledge, he says that God may or may not be. He relegates Him to the unknowable.

Comte denies that man has a soul ; so does Herbert Spencer. With Darwin, he considers "that the mental faculties of man and the lower animals do not differ in kind, although immensely in degree ;"* and concludes "that man is the co-descendant with other mammals, of a common progenitor,"† and that he

* *Descent of Man*, i., p. 179.   † *Ibid.*, ii., p. 369.

"like every other animal, has no doubt advanced to his present high condition through a struggle for existence;"* or as Herbert Spencer himself expresses it, through " the survival of the fittest." From this position he fearlessly draws his consequences. He infers that man is not responsible to anything higher than society for his acts ; that belief in God is acquired by education, and did not exist in the primeval man ; that our sense of right and wrong comes from experience; that "forms of thought (and by implication all intuitions) are products of organized and inherited experiences "†—"the absolute internal uniformities generated by infinite repetitions of absolute external uniformities "‡—that mind is "a product of evolution," and thought, of cerebral action This is Evolutionism in a nutshell. It changes ou whole view of thought, the soul, society, and God At the outset we felt compelled to diverge from i explicitly. Humanity without a supernatural order without a revelation, without a personal God, is to us an enigma, an unsolved and unsolvable problem. Admit these elements and their consequences, and the universe has a meaning, society in all its aberrations can be accounted for, and literature, its laws and history, becomes a profitable study, comprehensible in their light. Granting that humanity and the material universe are solely of the natural order evolved from primary forms of life, what is their aim? Why are we here restless, malcontent, with

* *Descent of Man*, ii., p. 385.
† *Principles of Psychology*, p. 571.
‡ *Essays*, Mill *vs.* Hamilton, The Test of Truth, p. 409.

an infinity of desires unsatisfied, living and dying in struggle, appearing for a moment, and then disappearing forever, going on, on, now merging into barbarism, now rising into civilization, our thoughts scarcely our own, we ourselves the creatures of fiction and fancy, the victims of a life-long delusion—and all for what? Mr. Spencer does not tell us.

"Absolute morality," he says, "means conformity to the laws of complete life."* A law implies order; an order, a purpose; a purpose, one purposing, a cause; and the cause purposing is the imposer of the law, the Creator to whom alone belongs the right of determining the laws of complete life. And what is complete life in Herbert Spencer's philosophy? He reduces it to a thing of time. The aim of life is with him as with Comte and his master, Saint Simon, industry; and complete life is a life blessed with temporary advantages. But how few of the world's millions enjoy this beatitude, temporary though it be! How few are content with their worldly lot! To the great majority, then, life is aimless and a burden. It is no day-dream; it is the agony of a nightmare. Literature is a raving maniac's utterances. What do I seek in speculating? The aim of life? But life will be past before I apply my results. The benefit of the many? The many will not understand my views; they will live and die struggling for the unattainable, each in his own way.

The moral sense by which this absolute morality is known, Herbert Spencer states to be "the experiences of utility organized and consolidated through all past

Essays, Prison Ethics, p. 224.

generations of the human race "—" certain emotions responding to right and wrong ; "* and Mr. Darwin undertakes to explain its acquired origin as being due to the fact that "the more enduring social instincts conquer the less persistent instincts."† "At the moment of action," he says, "man will no doubt be apt to follow the stronger impulse ; and though this may occasionally prompt him to the noblest deeds, it will far more commonly lead him to gratify his own desires at the expense of other men. But after this gratification, when past and weaker impressions are contrasted with the ever-enduring social instincts, retribution will surely come. Man will then feel dissatisfied with himself, and will resolve, with more or less force, to act differently for the future. This is conscience ; for conscience looks backward and judges past actions, inducing that kind of dissatisfaction which, if weak, we call regret, and if severe, remorse."‡ Whence, then, arises this remorse experienced in the gratification of desires that are at the expense of no society, and that are a source of pleasure to the individual—thoughts, for instance, that he knows to be wrong ? He is not amenable to society for them ; for he has injured no man. And yet he feels that he is guilty—that there is a court to which he is amenable.§ This can be explained only by the consciousness, more or less distinct, of the Supreme Judge who implanted in man's breast the moral sense. Furthermore, does not the fact of feeling that

* Letter to Mr. Mill in Bains' "*Mental and Moral Science*," p. 722, ed. 1868.

† *Descent of Man*, i., p. 83.   ‡ *Descent of Man*, i., p. 87

§ A. R. Wallace has pointed the same objection by the horror for lying—even where a lie would benefit them—of certain hill-tribes in Central India.—*Natural Selection*, pp. 353-355.

an injury is done to others, imply a sense of injury—that is, of what is just and unjust—in a word, of right and wrong ? In other words, the dissatisfaction, or remorse, is based on a sense of right and wrong. But Mr. Darwin argues that conscience—that is, the sense of right and wrong—proceeds from the dissatisfaction. Here is a vicious circle.

In good truth, there is an absolute morality beyond all cavil, as well as beyond all considerations of utility. It is universal. It exists in the rude, savage tribes, though distorted and misapplied ; the brilliancy of civilization cannot dim its light ; its fire is undying ; it glows in the breast of the most warped nature. Men may differ concerning the standard of right ; but that there is such a thing few deny ; and even these few, by their words and actions, prove its existence in them. Therefore, were man alone, the inward voice of his conscience would still speak to him ; it would point out to him the good to be done and the evil to be avoided ; its dictates should command his respect. Man would still find himself a responsible being. But what a weak barrier Mr. Spencer, in his opposite doctrine, places before evil-doing ! "If," the holder of such doctrine would argue, "I know that I can safely better myself at the expense of my neighbor; that the feeling to be over-come in doing so, the remorse to be smothered, is only a trait hereditary in me—as my features, my eyes, my hair—and that I am responsible to no one but him I injure, I am not going to stay my course ; it is a struggle for life, for enjoyment, for predomi-nancy ; it is his lookout: and I must enjoy life, since

there is no hereafter for me." Objections are as straws
before the torrent in the presence of such an argument, when the temptation is strong and the way
clear. And yet, Mr. Spencer imagines that he is
benefiting society in paving the way for such arguments and their practical results. He fancies that he has
the secret that will harmonize the elements of society.
It is told in two words—scientific training. That is
the panacea for all the ills to which flesh is heir.
The Cosmist would abolish all ideas of a God, of the
supernatural, of religious creeds, as superstitions, by
cultivating the mental soil scientifically, and thus
inducing habits of thought free from such beliefs.
Human society does not become better by such a
process. Suppress religion, and morality soon van-
ishes ; or tamper with morality, and little difficulty
will be found in eradicating religion. And with one
or other of these results achieved, let him who dares
attempt to control the masses. Mr. Fiske of Harvard,
the American exponent of Evolutionism, knows this,
for he says: "The cosmic philosopher is averse to
proselytism, and has no sympathy with radicalism
or infidelity. *For he knows that theological habits
of thought are relatively useful, while scepticism, if
permanent, is intellectually and morally pernicious ;
witness the curious fact that radicals are prone to adopt
retrograde social theories."* * That which Evolution'sm
would avoid is precisely what it brings about. It is
inconsistent. It destroys theological habits of
thought while acknowledging them to be relatively

* Lecture quoted in *Brownson's Review* for October, 1873, Art.
" Refutation of Atheism."

useful ; it fosters scepticism, knowing that it is morally and intellectually pernicious ; it encourages the radicalism that is prone to adopt retrograde social theories. We said that Evolutionism is more logical than Positivism. It walks correctly one step farther, then totters and falls.

With all its shortcomings, Evolutionism has attractions for the human mind, and is therefore to be regarded as more than a passing phase of thought. For the scientific mind, whose science is fragmentary, the simple explanation of the evolution of life possesses a fascination that it knows not how to overcome. The vagueness with which the theory is surrounded, the necessity under which the mind is of not examining the details too closely, and the host of fresh objections which it gives rise to against faith and revelation, have all tended to make it popular with a certain class of scientific men. The mysterious Unknowable to which Herbert Spencer relegates the inexplicables of science, and which is in the background of the energies of nature, possesses a charm for the dreamy sentimentality that has supplanted religion, to a great extent, among all classes outside the Catholic Church. The partial revival of Nature-worship will find in this mysterious energy a new bond to strengthen and rivet its claims on man's thoughts and affections, and will carry him far beyond the Nature over which Rousseau brooded, and of which Shelley sang.

In rejecting radical views of Evolutionism, we do not lose sight of the lessons it teaches. Darwin is the Newton of natural history. He has revolutionized

the whole study of nature. He has united in intimate bonds the present with the remotest past. Read
in the light of the doctrine of Natural Selection, this
world's story, with the story of all things upon it,
reads like a fairy-tale. Darwin has explained the
laws governing the variation of the species; he has
shown how potent a factor environment is in mod-
ifying transmitted organs and transmitted traits; he
· has thus accounted for the existence of rudimentary
parts in earth's flora and fauna, now useless but at
one time or other having had their special use and
function; he has brought out clearly the great law
in the animal and vegetable kingdoms of the power
of rapid multiplication in a geometrical progression,
the consequent struggle for existence, and the survival of the fittest. These are elementary truths
underlying all our studies in nature. They determine
the lines upon which science is at present constructed. We cannot ignore them if we would.

But there are limitations to this theory. To begin
with, it is by a misnomer that Darwinism is called
Evolutionism. Darwinism finds in Nature the law
of retrogression and of the degeneracy of species and
races as universally active as the law of progression.
The surviving type is not by any means the most
perfect type. It is simply the type most capable of
struggling against difficulties of climate, soil and all
other obstacles in the way of existence, and best
adapted to environment; in a word, the surviving
type is the fittest for time, place and circumstance.
Again, naturalists are compelled to admit a principle
of heterogeneous generation running all along the

various grades of plant and animal life, in opposition
to Darwin's theory of transformation by slight variations continued through ages beyond the grasp of
human conception.   Wigand, examining the subject
from the point of view of a botanist, holds strongly
by this principle, as the predominating principle in
the doctrine of Descent.*   Von Hartmann, looking
at it from the metaphysical point of view, finds room
for both principles.   He says :   " Heterogeneous
generation and transformism are placed side by side
in the series of processes of organic evolution, and it
would be equally inadmissible to want with Darwin
to exclude the first completely to the advantage of
the second, or with Wigand, the second to the advantage of the first."†   Finally, in both the animal and
the vegetable kingdoms, we everywhere meet with
variations of species and races ; but these variations
act within well-defined lines.   The laws of physi-
ology, as now understood, are opposed to the theory
that all forms of life are evolved from one or a few
primary forms.   Nature does not blunder.   The
germs of every species of plant and animal will develop along the lines of the species, in accordance
with a law as fixed as that which traces the heavenly
bodies in space.   Theorize how we will, there is no
getting over this fact.   The human germ from its
primary cell develops towards the formation of the
human being, and in every stage of its growth it is

* For a masterly summing up of the various schools of Darwinism, see Wigand, *Der Darwinismus und die Naturforschung
Newtons und Cuviers*, 1877, bd. iii, s. 290–315.

† *Le Darwinisme*, p. 297.

always the human being and none other. At no moment is the human principle aught else than the human soul. The formation of a human body is the evolution of a human animating principle along a clearly defined line, to a clearly defined result, subject to clearly defined laws.

Remembering these truths, we are in position to say that according to all that is known of the laws governing physiological phenomena, and according to facts as now observed and recorded by science, there is nothing to warrant any explanation of the specific origin of man as the product of evolution from lower forms of animal life. It is merely an inference drawn from another set of inferences and conjectures more or less plausible. We everywhere witness diversity of races among men and beasts, but we possess not a single instance of one distinct species originating another distinct species. M. Quatrefages gave the subject his most impartial thought in the spirit of a true scienist fully equipped to meet the problem face to face, and he has recorded his deliberate conclusion in these remarkable words : "Without prejudging the future, we have been obliged to acknowledge that the problem of the specific origin of man cannot be solved, or even attempted, with the scientific data which we at present possess." * Man's body may have been evolved from other animal forms in the distant past, or he may have been instantaneously created ; one inference has as much scientific support as the other ; in

* *The Human Species*, p. 129.

either case he is still a creature of God. To science in its present state man's origin is an enigma, and, Dr. Mivart truly remarks, "speculation as to this enigma is useless." * It is useless, because man's nature, come it to him ready-made, or be it the product of laws working through all time, is equally God's gift, and is none the less peculiarly and specifically man's own nature, as far removed in every attribute that makes him man from all other forms of the animal creation as the heavens are removed from the earth.

Be man's origin what it may, no theory of Evolution is adequate to explain the rational and spiritual side of his nature. We must look beyond the purely natural and phenomenal. Herbert Spencer acknowledges a power back of the Cosmos, guiding and directing: "A power of which the nature remains forever inconceivable and to which no limits in time or space can be imagined, works in us certain effects." † Dr. Alfred Russel Wallace, the co-discoverer with Darwin of the Theory of Natural Selection, in his latest word on the subject, goes to show that neither the mathematical faculty in man, nor the musical faculty, nor the metaphysical faculty, nor the faculty for art, nor that of wit and humor, could by any possible arrangement have been the outcome of Natural Selection ; but that all man's higher faculties point clearly to an unseen world guiding and directing the visible world. ‡ And we have seen how

* *On Truth*, p. 528.
† *First Principles*, p. 557 ; London Ed.
‡ *Darwinism, an Exposition of the Theory of Natural Selection*

inadequate is Darwin's explanation of man's sense of right and wrong. It is throughout a begging of the question.

Equally so is Herbert Spencer's genesis of the idea of immortality and the prayers and practices of religion. "The awe of the ghost," he says, "makes sacred the sheltering place of the tomb, and this grows into the temple; while the tomb itself becomes the altar. . . . And so, every religious rite is derived from a funeral rite." * Funeral rites have meaning only as religious ceremonies based upon belief in an hereafter, in a state of reward and punishment, in a Supreme Being who searches hearts, and in a moral sense knowing right and wrong and rendering man responsible for his every thought, word and deed. Degenerate races of men may have drifted away from belief in the primary spiritual sense of religious rites and ceremonies; individuals may have in their own consciousness reduced that belief to such a state of inactivity that it ceases to influence, and becomes for them as useless as the rudimentary organ that had ceased to operate in the species: but this no more militates against the existence and meaning and right use of that belief, than does the present uselessness of an organ bespeak inefficiency in all former stages of its existence. Come man's body how it may, every man has a distinct, separate, individual soul, that survives the growth and decay of his body, and lives through all eternity

with some of its *Applications*, 1889, Chap. xvii., "Darwinism applied to man.

* *Principles of Sociology*, vol. i., p. 446.

in bliss or misery according to the manner in which it followed its sense of right and wrong while animating the body. The new-born infant and the full-grown man, the illiterate peasant and the learned philosopher, the man-eating savage and the cultured denizen of civilized life—each has his own immortal soul. "No one outside of him can really touch him, can touch his soul, his immortality; he must live with himself forever. He has a depth within him unfathomable, an infinite abyss of existence; and the scene in which he bears part for the moment is but like a gleam of sunshine upon its surface." *

It is to obliterate this great truth as well as the whole structure of Christianity that extreme Evolutionists carry their theorizings beyond the domain of scientific principles into the regions of imagination and personal feeling. They find in the doctrine of Descent a substitute for the teachings of Christianity. Their enmity towards the Church is pointed; but they have never been stronger, more rabid, more numerous or more plausible than the Averroïsts of the fifteenth century, and where are the Averroïsts to-day? Even so will the anti-Christian Evolutionist live out his little day, and science will continue to advance in spite of his misreadings, and God's Church will continue the work of teaching man the same elevating truths she now teaches.

The sought-for reconciliation is not here. With a a morality the basis of immorality, a philosophy the

* Cardinal Newman, *Parochial and Plain Sermons :* Sermon on "The Individuality of the Soul." Copeland's Selections, pp. 133, 134.

destruction of thought, an industry the death of the higher species of literature and a religion that is atheistic, Evolutionism in the sense of Herbert Spencer has little in it that is ennobling to humanity.

CHAPTER XIV.

HEGELISM AND LITERATURE.

PERVADING the Relativism of Comte and Herbert Spencer, there is the Absolutism of the age, which also has its advocates.   Hegel is the philosopher of the Absolute.   To understand his philosophical position rightly, we must glance at the history of modern philosophy in Germany.

Kant is the founder of modern Transcendentalism. He taught that we can only know phenomena, that the noumenon or essence is beyond our knowing, that time and space are mere subjective conditions of thinking.   He created an abyss between the metaphysical reason and the practical reason, and then attempted to reconcile them over the chasm.   Upon his principles there was no reconciliation.   In throwing the shadow of skepticism upon metaphysical truth, in spite of his protests, he rendered moral truth no less uncertain, and soon found disciples who were more logical than he.   Fichte destroyed all objectivity, and, as we have seen, basing knowledge upon the Ego—*das Ich*—self,—he found himself incompetent to assert more than his own identity, accepted the situation, and settled himself into the conviction that the external world was only a projection of the Ego, that it received its shaping from the Ego, as a liquid from the vessel in which it is placed ; and he thus ended in subjective pantheism.   Schelling is known

as the philosopher of nature.   He conceived all
things absorbed in one infinite substance, asserted
universal identity, and thus ended in objective pantheism.   In identifying liberty with necessity, he
almost effaces the moral problem.   Art is practically
the summit of his system.

Then came Hegel.   He taught that all nature, both
the material and spiritual world, is a manifestation of ·
the Idea which he calls reason—*Vernunft*—in philosophy, and the world-spirit—*Welt-Geist*—in history.
"Reason. . . is substance as well as infinite power,
its own infinite material underlying all the natural
and spiritual life which it originates, as also the infinite form, that which sets this material in motion."*
That is, Hegel's Idea is his God.   It is an absolute,
impersonal, progressive, and ever-progressing Being,
with progress for its law, and freedom for its essence
and aim.   This is not the God of revelation, the God
of Christianity.   He is a personal God, having Himself for His own law, His own end and aim.   An
impersonal God is no God.   It is a mistaken notion
to consider personality as limiting.   It only distin-
guishes, characterizes.   St. Thomas calls it that
which is most perfect in all nature ; † and Boëtius

---

* "Durch die spekulative Erkenntniss in ihr wird es erweisen,
dass die Vernunft—bei diesem Ausdrucke können wir hier stehen
bleiben, ohne die Beziehung und das Verhältniss zu Gott naher zu
erörtern—die *Substanz* wie die *unendlich Macht*, sich selbst der
unendliche Stoff alles natürlichen und geistigen Lebens, wie die
unendliche Form, die Bethätigung dieses ihres Inhalts ist."—*Phil.
der Geschichte*, Einleitung, s. 12 ; *Hegel's Werke*, 9ter Band.

† Respondeo dicendum quod persona significat id quod perfectis-
simum est in tota natura ; scilicet subsistens in rationali natura.
Summa, i, i., quaest xxix, art. iii.

defines it as the individual substance of a rational nature.* In finite beings it is accompanied with the idea of limitation. In the infinite Being it is the completion of His nature. A God with an incomplete and imperfect nature is no God. That which is capable of increase or diminution is not infinite. Thus the Hegelian God is an idol of Hegel's own making.

History, according to Hegel, is the progress of humanity towards freedom. The essence of human progress he holds to be the clearer manifestation of the world-spirit. But the essence of spirit is freedom, pure freedom, potentially ; actually, freedom cramped by contingencies. Therefore, to use his own language, "universal history is the manifestation of spirit in the process of working out that which it is potentially."† The people of the East knew only *one* free person ; they were all his slaves. Pagan Greece and Rome realized the fact that *some* were free ; but they held slaves, and this marred their civilization. But Christianity taught for the first time to the Aryan race that all men were free ; that not *one* or *some*, but *all*, stood in the image of their Creator, equal before Him in their nature and essence. This is the drift of Hegel's argument. "The German nations, under the influence of Christianity, were the first to attain the consciousness that man as man is free ; that it

---

*Persona est rationalis naturae individua substantia. This defini-tion St. Thomas adopts. Ibid. art. i.

† In diesem Sinne können wir sagen, dass die Weltgeschichte, die Darstellung ist, wie der Geist zu dem Bewusstsein dessen kommt, was er an sich bedeutet.—*Phil. der Geschichte*, Einleitung.

is the freedom of spirit which constitutes its essence. The consciousness arose first in religion, the inmost region of spirit."* Freedom, then, is the aim of humanity. This is the focus towards which all nations converge. Freedom, and not lawlessness. Hegel makes the distinction; for he states to the effect that true freedom consists in the harmony between reason and the objective restraint of the law; that is, reason sees such restraint to be good and wholesome, and accordingly submits.

Here is a bond of union for all the elements of society. Every man, be he Pagan or Christian, loves freedom, seeks it if he has it not, and having it, rejoices in its possession. It ennobles life. It is one of the greatest blessings the individual can have. Beneath its invigorating influence, his whole nature expands into twofold energy. But before men unite, they must know why they are to make freedom the aim of their existence; for freedom is not a final cause. We are free for a purpose—that we may the better perform the functions of life. Are these functions to be performed for life's sake, or for an hereafter? In Hegel's philosophy, we are parts of the great whole—the all-absorbing Absolute, necessitated by our nature to seek freedom for freedom's sake, and for the benefit of those coming after us; and, after our share of the work shall have been accomplished,

* "Erst die germanischen Nationen sind im Christenthume zum Bewusstsein gekommen, dass der Mensch als Mensch frei, die Freiheit des Geistes, seine eigenste Natur ausmacht; diess Bewusstsein ist zuerst in der Religion, in der innersten Region des Geistes aufgegangen."—*Ibid.* Einleitung. Seit 22.

we will be merged into the primordial substance whence we emanated. Our reason tells us differently. Hegel has solved the easy part of the problem of existence, and therefore his philosophy is fragmentary ; and the philosophy that grasps not the whole meaning of life is necessarily false. "To forget in this life the care of the future, which is inseparably united with a Divine Providence, and to be content with a certain inferior grade of natural right, which an atheist can also hold, is to mutilate science in its most beautiful parts, and destroy many good actions." It is Leibnitz who so speaks.

Though Hegel comes nearest to the solution of the great difficulty of modern times, still he stops short of the real aim of life, and for substantial realities would give us empty phantoms. He, as well as Comte and Herbert Spencer, ignores the most strongly attested principles of thought and existence, and heeds not the loudest asseverations of human nature concerning its future destiny, the immortal spark that gives it life, and the personal God from whom it came. This doctrine of indefinite progressiveness and of instinctive finality, by which all nature, under the impulse of the Idea, tends to perfection, has no foundation in reason. For how can nature proceed towards an end it knows not?—As well might you say it can see by a light that does not exist. The philosophy of the indefinite can give only a literature of the indefinite. Its key-note is the vague. Aspirations unfulfilled, yearnings unsatisfied, life without a purpose : these are the normal themes of such a literature. If the Hegelian refuses to consider the indefinite future, and confines himself to the Idea animating society and constructing history, he can find no ideal beyond the actual world in which we live and move.   A critic of Hegel has well remarked : ''The philosophy of the Absolute in Hegel does not recognize the true ideal. The ideal for him is simply reality. The world is the system of ideas eternally developed by dialectics. There is to be found no practical ideal, no moral ideal.''*   The logical outcome of Hegelism from this point of view is realism in literature, and realism is the bane of literature.   A philosophy in its fundamental principle purely dialectic must needs induce reaction, and Hegelism is no exception. The reactionary phase most destructive of thought and aspiration is Pessimism.   Let us consider its nature and its influence.

CHAPTER XV.

PESSIMISM AND LITERATURE.

Schopenhauer is the philosopher of Pessimism. Let us ask him his solution for the problem of reconciliation between the secular and religious elements of society.   But first a word upon the Pessimism of the nineteenth century.   Leibnitz was emphatically the philosopher of modern Optimism.   He taught that all was for the best in this best of possible worlds.

* Harms, *Die Philosophie seit Kant*, p. 454.

During the eighteenth century his Optimism prevailed among the writers and thinkers of Europe. It entered as a soothing element into the philosophy of superficial complacency then prevalent. Shaftesbury and Bolingbroke basked in its sunshine. Pope, in his *Essay on Man*, feebly reproduced its main tenets. Hume picked flaws in it. Voltaire cleverly satirized certain aspects of it in his *Candide*. With the dawning of the nineteenth century a spirit of unrest and vague yearning hovered over sensitive natures. It was the throbbing of the new social upheaval. Châteaubriand was for a time under its influence—during which he wrote *René*—but he cast it off with the infidelity that threatened to blight his beautiful intellect. Byron inhaled its noxious vapors ; they rendered him cynical and embittered toward the world, and inspired *Cain* and *Manfred*. Lamartine took the malady in a milder form ; its presence may be detected in the melancholy tone pervading some of his sweetest poems. Heine felt the depth of human misery, and his muse sang the world-pain—*Der Weltschmers*—but his moods were many and he could not long remain a Pessimist. Lenau, in his wandering and careless life, was deeply impressed with the vanity and the transitoriness of all things ; their fleeting seemed part of himself.[*]

But the poet of Pessimism is Leopardi (1798–1837). A lifelong invalid, his body racked with pain, his soul ever stooping to drink of the waters of pleasure, and, Tantalus-like, ever finding them recede far-

---

[*] Es braust in meines Herzens wildem Takt,
    Vergänglichkeit, dein lauter Katarakt !—*Die Zweifler. Gedichte,* bd. i., s. 99.

ther and farther beyond his reach, he came to look
upon life as the greatest evil and death as the greatest
good, and he sang the song of the world's desolation
and unhappiness—*infelicità*—with the nerve and calm
of confirmed despair.   Life was to him something
wretched and dreadful,* a burden which he dragged
along with loud murmuring.   "He everywhere saw
lamentation, cruelty, cowardice, injustice, and weariness."†   And the vision was to him a source of dreary
delight.   "I rejoice," he wrote to his bosom friend,
Giordani, "to discover more and more, and to touch
with my hands, the misery of men and things, and
to be seized with a cold shudder as I search through
the wretched and terrible secret of the life of the uni
verse."‡   Life had for him no other worth than to
hold it in scorn.§

Elsewhere he tells us :   "We are born to tears,
. . . happiness smiles not upon our lives ; our afflic-
tions make heaven rejoice."‖   In the poem in which,
in a final groan of despair, he concentrated all the
sorrow, all the agony, all the defiance of his unhappy
life, he assures us that "on this obscure grain of
sand called earth . . . nature has no more concern
for man than she has for the worm."¶   Need we
wonder that he should envy the dead ?   His Pessimism grew into his soul till it became part of himself.

---

* Opere, i. 59.

† Licurgo Cappelletti : *Poesie di Giacomo Leopardi*, p. 38.

‡ *Epistolario*, i. 352.

§ Nostra vita a che val ?   Sola a spregiarla.—*A un Vincitore nel Pallone*, op. i. 57.

‖ *Il Sogno*, op. i. 84.   ¶ *La Ginestra*.

Patriotism, enthusiasm, aspirations for the good and the true in their highest and most ennobling sense, all came to a premature blight beneath the touch of scepticism, and his gifted soul stands out parched and arid as the barren sides of Vesuvius on which he was wont to gaze. His life and his writings form a complete contrast with the life and the writings of Manzoni. Each is perfect in his art ; but where one strikes the note of morbidness and blank despair, the other is joyous, hopeful, and patriotic. And the cause of this difference? Within the breast of the author of *I Promessi Sposi* glowed the fire of religious faith ; within the breast of the singer of *La Ginestra* that fire had become extinguished and was reduced to a cold burned cinder, such as underlay the broom-shrub he sang.*

While Leopardi was chanting the song of Pessimism, Schopenhauer (1788–1860) was forging its philosophy. And what is his solution of the problem of evil? How does he reconcile the secular and religious elements of society ? To begin with, Schopenhauer is a rabid opponent of Hegelism. He denies the Hegelian Idea. He sees no growth or development towards a better or a best in this world ; he considers it the worst possible world that could have existed, the domain of accident and error, into which man is born that he may live in misery and die the victim of a deceiving power that overrides all things and makes the individual miserable in the interests of the species. That power Schopenhauer

* *La Ginestra* is the broom-shrub.

calls Will.   This is neither the infinite personal Will
which we recognize as an attribute of God, nor the
finite personal will of the human soul.   In the philosophy of Schopenhauer there is place neither for the
soul nor for God.   Will he defines to be "the innermost nature, the kernel of every particular thing, and
equally of the totality of existence.   It appears in
every blind force of nature ; it manifests itself also in
the deliberate action of man ; and the great difference
between these two is merely in the degree of the
manifestation, not in the nature of what manifests
itself." *   This Will underlies all phenomena.   It
includes the operations of the material world as well
as those of man's consciousness—his hopes and fears,
his loves and hates.   In one sense it may be identified with the noumenon of Kant ; in another it is
more than the noumenon, or the Thing-in-itself. †
It is the ultimate reality of all things, the bond of
unity holding the universe together.   It is the real
source of all human action, personal and external
motives being the special conditions for its various
manifestations.‡   It works without end, and apparently without aim.   Pain and misery follow its
course.   Pain is the positive state of life ; pleasure is
its negative state.   The only real enjoyment in life
is that derived from intellectual culture.   All others,
when analyzed—and the philosopher enters into a
searching analysis of each and every source of pleasure to man—are found to be fleeting, unsatisfactory,

* *Die Welt als Wille und Vorstellung*, i. 131.
† Ding an Sich.
‡ Sully : *Pessimism*, p. 70.

and merely the absence of pain. This part of his system may be summed up in the words of Byron :

> "Count o'er the joys thine hours have seen,
> Count o'er thy days from anguish free,
> And know, whatever thou hast been,
> '*Tis something better not to be.*"

What remedy is there for this state of things? How may the misery of man be best ameliorated? The supreme remedy, according to Schopenhauer, is for all men and women to lead a life of celibacy, and thus hasten the end of human misery. In the absence of this universal understanding, it is the duty of each individual to resist with the whole energy of his nature the tendencies and impulses of the tyrannical Will which is the source of all his sufferings. In order to render this resistance effective, he seeks an emancipation of the intellect from the dominion of the Will. This emancipation is brought about, in the first place, by the practice of virtue, and especially of charity and pity for suffering and misery ; and secondly, by renouncing all the aims of life, and seeking self-control and resignation in the fastings and mortifications of asceticism. It is the remedy of Sakya-Mouni without the gentle spirit of Sakya to give it life. It is a seeking after Nirvâna. This is a consummation to which the proud and selfish spirit of Schopenhauer was certainly unequal. "He has," says Amiel, "no sympathy, no humanity, no love."*

But why dwell upon this system in the broad daylight of the nineteenth century? Has it not been

* *Journal Intime,* 16th August, 1869.

called "a philosophy of exception and transition?" *
It is because the exception bids fair to become the
rule.   It takes no deep insight into European thought
to detect its wide-spread influence.   "The whole of
the present generation," says Vaihinger, "is impreg-
nated with the Schopenhauer mode of thinking."†
Von Hartmann, while accepting the same Pessimistic
views, undertook to reduce their solution to a still
more scientific demonstration.   He also asserts that
creation is a mistake, the result of blind folly, and,
therefore, that death is preferable to life, not-being to
being.   He recognizes a power pervading and
unifying all nature and all history.   He calls this
power the Unconscious.   It is instinctive, blind, and
yet somehow it works with design.   It is ever struggling from the lower to the higher forms of life,
bringing with it increased capacity for pain according
as it grows into consciousness.   "It is an eternal
pining—*Schmachten*—for fulfillment, and is thus absolute unblessedness, torment without pleasure, even
without pause."‡ It is not to be confounded with
human consciousness.   The latter is subject to disease
and exhaustion, is conditioned by material brain or
nervous ganglia, and is liable to error.   The Unconscious is above all conditions of space and time and
matter, and is infallible in its actions.   Man is apparently free, but his work is laid out for him and he
is moved thereto by the Unconscious.   The Unconscious is the organizer of all life.   It moulds plant

* M. Caro : *Revue des Deux Mondes*, 1877, p. 514.
† See Ferdinand Laban : *Die Schopenhauer-Literatur*, Leipzig,
1880, p. 1.
‡ Sully : *Pessimism*, p. 129.

and animal each according to its kind. It determines the various forms of life rather than Darwin's principle of natural selection, which only accounts for physiological changes. The world was born of will and idea. Existence, Hartmann conceives to be created out of the embrace of the two super-existent principles, "the potency of existence deciding for existence," and "the purely existent." Now, "the potency of existence" is simply the Aristotelian and Scholastic "matter," and the "purely existent" is their "form." Hartmann is only repeating the time-honored idea that all things are the product of matter and form. Will, according to him, is the prime factor of human misery. But there is a scale in the capacity for suffering. The animal suffers less than man, the oyster less than the animal, and the unconscious plant less than all. Thus does suffering increase with the degree of intelligence. This has been formulated as follows : "Pain is an intellectual function, perfect in proportion to the development of the intelligence."*

The Unconscious is the guiding spirit of history. By means of the sexual impulse it founds the family. By means of the social instinct it founds the clan. By means of the instinct of "enmity of all to all," and the consequent struggle for existence, it consolidates the tribe and founds the nation. On, on it moves in its iron purpose through the ages. Individuals are sacrificed, peoples suffer, nations grow and decay and are blotted out from the face of the

* M. Charles Richet : *La Douleur, Étude de Psychologie Physiologique. Revue Philosophique*, Novembre, 1877, p. 469.

earth ; but unheeding, unpitying, onward still it moves. It manages so that the right men are born at the right time, that the right work is done at the right moment, caring naught for the suffering and misery entailed in the process. Such, in a nutshell, is the system of Hartmann.

And what is his remedy against all this pain? Does he also seek refuge in the teachings of Gautama? No; the consummation that Schopenhauer conceives in an individual sense, Hartmann apprehends universally. He would destroy selfishness by recognizing the illusory nature of all endeavors after positive happiness. He speaks of a world-redemption to which all men should tend and in which all pain shall be annulled. Here alone—"at the goal of evolution, at the issue of the world-process"—is to be found a reconciliation between Optimism and Pessimism. This reconciliation may be brought about by making the ends of the Unconscious the ends of our own consciousness ; by fostering a deep yearning for the peace and painlessness of non-existence till it becomes resistless as a practical motive ; and finally, by making a simultaneous common resolve to hurl back the total actual volition into nothingness.* To this night-mare of a Cosmic suicide does Von Hartmann reduce his philosophic dreams. In such theories the meaning and purpose of life are completely lost sight of. No wonder Amiel should write : "Everything has chilled me this morning : the cold of the season, the physical immobility around

* *Philosophie des Unbewussten*, absch. C., cap. xiv. S. 401-407

me, but, above all, Hartmann's *Philosophy of the Un-conscious.*"†

A cold, cold study, cold and dreary, and chilling indeed, is this. And were Pessimism confined to a few abnormally sensitive natures, and within the covers of a few books, we might leave it untouched and dwell upon philosophic issues of more general interest. But Pessimism is spreading its baneful influence over every department of literature. It has its organs of opinion and expression throughout the world. It has found its way into the books of the hour. You read it in their exaggerations of the miseries of life. It places arguments in favor of suicide in the hands of the coward who lacks the courage to face life's difficulties. It is the inspiring doctrine of socialism and nihilism. The philosophy of despair, it finds no worth in life, for it recognizes life only as a quest after one knows not what, ending in disillusion and disappointment. Do you not find this view of life pervading many a volume in verse and prose that makes up some of the most artistic literature of the day? It is the inspiration of the philosophic poems of Madame Ackerman. It indited *The City of Dreadful Night* of Thomson. It traced *El Diablo Mondo* of Espronceda. Its spirit animates the strongest creations of Tourgéneff.* In Russia there are fanatics who, under the cloak of religion,

---

* *Journal Intime*, p. 162.

† Take, for instance the character of Bazároff in his *Fathers and Children.* "If," says a Russian critic, alluding to the spirit of this book, "Bazároffism be a malady, it is the malady of our days, so widely spread that . . . . . stay its progress we cannot, for it pervades the very air we breathe."

carry out the godless and prayerless asceticism of Schopenhauer.* Bitterness in thought and feeling, and cynicism, and inanition are its legitimate fruits. It destroys the normal joyousness of the healthy soul. It is indeed a virulent malady. Thus has the rationalism of the day attempted to do away with God and religion. But men must have a formula into which they can translate their emotions. Religion has supplied that formula in prayer. Rationalism now appeals to science to supplant the religious formula, but science is unequal to the task.

Little good is to be looked for in a philosophy as purely subjective as Pessimism. "The world is my idea—*Vorstellung*—my intellectual perception. The world is my will." So reiterates Schopenhauer. And Hartmann tells us that there is no such thing as happiness, just as there are no such things as God and truth. All are subjective. Things are what we think them. Thus all thought, all science, the moral and material world, even God, in this system, are reduced to a mere act of consciousness. The philosophy that refuses to recognize object as well as subject as a primary element of thought is bound to end in just such a quagmire. The Pessimist's solution for the modern world-problem—the reconciliation between the secular and the religious elements in society—is the destruction of God, the soul, and all religion. He would make a waste and call it peace.

Another fundamental error underlying Pessimism is

* Leroy-Beaulieu, in *Revue des Deux Mondes*, Juin, 1875, pp. 600-610.

that it assumes pleasure to be the object of existence. Now, we are not in this world for the amount of pleasure it may bring us. Both Hartmann and Schopenhauer read in their master, Kant, a higher purpose. He taught them that morality is the chief aim of life; that man is here for the fulfillment of duty; that in this fulfillment is his supreme earthly happiness; that in the struggle to overcome himself he creates his own personality, and that sufferings and mishaps are so many stepping-stones by which man rises to the full growth and development of his nature. Kant might attempt to disprove the existence of God, but he could not destroy the moral purpose of life and the sense of duty in the human breast. And in these planks saved from the general wreck created by the *Critique of Pure Reason* we have the wherewith to scale to heaven's threshold and demonstrate the existence of God. The Pessimist may reject but he cannot destroy these elementary truths. In their light existence has a totally different meaning, and we begin to realize how vastly before pleasure stands duty.

But bad as the world is in the eyes of our Pessimists, the world still retains this sense of obligation, be it ever so ignored by philosophy. The world cannot move without the moral code. Renan, even while denying its obligations, acknowledges its necessity. "Nature," he says, "has need of the virtue of individuals, but this virtue is an absurdity in itself; men are duped into it for the preservation of the race."* Surely if virtue is an absurdity into which men are duped, then indeed is there no obli-

* *Dialogues Philosophiques,* intro. xiv.–xvii.

gation.   Then is there no such thing as sin.   This thought caused Amiel to ask : " What does M. Renan make of sin ? "   And M. Renan, with his characteristic flippancy, answers : " It seems to me that I suppress it. " †   If Renan is right, then he who rises up against this terrible illusion and seeks to destroy it —be the consequences what they may—is a true philosopher and deserves well of all men.   If Renan is right and Schopenhauer is right, then all honor to Pessimism for rending the veil of delusion and revealing the reality.   A simple remedy this of overcoming a difficulty, to suppress it, ignore it.   As though the dishonest debtor could satisfy justice by destroying the record of his indebtedness, or the man who injured his neighbor by word or deed could repair the wrong ˋby ignoring the injured neighbor !

Although the Pessimist in his speculations wanders so far away from our most elementary standard of truth and sense of right, still is he a keen observer and analyzer of men and things.   He states facts even while misinterpreting the facts.   And our safest method of refutation consists in separating theory from the facts and principles underlying the theory.   If we would understand any system we must stand at its central point on a common ground with him who holds the system.   It not unfrequently happens that the whole difference between two disputants consists in each giving a different name to the same thing.   To begin with, then, there is in the whole animal creation—man included—a tendency

† *Eh bien, je crois que je le supprime.*—*Journal Intime,* intro. xi.

that makes for the preservation of the race at the expense of the individual. There is a struggle for survival carried out along the whole scale of vital existence. We have seen this struggle reduced to a law in the doctrine of Evolution. There are in the human breast fierce passions which, when unleashed, play havoc with the individual and society. It is a natural tendency for man to lift his hand against his fellow-man in contention for supremacy. What other meaning have those immense armies now exhausting the energies and resources of Europe? So do the occupants of neighboring ant-hills wage war ; they also have their tribe and race feuds ; they fight their battles of extermination and subjugation. So far we are at one with the Pessimist. But here our roads diverge. Man with us is not all animal ; he is also a rational being. Those tendencies and impulses which in the brute creation are a matter of accurately defined instinct, which guides them and measures their use, are in man subject to his reason. And the dictates of his reason are distinct from the promptings of his passions or his natural tendencies. St. Paul recognized and clearly defined these two tendencies in his nature, and he called each a law : "I see another law in my members, fighting against the law of my mind, and captivating me in the law of sin, that is in my members." * It is this natural tendency and impulse that Schopenhauer calls Will and that Hartmann interprets as the Unconscious.

Dark as is the Pessimist's picture of the world's

* Romans vii. 23.

misery, it is scarcely overdrawn. The physical suffering, the untold pangs of the wounded and the
breaking heart, the groans of remorse, despair and
wretchedness, the havoc of war and famine, disease
and death—all ascending at every moment from this
revolving sphere of ours, in one agonizing wail c
pain, is appalling. The Church recognizes this
misery. She would have us consider ourselves as
exiles passing through "a vale of tears." *   In n
variety of ways she repeats the words of Job : " Man
born of a woman, living for a short time, is filled with
many miseries.   He cometh forth like a flower, and
is destroyed, and fleeth as a shadow, and never con-
tinueth in the same state." † She insistently im-
presses upon us that we are not to look for happiness
here below, for ours is a higher destiny.   One who
has faithfully interpreted her mind says : "Thou
canst not be satisfied with any temporal goods, because thou wast not created for the enjoyment of
such things." ‡ The Church alone holds the clue to
the miseries of life, she alone has the solution of the
problem of evil. Mallock gave his graceful but not
over-serious intellect to the study of this problem,
and what was the outcome of his studies ?   "Religious belief," he tells us, " and moral belief likewise,
involve both of them some vast mystery ; and reason
can do nothing but focalize, not solve it." §   After
questioning modern science, he finds himself forced
to seek the only satisfactory solution in the teachings
of the Church. Amiel, after wandering away from

* "Salve Regina."   † Job, xiv.
‡ Imitation, iii. xvi. 1.   § Is Life worth Living ? p. 269.

the Calvinism of his childhood loses himself in the mazes of German speculation; and after weighing all religious creeds, he finds nothing better than Christianity, for the reason that Christianity alone has a solution for the problem of evil. "Man must have a religion," he says; "is not the Christian the best, after all?—the religion of sin, repentance, and reconciliation, of the new birth and the life ever-lasting."* To the Church, then, which alone contains the fullness of Christian truth, let us go for the solution of the problem of evil.

Recognizing the sin and the misery with which life is beset, the Church does not say with Sakya-Mouni: "The great evil is existence." On the contrary, she holds existence to be a boon, since it is a pure and gratuitous gift from a good God. The misery and the pain, though inseparable in the present order o things, are still mere accidents of existence. She accounts for their presence by the doctrine of original sin. The whole struggle going on in every human breast between reason and impulse is an effort to restore the equilibrium in human nature lost by original sin. In her teachings there is no room for the question, Is life worth living? Life is a state of probation. It is within the power of every man to make it a blessing or a curse. Man is born into this world without his consent; he lives within certain environments, over which he has no control; acci-

* *Journal Intime.* Amiel was born in Geneva in 1821 and died in 1881. He was a man of rare talents, but his friends were disappointed in the sterility of his life. The blight of scepticism was upon him and paralyzed all his efforts.

dents befall him ; he is circumvented in many ways ; that which he most ardently seeks flies farthest from him ; that which he least covets is what comes most readily into his possession. But the measure of man's success in life is not the mere attainment of his desires. This is a life-lesson as old as human nature, but none the less a lesson that human nature is frequently ignoring. Conduct and motive are the two elements that enter into the fullness of human life and make of it a success or a failure. He whose conduct is upright and whose motive is sincere has not lived in vain. His frame may be racked with pain and disease ; adversities may befall him and friends forsake him ; these things disturb not the calm of his soul ; he turns them to account as aids to his spiritual growth. He knows that the be-all and end-all is not here. He recognizes a life above and beyond the plane of the natural, to which all men are des-tined and which all men can attain. This super-natural life is of the invisible world. We can neither touch, nor taste, nor see it, but it is none the less a reality. It is in us and about us. The light of faith reveals it to us in all its beauty and harmony and glory. Therein we read the meaning of the world, the plan and purpose of man. By prayer do we hold communion with this unseen world ; by the sacra-ments does the Church communicate to us saving grace out of this unseen world, and by hope do we live to enter upon a new and a higher life in this unseen world.

PART II.

THEORY.

CHAPTER I.

HAVING considered literature in its various relations with thought, with language, with such influences, whether of persons or times, as have affected it and given it a value of relation, we now proceed to dwell upon it in its intrinsic nature. It is evidently a power. It is one of the mediums invariably made use of in civilizing a nation. It possesses a formative character that, in the end, triumphs over material force, be its energy what it may. We have, then, to inquire what is the secret of this power.

A classic is the best representative of a people's literature. It lives through the wear and tear of time; it is enshrined in a nation's memories; it is an approved expression of its sentiments; it becomes a standard of excellence; it is admired; it pleases; it is the embodiment of the beautiful or sublime; and the more of one or the other it contains, the more genuine a classic it is.

"A thing of beauty is a joy forever."

14

It pleases, delights, touches our humanity according to the beauty of expression with which it clothes a thing of beauty, whether it be of the physical, intellectual, or moral world. So, also, a heroic deed or a magnificent scene is the basis of a sublime work. We must, therefore, as a preliminary inquiry, determine the essence of the beautiful.

All beauty is divided into three kinds. There is intellectual beauty, there is moral beauty, and there is physical beauty. The theories of the beautiful that have come under our notice seem to be constructed for one or other of these, to the exclusion of the rest. Evidently, beauty is not exclusively a material thing, or a moral thing, or an intellectual thing. Its essence is distinct from that of each. Beauty is not truth ; for truth is reality, and reality is not always beautiful. Neither is it goodness ; for each determines different faculties of the soul. Therefore, Cousin errs in saying that moral beauty is "the foundation, the principle, the unity of the beautiful." The moral and the good are identical. That which is formally good is intrinsically moral. Now, the good is necessarily the object of the will, and creates appetition ; whereas, the higher the order of beauty is, the less does the soul desire the object in which it resides, and the more content it is to rest in its contemplation. Again it has been asserted that the essence of beauty consists in "proportion and light." * The theory errs by

* Hill, *Elements of Philosophy*, p. 174. This is considered the doctrine of St. Thomas. But St. Thomas in making the statement, is only incidentally speaking of physical beauty. See *Summa*. Ia. Iæ. quaest. vi.,art. iv. ad. 1.

saying too much.   There is beauty in proportion ;
but there is more.   Not a particle of earth, air, or
ocean but has its ultimate atoms in proportion.   The
whole material universe is built upon proportion.
Destroy the combining ratio of the elements, and
order becomes chaos.   It is for this reason that where
there is beauty, there may be proportion ; but proportion constitutes the essence of beauty only inasmuch as it is a necessary attribute of material existence.   But where is the proportion of a moral act,
or of a well-put expression, or of a human soul, or
of anything without parts ?   The question is meaningless.   Nor is the matter bettered by making the distinction of Jerome Savonarola, who says :   " Beauty
results from harmony in all the parts and colors.
This applies to composite subjects ; in simple subjects, beauty is in light." *   Whether we take light
figuratively or literally, we must reject it on the
same ground.   It says too much.   Light is essential
to the discernment of deformity as well as of beauty
whether we look on the one or the other in the light
of day, or in the light of evidence, or in the light of
consciousness, or in the light of reason.   We are
also told that beauty is a " quality or attribute of
objects," and something relative.†   But the relative
connotes the absolute ; and if there is a relative
beauty, there must necessarily be an absolute
beauty.

* *Sermon on the Discourse of Jesus with the Woman of Samaria.*
Therein Savonarola denounces the materialistic notions of the artists
of the Renaissance.

† Bascom : *Æsthetics, or Science of Beauty,* lect. l., p. 8.

Beauty has an absolute existence, as truth has, as morality has ; and as we cannot say of these last that they are mere qualities or relative existences, neither can we assert the like of the first. Morality is independent of all action, truth of all knowing, and beauty of all existences, even as God, who is the Being infinitely true, moral, and beautiful, is independent of His creation. And as we have a moral sense and a sense of the true, or certitude, so we have a sense of the beautiful, which some call taste, and others, the æsthetic sense. Let us study the nature of this sense.

We perceive a thing of beauty, say an admirably executed picture. A feeling of pleasure possesses our soul, and we forthwith pronounce it beautiful. That feeling has the character of a dim recollection slightly awakened ; it is the feeling, more or less intense, that passes over us on recognizing an old friend after a long absence. Plato experienced it in his sensitive nature, and attributed it to a faint reminiscence which the soul possesses of a preëxistent state.* Wordsworth, who studied every phase of sensation, recognized the feeling, and revived the same doctrine :

"Our birth is but a sleep and a forgetting ;
The soul that rises with us, our life's star
Hath elsewhere had its setting,
And cometh from afar."†

There is in this feeling a recollection and a recognition. We are told that man is made in the image and likeness of his Maker. We know furthermore

* Phædrus, cap. xxix, p. 714.
† Ode on the Intimations of Immortality.

that all things proceeding from their Divine Author, are made in accordance with their archetypes in His mind; and therefore that they reflect some one or other attribute of His Divinity—that same Divinity, be it remembered, in the image and likeness whereof we have been created. Therefore, that pleasure experienced on beholding a thing of beauty is due to our recognition of the type of perfect implanted in our natures by the creative act; our power of recognizing being developed in different degrees, as the faculty of knowing or the moral sense is different in each individual. In recognizing, in the object presented to us, a dim reflection of the standard within us, our æsthetic sense is awakened. Therefore, actual beauty does not exist independently of ideal beauty. The former is only the expression, more or less perfect, of the latter, and without it is not known to be beauty. Dr. Brownson has shown, after Kant, that every object, empirically considered, is known only in its relation with the ideal.* Each connotes the other.

Turning to the object we call beautiful, we ask: What is there in that object that makes it beautiful? In the case of the picture, we must say that it is not the colors; for another might have placed the same colors in the same proportion, and yet not produce the same effect. Thus there is a vast difference between a real Raphael and a copy. So, too, with human countenances. One face has all the contour and proportion of parts of another; and still we turn from the one with disgust, and are ravished with feel-

* Works, vol. ii., *Refutation of Atheism*, ix., pp. 56, et seq.

ings of awe and respect on beholding the other.
The same difference is found in two poems. One
writer describes a landscape in language select,
grammatical, appropriate; we read it, and put the
book aside with indifference. Another writer paints
the same scene in a few happy phrases, apparently
thrown together with less care; still the effect is like
magic; we read and re-read the piece; we exclaim:
"Magnificent! How grand! What a beautiful word-
picture!" Now, in all these instances, one word expresses the whole difference. That one word is
EXPRESSION. Its presence gives the beauty; its absence leaves dead colors, dead words, dead features.
And it is that expression alone in every beautiful
object that has power to awaken the sense of the
beautiful in the soul. Hence the success of an artist
depends upon his power of infusing expression into
his work. And the secret of our pleasure in admiring his production is, that it brings before our consciousness the ideal in our minds.

Here an interesting question arises. In describing
the material universe, is all that goes to make up the
expression of it, whether on the canvas or in the
poem, in nature or in the artist's mind? It is obvious
that we are in sympathy with nature. When man
fell, nature also was cursed. It is further plain that
inert matter does not arouse our sympathy, has for
us no expression. A thing is intelligible in proportion as it is intelligent: this is the law of intelli-
gibility; and, as Balmes has shown,* we might live

* *Fundamental Philosophy*, bk. I., ch. xii., which is also the doctrine of St. Thomas.—*Summa*, I. 87, 1.

forever in presence of the material universe and be no wiser concerning it, if we did not have an idea of it. But the idea of the universe is not its expression as given in its beauties and sublimities. We analyze a piece of granite. It has for us no other expression than the names we impose on its component parts, and the combining force that keeps them together. It seems to us that there is something more significant in the sleep of winter, in the awakening of spring, in the activity of summer, and in the repose of autumn, than is to be found in death and inertness. To say that the expression of these phenomena was God in Nature, would be to make Him an integral part of the universe, the soul of the world; and, with Emerson, we would be obliged to recognize no God who is not " one with the blowing grass and the falling rain." But the Divine Artist that fashioned the universe, also infused therein a trace of His own beauty—a reflection of Himself, once clear and serene as the undisturbed lake of crystalline waters ; but since the fall, it is a mirror that has been cracked, broken, and bedimmed. That which speaks to us in Nature is behind the hill and dale and starry sky, on which we fix our gaze. It is the ideal which the Cosmos actualizes. He who holds in His Divine Essence the types after which the physical world and we are created, has established between us and it this harmony and sympathy. We may then conclude that the expression of Nature is external to the mind of him who contemplates it; he imbibes it by degrees, and reproduces all he has received in his master-piece. Were all that expression in himself primarily its outward embodiment would have been a Divine act. He imitates creation in expressing, according to the strength of his genius, the ideal in his soul; but the expression he gives out has been communicated to him from the ideal in Nature. Therefore, that modern subjectivism which would impose the various moods of an author upon Nature, and interpret its expression as the expression of these moods, is based on a false principle. The prophet imagined God present in the whirlwind; but God was not there: it was under the calming influence of the gentle breeze that He made His presence felt.

To sum up: We speak in sign and symbol. The ideal in our mind is symbolical of Him who created it—the Beauty ever ancient and ever new—whom we now see "darkly, as through a glass." Everything perfect in its kind has a beauty of its own; it is the created ideal modelled after the eternal and un-created ideal in the Divine Mind. When the Supreme Being first called things from nothingness, He created each perfect in its kind. After the fall, every creature of earth became subject to degeneracy; but as in the nobler specimens of animal life there is a reversion to that first model, so that instinctive reversion recalls the type of perfect—the ideal after which it was fashioned—and we speak of such specimens as beauti-ful. The beautiful, then, is the expression of the Word. From one Word are all things, and this one all things speak.* The splendor of that Word it is that we admire in the glowing sunset; that steals into our soul in the lovely landscape; that, beaming from the truly beautiful countenance, inspires awe and respect; that elicits the burst of admiration on witnessing the heroic deed.

* *Imitation*, bk. i. ch. iii.

CHAPTER II.

THE CONSERVATIVE PRINCIPLE OF LITERATURE.

WE are now prepared to consider the element in a classic that causes it to outlive the people whose genius gave it birth. We have found that according as it embodies the sublime or beautiful with a corresponsive sympathy—that is, in proportion as it reflects the splendor of God in His creatures—in proportion as it *speaks the Word*—it is an immortal production. The mere outward expression, no matter how graceful and polished it be, does not guarantee immortality; long ago did the poet tell us as much: "Mortal works shall perish; much less will the bloom and elegance of language survive. . . . , It is not enough that poems be beautiful; let them also be affecting."* Not that a classic can dispense with grace and polish of expression. The form should be adequate to the thought. A beautiful idea must needs be cast in a beautiful mould. Destroy the form in which the idea is fully expressed and there remains but a vague conception or a broken utterance.

* "Mortalia facta peribunt:
Nedum sermonum stet honos et gratia vivax. . .
Non satis est pulchra esse poëmata; dulcia sunto."
Horace, *Ars Poetica*, 68, 69, 99.

It is the soul of language that makes the language undying. That soul is the ideal as interpreted by genius. When it reflects the splendor of the Divinity, it becomes enshrined in its beauty, and lights up dark ways through the ages, as the moon gives light and comfort with the borrowed rays of the sun. It is this splendor, reflected in language vigorous, fresh, and polished to a high degree of beauty and fitness, that has preserved the ancient classics. It is this same splendor that glows in all that is best in our modern literature. Read the all-pervading thought of each of the world's three great poets. How runs the key-note of their themes?

That which flavors the Homeric poems with the divine afflatus, is surely not Achilles' wrath, or Hector's prowess, or the Grecian quarrels, or Ulysses' cunning. Pervading all this—pervading the inner thought of those noble epics—is an innate feeling of helplessness, giving vent to the frequent outburst of natural, unaffected piety, in which the stoutest heart confesses dependence on the heavenly powers, and calls on their assistance to shield him or to guide his shaft. The truth constantly recurring in every variety of note at the blind bard's command, is that all men have need of—yearn after—the assistance of Heaven.

We open the *Odyssey* at random. We read how Odysseus is recognized by the gods as beyond all mortals in understanding and in piety.* He is known to men as Odysseus of many devices.† But

* *Odyssey*, i. 66, 67.
† Ibid, x. 456.

in all the buffetings of fortune to which he has been subjected, he is careful to refer the goods and ills of life that have befallen him, not to his own merits or devisings, but to the will of the gods.* And the great lesson which this noble poem seems to inculcate, is summed up in these words : " One thing the god will give and another withhold, even as he will, for with him all things are possible."† The underlying conception is the inadequacy of man's self-help and his dependence upon the unseen world.

It is a great mistake to consider such interventions of the deities mere "poetical machinery," as though they were scaffoldings—simply aids to construct the poem—and not, as they really are, an essential part of its existence, the principle of its vitality The sylphs and gnomes in Pope's *Rape of the Lock*, the enchantments in the *Jerusalem Delivered* of Tasso, and the mythological aids in the *Lusiads* of Camoens, may bear such an explanation—may be regarded as mere accidentals, not at all affecting the main expression of their poems — but the heroes of the Homeric poems are as earnest in their devotions to their titular gods as is the Christian to his patron saint.

In Dante's great poem, mingled with an ardent love for his country and a strong faith in the tenets of his religion, is a third element which absorbs these two ; it is an insatiable thirst for knowledge—an ardent passion for philosophy, which he personifies

* *Odyssey*, xiv., 197, 198.
† Ibid, xiv., 444, 445.

in his Beatrice—and from the union of all three elements has sprung the *Divina Commedia*. Now, the
lesson he constantly repeats is his inability to know
things of himself, and the dependence of all knowledge on the divine Idea :

> "——That which dies not,
> And that which can die, are but each the beam
> Of that idea, which our Sovereign Sire
> Engendereth loving."—*

In Shakespeare there is plainly asserted, in the
grand array of passion personified in his master-
pieces, an overwhelming feeling of retributive justice
and of an all-ruling Providence, which is imparted
rather by insinuation than by any direct assertion ;
and that feeling he himself has summed up in his
own masterly words :

> "There is a Divinity that shapes our ends,
> Rough-hew them how we will." †

Thus it is we find all thought, all genuine literature,
as well as the universe itself, mirroring forth the Divinity. All point to one creative source ; *all speak
one Word.* Back of the outward word, behind the
form and construction in which a classic is clothed,
is something more than the mere incidents and circumstances with which it deals. They are transient
and contingent ; but this element partakes of the immutable and the necessary, for it is of essences. It is
absent from all mere copy-work. He who undertakes to describe for description's sake, or who sim-

---

* "Ciò che non muore e ciò che può morire
Non é se non splendor di quella idea
Che partorisce, amando, il nostro Sire."

Paradiso, xiii, 52-54.

† *Hamlet*, Act. V. sc. ii.

ply remembers and repeats, or who makes art the whole aim of his writing, enshrines not the pages of his book in this conservative principle; for he has not a vivifying idea, and still less an ideal. The ideal, then, is the conservative principle of all literature. *A literary production is entitled to be considered a classic in proportion as it fittingly expresses the ideal as conceived by an age or nation.* This law supplies a safe canon by which to determine, at least approximately, the classic merit of a literary work.

CHAPTER III.

THE RELIGIOUS BASIS OF LITERATURE.

PRIOR to the creative act, the archetypes of things spiritual and material existed in the Divine Mind; and as that is simple activity, they and It were one. Then God was all. But God saw these archetypes in the Word, and by the Word did they become actual existences distinct from the Divinity. Their ideal therefore is the expression of the Word. But all literature has its significancy and power according to the clearness with which it expresses the ideal; and the nearer the ideal approaches the Word— the higher it leads upwards thereto—the more powerful is its expression. It is not by reason of man's being created that he is a religious being. The cattle of the field are equally creatures of God, but they have no religious susceptibilities. Religion is meaningless when applied to them.   It is because man has been created with a soul capable of reasoning, loving, and recognizing its First Cause and its Final End, that he is a religious being ; for it is by reason of that noble consciousness that he communes with God.   But the recognition of God he has through the Word, and through the Word also does he address God.   Nor is there any other way even for the Divinity to com-·mune.   The Father speaks with Himself through His Word, and with men through His Holy Spirit.   But without the Word there were no Holy Spirit.   Therefore religion has its origin in the Word.   And it is to be looked for that the highest forms of literature will be inspired by the relations of man with his Maker.

1. The basis of literature, then, in its supreme efforts, is religion ; for while literature has its roots in humanity, it draws its life and nourishment, and receives its strength and greatness from religion. Every priesthood has been its preserver and pro-moter.   Under the inspiration of religion have the sacred books of all nations attempted to explain the mystery of man—his origin and destiny—and to reconcile heaven with earth.   Within its sanctuary have canticles of praise and adoration wafted their agreeable incense to the Supreme Power.   The poet, the philosopher, the orator, the historian, are one and all influenced by its doctrines in their writings and actions.

Literature deals with the elements of humanity. It appeals to some, it studies others ; others again it exemplifies.   Now religion pervades every part of man's nature.   Its hand moves over the fibres of his heart, and changes their native discord into harmonious music ; its voice chides him in wrong-doing, and speaks the word of approval when he has achieved the good action ; its doctrines shape his course through life ; whilst its ceremonies surround him in the cradle, are the pageants of every important step he takes, and still solicitous for him, accompany him to the grave. Only in the undimmed light of faith which it sheds around him, does he know himself, the inner recesses of his nature, his various relations and his destiny. Without that light he is a purposeless being, groping in the dark through the labyrinthine ways of life ; whereas its presence in his soul shows his every action to possess a bearing and a significancy which time cannot measure, and eternity alone can fathom. Here is a powerful determining principle in the life of man. It is the office of literature to consider it as such ; and as such has it been considered. All the creations of genius—*Ulysses, Æneas, Hamlet*—have acted under the influence of their religious tenets. Hence it is that fates and furies and titular deities figured so largely in pagan literature, and that the wise course of an all-ruling Providence is traced upon the pages of modern Christian authors.

2. But the tendency of the age is to do without religion, and—must it be said ?—without God. Taine expresses this tendency when he tells the English people that their God inconveniences them.* This might be true if God were, as Taine and his master

* Votre Dieu vous gêne ; il est la cause suprême, et vous n'osez raisonner sur les causes par respect pour lui.—*La Littérature Anglaise* l iv.

Comte hold, a fiction of the brain and a prejudice of education. Now, one of England's most gifted son's * did consider God an inconvenience, and lived without taking Him into account ; but he ended by making a human remains—a reminiscence—the limit of his thought. He who considered the Infinite Being too narrow for his thinking, in the limited nature of a woman discovered the source of inspiration, the supreme good after which his soul yearned ; in a word, his all. Not being able to destroy the instinctive aspirations of his soul for its Creator, he makes to himself an idol of one no greater than he,—frail and mortal like him,—and lavishes upon her all the worship due the Divinity.† Man is finite in his nature and personality ; his intellect cannot compass the infinite ; it only apprehends it ; still the infinite is ever present to him ; in thought he moves through it ;‡ he catches glimpses of its sublimities ; he sings of its glories. But its immensity does not weigh down his soul. He calmly faces it ; and while contemplating it, questionings arise in the human breast, which prove that the infinite is not a creature of the human intellect ; for humanity comprehends it as little as it does its own existence. Humanity is more logical than the atheist. Leaving him to his cavillings, it recog-

---

* John Stuart Mill.

† "Speaking of his wife, he says : "Her memory is to me a religion, and her approbation the standard by which, summing up as it does all worthiness, I endeavor to regulate my life."— *Autobiography*, p. 251.

‡ Penser, c'est se mouvoir dans l'infini.—LACORDAIRE *Confér ences de Toulouse*, p. 8.

nizes One to whom creation is no enigma, and who holds infinitude in Himself.

This tendency to do without religion in literature and in life, is based upon the assumption that human nature is self-sufficient. Under another order of things man might have been so created that he would be content with the finite and the tangible, would never know or feel a want beyond what they could supply, and would live satisfied with the sufficiency of his nature. But constituted as he now is, man's destiny is completed only in the sphere of the supernatural order. And this order it is not in his power to abandon. To live in it is his destiny, and he can be suspended from it only by the Being who traced out for him his course. He may live as though there were but the natural law ; but he is never exclusively confined to its action. It is supplemented and its efficiency increased by the law of grace. Being possessed of a free will, man is a meriting being. Every deed he performs—every intention he forms—is taken into account. That is an erroneous view of things that represents God as aloof from His creatures ; He is ever intimately present to the soul, by the preservative act with which He is present in the Cosmos, and by the sanctifying grace with which He binds every rational nature willing to be bound more closely to Himself.

The assumption of the self-sufficiency of human nature is due either to the rejection or to the misunderstanding of the teleological order. Men bring into moral and metaphysical discussions the habits of reasoning contracted in treating the physical sciences :

and as in these latter, since the days of Bacon, they have discarded the doctrine of final cause, in dealing with the former, they omit the idea of design. They see no purpose in life beyond the immediate supplying of present wants ; they are content to regard themselves as the product of an unconscious force ; with Strauss, they "no longer recognize a self-conscious Creator." *   But to deny a final cause is to deny all design, and therefore a designer. This is a practical denial of an efficient First Cause; and leads either to pantheism, by making all things manifestations of the great All, or to atheism, which reduces this great All to a blind force, consisting of "the one essence of forces and laws which manifest and fulfill themselves."†   In either case, the absence of design implies the absence of cause ; and he who refuses to admit final cause is logically compelled to deny a First Cause, and to eliminate altogether from his philosophy the problem of causation. And this the Positivist has done.

But those who, while rejecting final causes, would still adhere to a First Cause, say that because man works with design, gives no reason to infer that the great Primal Cause would do the same. "This," they say, adopting the language of Strauss, "by no means follows, and Nature herself proves the fallacy of the assumption that adaptation can only be the work of conscious intelligence."‡   This position has only one

---

* *Der Alte and der Neue Glaube*, III. , § 65.

† So Strauss defines Cosmos.—*Der Alte und der Neue Glaube*, II., § 41.

‡ *Ibid.*, II., § 36.

logical outlet, and that same is a mere hypothesis : it is that Nature is the origin of our intelligence, and imparts to it all its characteristic qualities. To say so is to identify Nature with the God of nature ; the two are made one ; and all that we see and apprehend are manifestations of the great Be-All. We reject the assumption, because it reduces our reason to an instinct, leaves us with no control over ourselves, destroys all freedom of action ; and in doing so, contradicts our innermost convictions. One man performs an action, another at the same moment is doing the contradictory of it ; where one affirms the other denies; but the great Be-All is simultaneously acting and asserting itself through both ; that is, it contradicts itself ; which is admitting that it can annihilate itself and still continue to be. Here is neither law nor force ; here is only absurdity. Now, as reason will not admit an absurdity as the basis of nature, the source of life and the inspiration of literature, let us look elsewhere for an explanation that will reconcile exception and rule, the atheistic tendencies of the age with the instincts of humanity.

3 There are traces of an intelligent being working with design in the material universe ; there are consciousness and instinct in the insect as well as in the brute creation ; and in man, besides consciousness and instinct, there is a rational soul capable of loving, of making abstractions and generalizations, and of evolving in language continuous and connected thought. Now, while brute instinct shares with the human mind, a certain capacity for particularizing, it is the exclusive property of the latter to generalize,

to deal with essences and to possess science; the one can never be confounded with the other. Here it may be said that this proves nothing; for man, though superior to other visible forms of creation, is still one with "the Cosmos whence he springs, from which also he derives that spark of r ason which he misuses."* To this we reply : Man has conscious power of adapting a means to an and; and he can vary both means and end. All other forms of animal life are limited in their power of adapting means to an end, to the extent of preserving their life and their species. With them it is an instinct, guided and directed with little more freedom of action than is the machine by him who makes it. But this guidance is not in the gift of the Cosmos ; for according to those who object to the distinction, the Cosmos is bound by her own laws, and cannot make exception to them. She cannot give and take at the same time. If the brute and the human intelligence are one in kind, then ought they be governed by the same law. But since it is otherwise—since man, over and above the organic and emotional powers which he shares with the brute, possesses a pure reason in which the brute has no part—we conclude that the source of action, for reason as well as for instinct, is other than the Cosmos. The Power that placed in man's hands complete control over his actions and their motives, holds that control in His own hands, with all other things of life, and makes the bird build its nest and the beaver construct its dam, in the same fashion to-day as they did a thousand years ago, and as they will a thousand years

* Strauss—*Der Alte und der Neue Glaube*, II., § 41.

hence. Now, as an effect can never contain more than its efficient cause, for the latter must always be more perfect than the former ; and since man has design in his actions, that Power which is the Primal Cause of all things must also have design, and must have therefore created for a purpose.

Man has therefore been created with a destiny to fulfill. And such is the testimony of his conscious-ness. This is the meaning of those yearnings after he knows not what, that sense of dissatisfaction he is continually seeking to confine, that effort with which he is ever grasping at, never seizing, an ideal standard of goodness and beauty. And the fact of this unset-tled condition and constant struggle proves that man's destiny is not fulfilled in the plane of the natural order. If he lives in forgetfulness of any other, it is because the finite order is ever present to him, and it is always within his power to enjoy the good it offers him. Still, in the midst of this enjoyment—surrounded by everything calculated to gratify the heart—a Solo-mon will cry out : "Vanity of vanities, and all is vanity ;"* while saintly characters, in poverty and privation,—midst annoyance and suffering,—rejoice that it is even so, and exclaim, "Thy will be done, O Lord." There is underlying all this a fact of deep im-port. Its explanation solves the problem of man and nature.

Creation is finite ; the Creator is infinite. In the understanding of their relation is the solution sought. And that relation is one of two-fold union. Besides their dialectic union in the creative act, and in con-

* *Ecclesiastes* i. 2.

servation which is a continuation of that act, they are still more intimately brought together by a mystical and substantial union of the Divinity with that one of His creatures which embodies in itself both the spiritual and material elements of creation. This union is accomplished in the Incarnation. *And the Word was made flesh.** Therein is man generically united with his Maker; thereby is he raised above the sphere of the purely natural order into a higher and better grade of existence; and it is only in that higher place he can work out his destiny. It was so prior to that supreme union. In anticipation of it was man then saved. It is so at present. Only by reason of its merits can he attain to eternal life.

In the Incarnation of the Word is the secret of life. It explains the mystery of man. It gives meaning to those yearnings of his soul that seem never satisfied. They are aspirations for the infinite Being. Humanity, in the hypostatic union with the Divinity, has tasted the Supreme Good, and ardently desires to rest in its enjoyment. That the individual does not always wish for the consummation of this union that he may even show a repugnance for it—argues nothing against its reality. It arises from his present position in the Cosmos. As has already been remarked, man's nature is always present to him; his perception of the supernatural order is faint, because though individually predestined to it, the act of union has been accomplished generically; he therefore finds repugnance in turning from the clearly asserted order of genesis, to the more vaguely though

*St. John i. 14.

no less truly defined sphere of palingenesis. Hence it is that so many ignore the latter, and live but for the former. Hence too, the repugnance mystics say they experience when first brought to the contemplation of the Divinity.

4. Thus, the incarnate Word is the principle of creation ; therefore of life ; therefore of literature. Having been dignified in His Divine Person, humanity imbibes therein the elements of its material and spiritual progress. There is no true civilization except through the Word. But literature goes hand in hand with culture, refinement, civilization. Indeed, it is one of the chief elements, and standards of civilization. As such, it also shares the influence of the Word. In its own imperfect way it speaks the Word. But the Word asserts Its influence through religion. Therefore, in considering the nature of things, we find religion an essential factor in the development of thought. Its spiritual action determines man's real condition. It looms upon his horizon, tingeing the rising and setting of his ideas, and throwing a world of light upon some of the grandest views that ever illuminated the ways of his life. The tendency to secularize man and teach him to ignore the supernatural order is ill-founded. It would extinguish the life of his life. It takes man to be what he is not, and accordingly warps his whole being into a false system of action. Under the hand of secularization the music of his nature becomes noise ; its harmonics speak discord ; and his existence, instead of mingling in sweet accord with the rhythm of the spheres, recoils upon him in infinite torture. Out of place, then, is any theory of life that would banish the religious element from education.

And for this reason, the suggestion of Strauss to substitute poetry and music for the Bible and religious worship, is to be rejected. What this arch-priest of unbelief says of the difficulty of understanding the Bible is true enough. It is in itself a life-study. Still, it is one of the mediums by which God has deigned to express His Will to man ; and in His Church He has deposited the true sense and the authority to explain.   But poetry and music are poor substitutes for prayer and reliance upon a Providence. Prayer has always been efficacious. It dries up the tear of misery ; it soothes the pain in suffering ; it strengthens the wavering will ; it influences zeal ; it makes man strong to go forth and earnestly do his duty, were it to carry him to the ends of the earth; it raises him above his native weakness, ennobles his character, and spiritualizes his nature. Withdraw from men the power of prayer, and naught is to be witnessed but the cold selfishness of worldliness, and the unimpeded impetuosity of passion. It is to open the floodgates of vice and corruption upon society. The starving poor man will no longer keep his hands from the property of his more fortunate neighbor. The feeble widow finds no further comfort in providing for her helpless children. Under the influence of prayer, she has toiled by day and watched by night in order to give them the necessaries of life. But since her eyes no longer look heavenward in faith and hope, and her tongue has refused to call upon God, and her knee has ceased to bend to His name, she seeks rather herself, and solicitude for her little ones grows daily more faint. But this is a class of people that has not entered as an element into the calculations of Strauss. And yet the poor and miserable constitute the large majority of mankind. Fares it better with the favored few?

Man owes it to society to cultivate his senses. Through these all art appeals to the imagination. In their cultivation he finds recreation ; their enjoyment gives him rest from the more serious functions of life. But assuredly the portals of the soul do not make up the whole man ; their improvement and exercise must be the least part of life. *Ernst ist das Leben, heiter ist die Kunst.** Life is earnest, for it seeks in time the repose of eternity ; art is serene, for in expressing the ideal it has already touched upon that repose. Man, then, cannot rest in art. He must be up and doing. Higher motives regulate the cultivation of sense and intellect. It is well to commune with the great masters of thought, to become penetrated with the words of wisdom that have dropped from their pens, and to take in the glorious pictures of life and death, of time and eternity, of happiness and suffering, with which their pages are filled. But all this is not done for the sake merely of reading or of polishing the intellect. These men did not write with any such intention. They wrote because a great thought oppressed them, and they considered it worth man's knowing. Ideas are not simply to amuse. They do not confine themselves to the library. They become facts as soon as they filter into the general intelligence, Wycliffe's wranglings with the regular clergy, and his theorizings about dominion and power, substantiated themselves in Lollardism and the insurrection of Wat

* " Life is earnest, art is tranquil."—*Schiller.*

Tyler.   Luther's doctrines received their logical expression in the Peasants' war in Germany.   Voltaire's irreligious teachings found form in the revolution of '89.   Ideas are of value only in proportion as they strengthen man in the battle of life.   But the ideas of the great masters—of Plato, of Aquinas, of Dante, of Shakespeare—have power to move by reason of the order of things that Strauss would reverse.   They have all come from above.   They have meaning only in the belief of a spiritual world and a future life. They cease, therefore, to be motive-powers with the disciples of unbelief.   They may still continue to supply food for the fancy and to please the æsthetic sense ; but they have lost their power of giving direction to life.   For this, man has to fall back on self-interest. In self has he to find inspiration.   Towards self will his aspirations converge ; for according to the new philosophy, in self does the Cosmos find its consciousness.   But man's soul thirsts for something more than self.   Nor will music supply that desire.   The influence of music is not to be ignored.   It awakens sweet reminiscences ; it raises man out of the consciousness of suffering and misery ; it makes him forget the cares of earth ; its rapturous tones entwine themselves in the soul, and sway it to and fro.   Recreating and instructive may be the opera ; soothing is the symphony ; delightful is the well-executed sonata ; soul-stirring is the simple national air ; but when the sonata is played, the ballad sung, the opera over, man finds himself fallen back upon the rugged ways of life ; his nerves have been calmed, and his imagination pleased, only to make all the greater the contrast between the ideal life into which he was transported, and the actual life which he has to face. The shock thus given to his nerves tends rather to irritate than to soothe. And if beset with difficulties in his struggles for the comforts of life, he worries and makes himself miserable. Nor is he who is rich in the world's goods and beyond the necessity of toiling, any the happier under the new order of things. He is liable to make pleasure the business of life. And no man is more miserable. A sense of weariness, of which he never can rid himself, so interferes with his enjoyments as to render life insupportable. That is a shallow view of man that would limit his education to the cultivation of imagination and sensibility. Beneath the delicate nerve, the exquisite taste, the refined sentiment, will lie whole wastes of human nature, giving out briars and thorns ; will smoulder unchecked the fires of passion ; and it will require but the occasion to make of the one so educated a moral wreck.

That which unbelief would substitute for religion is the creature of religion. The Church is the inspiration of all that is grand in music. Beneath her shadow has it grown into its present noble proportions. The notes of its gamut speak its origin.†

* They are said to have taken their names from the first syllables of words in the first verse of the beautiful Church hymn in honor of St. John the Baptist :

Ut queant laxis *re*sonare fibris
*Mi*ra gestorum *fa*muli tuorum,
*Sol*ve polluti *la*bii reatum,
Sancte Joannes.

Guido Aretino, a Benedictine monk, who flourished about 1030,

And when it leaves the influence of the Church—
when it becomes secularized—it grows sickly ; it
can only give us the effeminate strains of an Offen-
bach. In order to be satisfied with such music,
men's souls must cease to reverberate with the
echoes of Palestrina and Mozart and Beethoven ; the
solemn grandeur of the Gregorian Chant must no
longer please ; the sublime and the beautiful must
have vanished before the frivolous and the fantastic.
So, too, with the poetry and general literature without a religious basis ; they will prove abortive.   They
will give a false direction to education, and in their
misapprehension of the ideal, they will ignore the
infinite, circumscribe themselves in the finite, and
live content in the expression of the tangible, the
sensuous and the material.   Flashes of great thought
may sometimes shine forth in them ; but they belong not to them ; they are reminiscences of the
literature that was inspired by religion.

is said to have so applied them.   Friar Peter d'Ureña added *si* to
the scale about 1520.

PART III.

PRACTICE.

CHAPTER I.

EVERY age is characterized by some intellectual trait. It has been already perceived that the prevailing tone of ours is scientific. Progress in industry and the mechanical arts is more highly prized than purely literary ability. Not but that there is much still written which is labelled literature. But few, very few indeed, of the many thousand volumes that are yearly flooding the reading world bear the impress that ranks them among the enduring monuments of intellect; very few deserve the title of classics; the greater number are explosive bubbles on the stream of thought. They are so, not through any lack of talent, but rather through its misapplication. The reason of this is to be found in the spirit of trifling that possesses the age. Time is wasted and energies are expended in the endeavor to move over a large surface of attainments; and as slight account is made of profoundness of knowledge, the results are not at all in keeping with the motive-power applied. Men are too Pilate-like ; they ask what the truth is and wait not for an answer ; or, with Tennyson, they postpone it to the other life ;

> " What hope of answer or redress ?
> *Behind the veil, behind the veil.*" *

They forget that investigation is a law of our intellects,† and that the truth can be found by every earnest searcher before he passes behind the veil. There is not enough of the steadiness of purpose, profound thought, and diligent preparation that are necessary to achieve permanent success.   Writers aim too low ; they no longer seek the sublime and beautiful ; they are content with the pretty and the startling ; they have found the labor of art-study too irksome, and have thrown off its invigorating discipline as a cramping yoke ; in a word, they have ceased to be literary artists.   For in the marshalling of words and the evolution of ideas, the greatest effect is sought to be produced, and therefore artistic skill is required for the arrangement best calculated to give the desired result, and must be inborn, as in the man of genius, or acquired, as by the man of talent.   Glance over one of the Shakespearian master-

---

* *In Memoriam, lv.*

† " Next, I consider that, in the case of educated minds, investigation into the argumentative proof of the things to which they have given their assent is an obligation, or rather a necessity.   Such a trial of their intellects is a law of their nature, like the growth of childhood into manhood, and analogous to the moral ordeal which is the instrument of their spiritual life."—JOHN HENRY NEWMAN. *Grammar of Assent*, p. 182.

pieces. In that apparent abandonment to the inspiration of the moment, during which from his magic pen drop some of the loveliest flowers of poesy and the sweetest words in language, which reveal new worlds of thought and sentiment—in that total absorption in the spirit of his piece to the seeming neglect of the diction he employs, so that what is apparently a random expression turns out to be most essential ; in that entire subserviency of all the parts to the end proposed ; in all these traits of that grand whole producing the desired effect upon the reader, playing upon the multitudinous chords of his heart, and calling forth at will notes of pleasure and pain, we have unmistakable evidence of the perfect artist, possessing the secret of hiding his artistic efforts. And so, on a like examination of one of Pope's pieces, in the rounded finish of every expression, in the exquisiteness with which a figure is set, and the apparent solicitude lest any word should be misplaced, we find palpable evidence of effort to have everything tend in the best manner possible to produce a desired effect ; the piece wears on its face traces of art. So it is with the labored finish of Sallust ; with the exquisite expression of Fenelon ; with the Attic grace of Xenophon ; with the sublime eloquence of Bossuet. All point to study, thought, labor, art. For the literary man is it true, as for the mechanic, that he must earn his bread in the sweat of his brow.

And genius is no exception to the rule. Carlyle defines it "a capacity for work." Michael Angelo calls it "eternal patience." Augustus Schlegel says that though it is "in a certain sense infallible, and has nothing to learn, still art is to be learned, and must be acquired by practice." Therefore, genius is not indolence, nor eccentricity, nor a license to dispense with all labor. True, it is a gift from heaven, and like all heavenly gifts, generally placed in a frail vessel thrown among us at random ; but invariably for a purpose and in obedience to a law.

We have already defined the characteristic of genius to be a power of simplifying, of taking that view of a subject in its rounded completeness that makes it more easily understood, of possessing one idea, in the light of which all others are resolvable. Hence a universal genius is never spoken of except by exaggeration. Genius in one department of knowledge as a rule excludes genius in another. Thus we have the mathematical genius, the military genius, the philosophic genius, the genius in sculpture, or painting, or poetry, or architecture ; but we never mention a genius in all, and seldom in any two of these branches together. "But," it may be urged, "the possession of only one idea implies intellectual weakness ; the man with many ideas has the superior intelligence." The truth is the opposite. Contemplate the Supreme Intelligence for a moment. It sees everything ; It possesses all knowledge in the light of an idea, which is Its own essence. Everything is contained in that idea, that Divine essence ; *and the more perfect created intelligences are, the more closely do they resemble their Creator, the less is the number of their ideas, and the more they see in the light of these ideas.* * This is the law of all intelligences. Superior intelligence be-

* " Unde oportet, quod ea quæ Deus cognoscit per unum, infe-

longs not to a caviller, a disputatious person, a hair-splitter; these classes give indications of narrow-mindedness and weakness of understanding. We make use of argument to supply our deficiency of comprehension. We are discussing some property or relation of a triangle; we are puzzled over it; we can proceed no further. A mathematical genius comes along; he draws a line or two, and resolves the figure into its simplest elements; in a few words, he throws a flood of light upon the subject-matter, so that we are surprised at our own lack of comprehension, and we exclaim: "How simple! Why did we not see it before?" Again, we are perplexed over a proposition in some old author; we see not its bearings; we throw it aside as a dry and barren idea, and we wonder why any man in his sound senses can sit down and seriously write such language. A genius takes up that idea; he makes it the nucleus of an essay or treatise, in which he traces its relations through all departments of thought; in his hands it becomes the central point whence emanates an illumination that reveals the secret of a thousand things hitherto incomprehensible. What was barrenness before, becomes the germ of a whole world of thought. It is ever thus with genius. We all of us bask in its sunshine. Its slightest conjectures become established truths for us. Its proven ideas we take as our first principles. Its views we make the standard of our own. It discovers and invents, and

riores intellectus cognoscant per multa; et tanto amplius per plura, quanto amplius intellectus inferior fuerit."—*Summa*, prima prima uv.æst. 66 art. 2.

16

we apply. We add the weight of its assertions to support the deficiencies of our own weak arguments. "The master says so," is often enough our saving clause and our most convincing proof. Reason is infallible under given circumstances ; but the instinct of faith is always strong within us. It is the secret of our progress ; for were we obliged to refer all truth back to first principles, taking nothing for granted but the self-evident, the march of ideas would be slow ; we would be always beginning, always making the same discoveries, and much that is now the glory of intelligence would be still buried in the unknown.

It is the privilege of the genius to perceive a new idea dawn upon his age before the common mass of thinkers. His superior intellectual position widens the horizon of his ignorance, and he feels a want the sooner. Hence the fact, of such frequent occurrence, of two or more making the same discovery about the same time. Their attention is drawn by the exigencies of the case in the same direction, and even before they know definitely what it is they are going to discover—before the want arising assumes a definite shape, they feel it steal upon them, so to speak ; and often, groping their way in the dark, they hit upon it accidentally, not recognizing its value for future times. Scheele and Priestley discover oxygen in the same year ; Newton and Leibnitz discover the calculus independently of each other. Leverrier and Adams about the same time are computing the elements of the planet Neptune, the discovery of which Airy considers "the effect of a movement of the age" ; Wallace and Darwin, unknown to each other, on the same day, decide to publish the doctrine of Natural Selection ; and in 1868, Lockyer in England, and Janssen in Hindostan, under circumstances entirely different, conclude that by means of the spectroscope they can, on any clear day, study the solar prominences, visible to the naked eye only during total eclipses. Such are a few of many instances that go to show one phase of intelligence working.

Writers on genius have much to say about originality. It consists not so much in saying something that nobody ever before said, as in moulding an idea into shape, and giving it a hue that stamps it as characteristic. " The bard of Eden." says Chateaubriand, speaking of Milton, " after the example of Vergil, has acquired originality in appropriating to himself the riches of others, which proves that the original style is not the style that never borrows of any one, but that which no other person is capable of reproducing."* The great genius is not over-particular about the materials he uses. He picks up those nearest to hand ; he stamps them with the impress of his genius ; and so fashioned, they ever after pass as his, and his alone. The conception of no one of Shakespeare's plays is his. It lived in history and tradition long before he made it the heirloom of humanity. The history of *Athalie* was read in Scripture ages before it became, under the hand of Racine, one of the flowers of French letters. The appearance of an idea in two or more authors proves nothing beyond mere coincidence. Two minds may arrive at the same result by entirely different methods of thought. Truth is one, as the Author of truth is one ; and only small fry

* *The Genius of Christianity*, ii., bk. i., ch. iii., p. 221.

ments of it are realized by the most powerful minds. The rill, feebly following the ravine's course, the torrent dashing down the mountain's side, and the expansive river majestically winding along the plain, bearing on its bosom a nation's treasures—each and all, however distant be their sources, originally came from the same ocean to which they return, and in comparison with which the greatest of them is insignificant. So all truth, all beauty, all excellence, have their creative source in God, the Divine Fountain-Head, in whom they will again find a resting-place and a home. What wonder, then, that as the same shower replenishes many springs, the same truth should sink into more intellects than one, and flow therefrom tinged by their individual peculiarities.

The source from which the literary artist draws materials to work upon, is as varied and universal as Nature. The intellectual, the moral, and the physical worlds are alike open to his observation and study. Life, savage and civilized ; the past and the present ; the empirical and the ideal ; beauty and deformity ; virtue and vice ; nobility and baseness ; pleasure and pain, all present themselves to him ; from all he must cull, and from the clashing of opposites, and the harmony of compatibles, and the influencing agencies in the physical and spiritual orders, weave an artistic whole that is so connected in parts, and so much the expression of an inspiring principle, that it becomes a thing of undying fame for all time. His aim—the aim of all literature—is to solve life's problem. No easy one it is, considering man's numerous and complex relations with his

fellow-man, himself and his Creator ; the thousand
passions that alternately roll over his soul, and lash
it into so many moods ; the contradictory influences
under which he moves, and the rigid logic with
which every event works out its result, either here or
.hereafter.

The production of a literary artist is the image of
himself, inasmuch as it possesses a soul and a body.
In nature, it is not the body that shapes the soul ; it
is rather the soul that gives form and activity to the
body.   We lay stress on the same distinction in a
work of art.   When Cousin tells us that " method is
the genius of a system,"* he makes method usurp
the place of principle. The principle is the soul of the
system, and therefore its genius.   It determines both
system and method.   We made this distinction at the
outset ; we again call attention to it here, as the opposite doctrine has respectable names on its side. It
has been seen that there is no artistic master-piece
without expression ; there is no expression without
unity ; and there is no unity without a common bond,
in which all the parts unite, and therefore without an
animating principle to keep them together.   In the
construction of a work, then, the first thing the literary artist must do is to determine the principle that
gives it unity, and therefore life.   He must observe,
study, meditate. His subject-matter, when well di-
gested, will determine his method of treatment. And
if he has no subject, no aim, no idea to develop, no
proposition to prove—

" S'il ne sent point du ciel l'influence secrète,"—

* *History of Philosophy*, vol., I. p. 320.

if all is random and confusion, he had better wait. It is a loss of time to undertake that which pride, rather than ability, dictates. "Life is short, art long, occasion passing, experiment dangerous, judgment difficult."* There is a work for every man; each has his function in life. Let not him destined for hand-work assume to do the labor that belongs to him selected for brain-work. Let each hold to that for which he has natural aptitude; in that alone lies the secret of his success.

Thought, sentiment, enthusiasm, unite in giving soul to a work. A great source of labor is the mechanism of construction of the body. Language is the material with which the literary artist works. He must aim at the accurate wording of his propositions. He must therefore seek to be complete master of his language. He must know the force and bearing of every word. He must study the great masters. We cannot judge of a musical instrument by the grating notes which a beginner draws therefrom; it is only when the consummate master elicits sweet and rapturous variations that we appreciate its power. The tyro in literary art should learn from those who have made it the vehicle of profound ideas and happy expressions the power there is in it, its richness of idiom, the flexibility with which it bends to the humor of the author—now plain and simple, now full-flowing and pathetic, again vigorous and energetic, in all cases variety of style yielding to variety of thought. But nothing can take the place of con-

* Vita brevis, ars vero longa, occasio autem præceps, experimentum periculosum, judicium difficile."—HIPPOCRATES, Aph. i. i.

stant practice. It is only that beating and hammer-ing on language—that turning it into a thousand moulds—that correcting and refining of its diction, which can make it bend to every grade of thought, and express every shade of meaning.

Above all, the literary artist should guard truth as a sacred trust, and never sacrifice any jot thereof to a smooth turn or a rhetorical figure. There is no beauty without truth. Real art grows sickly, rank, defective, in the unwholesome atmosphere of falsehood. Let the artist be so possessed with his subject-matter that he will see in it "the truth, the whole truth, and nothing but the truth," and he will always find fitting expression for his views.

> " Prune thou thy words, the thoughts control,
> That o'er thee swell and throng ;
> They will condense within thy soul,
> And change to purpose strong."*

CHAPTER II.

LITERARY MORALITY.

MAN has more than art-power and intelligence; he has soul, and that soul is the seat of a multitude of contradictory passions. As such it is called the heart. In literature, the whole man speaks ; there-fore the heart has a say in the production of thought, and in sensitive natures determines motives, and

*J. H. Newman, *Verses on Various Occasions*.

gives a coloring to the labor of their life.   Genius is
generally accompanied with refined sensibility, and
is therefore influenced in a special manner by the
heart.   Is the author who is ruled by his sensibility
crossed in life ?   All his darker passions are aroused ;
he grows embittered against society ; humanity is a
monster ; the Divinity even is the impersonation of
cruelty and injustice.   He recoils from friends ; he
recoils from himself.   He lives a misanthrope.   The
hiss of black hatred resounds through his works.   Is
he happy in his career, surrounded by endearing
friends, who wield a wholesome influence over him ?
His writings everywhere reflect the sunshine in which
he basks.   Nature is all beauty ; society a joy ; life
a pleasant dream, and God good.   Thus are impressions ideas to him ; and it not unfrequently happens
that what, in his seeming, is the logical deduction of
a severe course of reasoning—a purely intellectual
process—is but the silent work of an undercurrent of
sentiments welling up from the inner recesses of his
heart.   And so sentiments influence thought, expand
the intelligence, raise man above himself, and inspire some of the sublimest passages in literature.
Where an author throws his whole soul into a subject, he is most forcible.   The most soul-stirring
passages in literature are the result of a play of feeling, a personal reminiscence, an overflow of sensibility.   There is in the reading of such passages the
electric influence of soul upon soul, the source of
sympathy between author and reader.

As literature proceeds from the whole man, so it
addresses itself to the whole man.   There is in it

truth for the mind, beauty for the æsthetic sense ; and
there is also in it that which appeals to the heart.
When the genius rises above the crampings of systems, and personal likings and dislikings ; when he
soars clear of all prejudice and the turmoil of passion,
and seems to catch a glimpse of the real relations of
things, and a stray beam of the created light of truth,
such as primeval man lived in prior to the fall, lights
up his soul, he is invariably in harmony with the good,
the true, and beautiful. But man is fallen man,
and his moral nature is sadly impaired. Human
nature is corrupt human nature. Passion is active.
It blinds : it leads reason captive. It never dies ; it
only sleeps, and is easily aroused ; and when aroused,
it is in continual struggle against man's better judgment. It behooves the writer, then, to be calm and
collected, to know fully what he is about, and to say
to himself : " Are the consequences of this work to be
for good or for evil ? Is there anything here that I
would regret in after-life—anything that I would wish
recalled on my death-bed ? " And at every sacrifice
he should prune whatever in the remotest degree
would be the germ of ruin to a soul. Having satisfied himself on this negative test, he should further
say to himself : " As a work of literature, this book is
addressed to fallen human nature ; and fallen human
nature ever tends to fall lower in the moral scale ;
but it should be the aim of every book to raise up
that nature, to draw out its nobler and better parts.
Is this the function of the book I now write ? Will it
make man look more kindly on his fellow-man?
Will it help him to think on his Creator the more,

and draw him closer to Him? Will he be a better man for the reading of it?" And if the writer can answer these questions with satisfaction, may God bless him ; he is a benefactor to humanity ; he is deserving of laurels; his book through all time will be doing good ; and in eternity alone will he be able to reap the reward it has sown for him. It is within the power of every literary artist to thus control himself, and express the true and the good in spite of his individual feelings. The higher genius always makes his prejudices subservient to his art when he cannot keep them altogether out of sight. It is littleness that bustles and cries out, and makes a great noise about grievances, exaggerated or imaginary.

In literature, then, it is of extreme importance to draw a line of distinction between the moral and the immoral. As in nature there are flowers and fruits fair to the eye but rotten at the core, so in the garden of humanity are there to be found, under an accomplished exterior, a bad heart and a vicious character, such as might be the product of a cultivation based merely on Chesterfield's *Letters*—that elegant code of polite scoundrelism—such as led Shakespeare to say :

"That one may smile, and smile, and be a villain ; "

so, also, in the domain of literature, there often lurk behind the garb of an elegant diction ideas and sentiments the most contaminating. The great and infallible criterion whereby to distinguish, is the Divine and immutable law of morality, such as is the rule of man's actions, and as he will be judged by—the Decalogue. A literary production should never at-

tempt to infringe this law by directly teaching doctrines, insinuating a spirit, or acting upon and draw-
ing out feelings to which it is opposed. The very
instinct of literary art looks to this criterion : for in the
departments requiring most artistic skill, viz., poetry and fiction, the basis of nearly all, and of all the
most excellent and successful efforts, is also the basis
of the moral code. A thread of love is woven into
their ground-work. But that thread is frequently so
tattered and soiled with human passion, its Divine
origin is no longer recognizable. Yet love is the
golden chain that binds humanity in a bond of brotherhood, that keeps society together, that connects earth
with heaven. It is the law not only of man, but of
God. It is the principle of His Triune Personality.
Without it, Nature would drop back to its original
nothingness, and its Creator would cease to be ; for
God is Love.

Writers of poetry and fiction seem to forget this
elevated character of love, and give the sacred name
to blind passion. They spin a thread of fate from
the fiction of their brain, and weave it about their
characters, and call it destiny or elective affinity, as
though every individual were not responsible and the
master of his own choosing ; and thus they sow
broadcast the seeds of free-loveism, again abusing
the sacred name. They deck up monsters of vice in
all the fascinations of youth, beauty, engaging manners, and splendid fortune ; they

"——make madness beautiful, and cast
O'er erring deeds and thoughts a heavenly hue of words,"

and represent such creations wading through crime

to the enjoyment of earthly happiness, and call on the reader to sympathize with them in adventures and sufferings brought upon them by their own vicious ways. The reader responds ; from sympathy he passes to liking, and from liking is soon involved in like deeds. Say he does not fall so low ; still the reading of such works blunts his finer feelings, prepares him to consider unmoved, perhaps even complacently, crimes the bare mention of which should have been a horror to him, and thus suppresses the growth of his better nature. It especially destroys genuine sentiment.

There is too much of the lackadaisical in our modern literature. Authors abound—especially writers of fiction—with whom life is reduced to a sentiment ; thought is a sentiment ; love is a sentiment ; religion is a sentiment ; and often God is regarded as nothing more than an object of pious sentiment. This is sentimentalism. The offspring of exaggerated and unnatural feelings, it fosters them in the reader of delicate sensibility to the ruin of all humane impulses. He becomes unreal. His heart grows hardened. It may seem paradoxical, but it is true that sentimentalism hardens the heart. It is but a passing thing ; it evaporates soon, and seems, so to speak, to leave after it a sedimentary deposit which shrouds the better feelings. See that young lady transported to ecstacy over some meaningless expression, and paying the tribute of a tear to some high-wrought, fanciful, and improbable incident, picturing affliction and misery where they never could have existed. She is distracted by the untimely intrusion of some poor, infirm, suffering, needy one, a true object of pity and charity. He asks an alms. In that half-scowling, perturbed look with which she gives the scanty mite or the curt refusal, we perceive no indications of a heart softened on beholding a brother in actual distress ; the unholy tears she had been previously shedding seem to have extinguished in her the last spark of real sentiment, and encased her heart in selfishness. This is a scene of daily occurrence. Man is but too prone to be unreal, and to deceive himself on his nearest and highest interests ; the grand aim of literature ought to be, not to hide these interests from his view and sink him deeper in delusion, but rather to raise them out of the daily cares in which they lie buried, place them before him in their most attractive form, and inspire him with practical and ennobling sentiments regarding them.

"It is unlawful to influence when it is not permitted to convince ; where conviction is a deception, persuasion is a perfidy." *   An incontrovertible truth, rendered doubly strong when we consider the usual attitude of readers towards an author. They are frequently credulous and unthinking ; and some read to beguile an idle hour, or even to be lulled to sleep ; some crave light reading, and abandon themselves to the scenes, incidents, and impression of the novel or poem with the repose of one listlessly gliding down a smooth stream, calmly enjoying the varied beauties that present themselves on its banks ; some

* No es licito persuadir quando no es licito convencer ; quando la conviccion es un engaño, la persuasion es una perfidia.—BALMES; *El Criterio*, p. 299.

few read to gain a further insight into the workings of the mind and heart than can be learned within the narrow circle of their own experience ; but they are far between who vex and weary their minds in separating the salutary from the baneful. He, then, who would avail himself of the confidence placed in him by the large majority of his readers, to insinuate aught in his work that tends to inflame the passions, who would diffuse a misanthropic spirit through its pages, who would elicit sympathy in an unhallowed cause, or tamper with the truth, or gild false maxims, is guilty of a breach of good faith towards his readers ; he becomes a public evil ; he is, indeed, a seducer of men and an agent of hell.

The reader has a duty to perform here. He should be select in his reading. He should neither patronize nor encourage a bad book. Supply is always in proportion to demand. Let the bad book drop. Cease lauding it as a matchless literary production. Show it up in its true light. Show it to be false in sentiment, false in fact, false in principle, and it will soon pass into oblivion.

The critic's is a noble position ; it is also a responsible one. He ought to be the faithful sentinel and and servant of humanity, ever on the lookout, ever quick to report the signs of the times and the spirit that actuates a work, fearless in exposing shams, just in his estimates, and at all times truthful. But truth compels us to say that the press weakens its own power by its negligent criticisms, by the subserviency with which it does party work, and by making use of false standards in judging of a literary production.

There are honorable exceptions. The critical opinion of a book is not always the just estimate of its
value. The professional critic is usually a man over-
powered with work, and, when he is best disposed,
he seldom has time to read a book to the end ; he
has to be content with dipping into it and recording
his impression as favorable or unfavorable. He may
have found the drift of the work good, and it really
may be so ; but in an uncut page there may also lurk
poison intellectual or moral whereof he knows nothing.
Hence all criticism is based on probability, more or
less reliable, according to the known judgments of
the critic in other cases. That criticism is the most
probably correct which agrees in the main with
others from different quarters, representing opposite
or divergent interests. Criticism, like medicine, is a
matter of empiricism. There is nothing infallible in
its judgments. There are no standards, except of a
vague nature, by which all can be ruled ; and even
were there, each critic would apply them differently,
according to the cultivation of reason and taste. We
say reason and taste, for a literary work is not
judged by reason alone. A scientific work is either
true or false, and its value is determined accordingly. Not so a piece of literary art. There, it not unfrequently happens that where the reason condemns,
the æsthetic sense approves. The language of soul,
heart, sentiment, is not the language of intelligence.
The feelings may speak one thing, the judgment
another. St. Augustine, in his younger days, shed
tears over the love of Dido. His maturer judgment
condemns his folly ; for it finds that love opposed to

morality, and he again weeps over the tears he
formerly shed.   And so, throughout literature, in the
greatest master-pieces, there are passages based
upon deeds our judgments condemn, and we shrink
from with horror ; and yet we learn them by heart ;
we are enthusiastic in their praise ; we recite them
to our friends.   They please our æsthetic sense ;
they move our sentiments.   We see perfection approached in their artistic execution.   And this suggests a question delicate as it is important : What
works may or may not be safely read in literature?
We lay down but a general rule :

I. Every literary production that promotes, encourages, and strengthens truth and virtue, may be read
with profit to soul and intellect.

II. Every literary production not opposed, in its
spirit and bearing, to truth and virtue, and implying
the necessity of both one and the other, may be read
with safety.

III. Every literary production, be its artistic qualities what they may, that scoffs at religion, disregards
truth, looks upon morality as a prejudice into which
men have been educated ; that speaks lightly of any
of these : that throws any, the least, aspersion upon
them ; that even, in a negative manner, by losing
sight of them, and treating subjects as though these
eternal principles were not, thus insinuates that life is
good without them—every such production is to be
condemned, and its reading discouraged.

It will not do to quote the maxim : "To the pure all
things are pure."   It is a sophism.   Virtue can never
regard vice as a virtue, and it may or may not be

contaminated by coming in contact therewith. It is not given to everybody to be able to draw good out of evil and turn all things unto a spiritual purpose. There is another maxim much more to the point. It is, that evil communications corrupt good manners.* Individual experience is of no avail here. True, one man may have read a bad book without its injuring his moral character in the least; but how knows he that his neighbor, to whom he recommends the same work, has the strength of character to withstand its poisoning influence?

In all departments of thought there is a pure and invigorating literature. There is also a literature of doubtful morality. Finally, there is a literature positively immoral. Nor is it to be wondered at. Being the embodiment in language of what there is most intimate in man—part of himself—and often the production of a misinformed mind and an erring heart, it is to be expected that a large ingredient of untruth and immorality run through it. From the imperfect, the weak, and the erring, we cannot hope for the perfect, the strong, and the infallible. These truths will be all the more evident from a further search into the scope and function of literary criticism.

CHAPTER III.

LITERARY CRITICISM.

CRITICISM goes hand in hand with art. It is the educator of art. It restrains impetuosities, prunes extravagances, develops stunted parts into due pro

---

* 1 Cor. xv., 33.

17

portions, and initiates into the canons and practices of good taste. Criticism is not simply fault-finding. Mere intellectual cleverness can pick flaws. Every human production may be quarrelled with on the score of defects or imperfections. Our rhetoricians tear our master-pieces asunder, show how defective is their language, how inconsistent their action, how rambling their plot or the train of their thoughts, and end by leaving the pupil under the impression that our greatest writers wrote their own language very badly indeed. Generations have been, and are daily, taught, nothing else of our classic authors than that they violated this rule of grammar or sinned against that canon of rhetoric. It never occurs to teacher or pupil that the grammar might be erroneous or the rhetoric arbitrary ; that a standard of expression in one stage of a language need not be the standard in another stage ; that a sentence may seem very defective when torn from its context, and may be the only proper form when read in the page from which it has been abstracted, and that the final tribunal of appeal in all matters of correctness and taste regarding language, is the general custom of the great writers of the language. Prim phrasings may be good ; but the thought that burns for utterance does not express itself in prim phrasings. It sweeps through the soul, making a music all its own, in language possessing a rhythm and a force all its own, not to be measured and weighed with the weights and measures supplied by grammarian or rhetorician, and all the more forcible because of the apparent irregularities.

Criticism is the careful examination of a work in

order to determine its nature and scope, how far it speaks the truth, and what standard of taste and excellence it has attained. As we have already perceived, a book-notice based upon a glance at the table of contents and a hasty perusal of the preface, is not criticism. Neither is it criticism, simply to search for what is not contained in a book; nor to commend a book merely because of the pleasure it gives without paying due regard to the truth or falsity of the opinions or principles upon which that pleasure is based ; nor to carp at that which may run counter to one's prejudices or preconceived notions, for one's prejudices may be unreasonable and one's notions may require revision. True criticism rises above party and prejudice. It is search made with a mind ever docile, ever open to instruction. It is truth-loving. It examines both sides of an issue. It will state the points telling against a cherished opinion as well as those in favor of it. It is conscientious. Under no circumstances will it suppress any jot or tittle of truth. It is honest. What it says, it says for the sake of truth pure and simple ; it therefore disdains to trifle with the truth or with the sincere mind inquiring after truth.

Criticism is twofold : it is analytic and synthetic. Analytic criticism resolves a subject into its component parts. It takes account of the various elements that make up a work. It notes the extent to which other men's thoughts enter therein ; to what degree it reflects past and present influences ; which of its ideas are of home and which of foreign origin ; and of the home, which are personal and which national. It traces the work back to its sources. It analyzes style, method and principles ; the style, in order to note how far it is in keeping with the subject ; the method, in order to determine the degree of ability with which the author has handled and utilized his materials ; the principles, in order to ascertain how far he understands his subject-matter.

Here we are landed at synthetic criticism. This consists in the reconstruction of the work out of its component parts ; or rather, it is building up in the mind of the reader, a just conception of the work, after it has been thoroughly analyzed. This is the more difficult portion of the task of criticism. It implies that the critic has formed unto himself an ideal. The accuracy of his ideal will depend largely on his acquaintance with what is best among the writings of different peoples. An exclusive knowledge of the literature of his own language will not suffice. Each nation has its ideal of excellence in style and method. The element that may be lacking in one literature is to be found in another. The prose of French literature is far superior in clearness and epigrammatic precision to the prose of German literature ; but, other things being equal, a page of German literature is, as a rule, far more thought-suggesting than a page of French literature. And so we might compare all our modern literatures and find in one the excellence that another may be deficient in. It is only by an acquaintance with several that the modern critic can form unto himself an ideal embodying all excellences. Having set up his ideal, he makes comparison of the work under review with others of the same kind and notes the points of difference and resemblance. He dwells on the parts in their relations with each other and with the whole. He notes how far the book falls short of his ideal ; what subject-matter it actually contains, and what it lacks in order to be more perfect.

The critic's duty is not yet accomplished. There still remains for him to label and classify the book and give it its proper niche in the world of letters. Has the book the notes of a master-piece that will endure for all time ? Has it a vivifying idea ? Does it reveal a soul ? Or is it a book of the hour, made to satisfy some want or some craving of the hour, and then pass into oblivion ?—These are questions that no critic can settle, and few can give approximate answers to. A more pressing question still, is this : Does the book reflect or embody the Time-spirit ?— It is essential that the critic know the various currents of thought that flow through the age. He should be able to distinguish between the main current and the various subsidiary and counter currents that are induced thereby. He should know whence they come, whither they flow, how they move, whether slowly or rapidly, whether directly or meanderingly, and on what plane. He should know what authors drift in each. For this he requires a clear vision and a delicate and highly cultured sense of literary appreciation. Then there is a twofold Time-spirit. There is the Time-spirit that guides, directs and providentially ordains the onward and upward progress of a nation or an age in the path of civilization. It is this spirit that makes for liberty of thought and liberty of action with such rapid flow in the

present century. Men misinterpret its meaning ; men
misapply its inspirations ; men pervert its ordi-
nances; in its name men violate obligations the
most binding, trample on rights the most sacred, and
ignore duties the most pressing ; but withal it is none
the less Heaven-sent, for liberty is truth.   Then there
is the Time-spirit begotten of men's evil passions.
It counteracts the good ; not unfrequently like a torrent does it bear down all other spirits before it, and
becoming predominant, inspire the most active and
fertile intellects of the period.   In this manner did
the paganizing spirit of the Renaissance possess
Boccaccio.   So did the sentiment of the vague so
prevalent in the early part of this century for a while
hold Chateaubriand within its grasp ; so did the secular spirit of the present century possess Goethe.
With the Time-spirit in all its phases must the critic
be familiar.

Every author leaves unsaid a certain amount which
his readers supply in the perusal of his book.   It is
the common ground work of their thinking, upon
which author and reader stand and meet and are at
home.   It never occurs to the author to repeat this
unwritten body of ideas.   It is in the air ; it is the light
by which his thought has meaning and relevancy ;
it is of the very essence of the Time-spirit.   The
moment this subtle, all pervading atmosphere of
thought is lost, the book ceases to be intelligible in
the same degree ; it becomes like unto a manuscript
from which some sentences have been effaced, and
the reader is obliged to supply the deficiency by

conjectures more or less happy. He who reads *Paradise Lost* without being familiar with the times in which Milton lived, the frame of mind in which he wrote, and the temper of those to whom he addressed his sublime song, has still to learn the scope and meaning of that great poem.

Criticism has other and higher duties. These are mainly of an educative character. It is eclectic in its method. It sifts the wheat of literature from the chaff. It seeks to bring the popular intelligence into touch with the best thoughts of the best authors of all times. By placing within general view its ideals of thought and expression, it becomes a factor of true culture. It teaches us how to read and interpret our world-authors. It throws upon their methods, their persons, their times, their modes of thinking, a flood of light, which enables us to understand and read correctly what had hitherto been many a dim and blurred page. It gets at the heart of a book and shows it to us palpitating with the life-blood of a vivifying principle coursing through it, and we henceforth are possessed of the meaning and import of that book. Sainte-Beuve, that prince of critics, in his polished and beautiful essays—*Causeries du Lundi*—possesses the rare talent of renewing one's interest in an author, and causing one to re-read the author with a pleasure that one had hitherto not known. Take, for instance, his essays on Bossuet,* on Bourdaloue,† on Joubert, ‡ on Pascal, § on La Fon-

---

* t. x., pp. 145–174.   † t. ix., pp. 210–240.
‡ t. i., pp. 126–142.   § t. v., pp. 413–426.

taine.* These are all subjects within his grasp, and he charms one in his talks about them. Sometimes, he talks about a subject that is beyond his reach ; such is his essay on Dante † in which he fails almost as hopelessly in his estimate of the great Italian as did Voltaire.

Three primary elements enter into literary criticism : the author, the book, and the critic. The author exercises all the powers of his soul and puts into his book a certain amount of his personality. The whole man speaks and appeals to the whole man in the reader. A soul vibrates behind the printed page, and the reader's soul vibrates in a responsive thrill. This is especially true of literature in its highest and best form. But in order to produce such literature, the author should exercise his faculties in the order of their pre-eminence. His will-power should control his pen so that it inscribe nothing contrary to the eternal principles of morality. His reason should retain its supremacy and direct the imagination in its flights. He should always hold sensibility subordinate to reason and imagination. In the harmonious working of all the faculties is the healthful book wrought. This is the book that becomes a joy to the soul. With such a joy does one disport in the sunlight that plays upon the page of Homer. In Shakespeare also does one find a healthful balance of soul which enabled him to fashion his world precisely as the world we live in is fashioned, with its smiles and its tears, its comedies and its tragedies.

* t. vii., pp. 412-426.   † t. xi., pp. 166-179.

There is a joy running through the pages of Walter Scott as refreshing as the morning dew. This complete sanity of authorship accompanies genius in its highest and best flights. Where there is a lack of harmony in the faculties, there is an absence of healthfulness in the book. In the stead is to be found a morbid sensitiveness running through the whole gamut of feeling, from *Kubla-Khan* and the nightmares of Poe to the melancholy of Lamartine and the cynicism of Carlyle, from the soul-disease of *Manfred* to the world-pain of Heine and Leopardi. It is not the whole man that speaks ; it is passion, prejudice, exaggerated feeling. The soul-response cannot be healthful ; it can give out only the harsh notes of despair, discontent, and revolt.

Next, consider the book. Its object is truth ; whether it be truth in the moral, physical, or metaphysical order—in the domain of history, or in that of poetry and fiction—truth it is pure and simple, the truth and the whole truth. Now, there are many ways of looking at truth, all of them depending upon the habits of thought of the author :

1. There is the rhetorical method, in which the author looks at truth, not for truth's sake, but as it speaks to his rhetorical sense. He measures the value of things, not according to their intrinsic worth, but by the effect they are likely to produce in a well-balanced antithesis or a clever metaphor. The note of sincerity is totally absent from such composition. The reader feels all along that had the opposite or the contradictory proposition been as favor-

able to the construction of a clever sentence the author would have made use of it equally as well. This is the feeling that accompanies the reading of those brilliant flashes of rhetoric, the *History* and the *Essays* of Macaulay.

2. There is the fantastic method of regarding a subject; it is sometimes inaptly called the poetic method.   It consists in overlooking all other aspects of a subject than those that strike the fancy.   It would see in Puritanism only its fanatical feature, and in Catholic ritual only the candles and incense and gorgeous vestments.   It never penetrates beyond the superficial traits that speak to the eye and harmonize with the natural taste.   It has never grasped the deeper meaning underlying the outward show. Sensibility is the predominant faculty in this method.

3. There is the logic method, which cannot think a thought without a therefore.   It bristles with syllogisms.   It has a show of clearness in arrangement of subject-matter.   Its points, and divisions and subdivisions are numbered and ordered.   It seems possessed of depth and carefulness, and apparently it exhausts its theme.   But it is all a seeming.   It is shoal and shallow.   Far from exhausting, it has simply contrived to steer clear of the real difficulties. It is the most deceptive of mental habits.   It takes the genius of an Aquinas to fathom a subject and reach all its difficulties with such a cumbersome method.   The genius of a Spinoza was shattered upon its shoals.   The syllogism is useful as a test ; the mind should always be logical ; but with great

thinkers the logic runs along in an undercurrent
even as it does in all sound thinking.

4. In opposition to this logic method is the piece-
meal method of thought. It does not seek consec-
utiveness. The mind stands aloof from the works
on which it feeds ; it jots down the suggestions
that come, be their relevancy what it may. It is a
method of moods. It does not pretend to consistency. Its opinion of to-day may not be that of to-
morrow ; and still it makes no advance. It moves
in circles. Such a mind was Emerson's.

5. There is the metaphysical method. It endeavors
to grasp the essence of things. It makes straight
for the heart of a subject, and in doing so it is likely
to walk rough-shod over the refined phrase and all
that goes to make up the urbanity of style. Imagination there may be in abundance, but sensibility
and patient culture are lacking.

6. There is the moralizing method begotten of the
mental habit of prosing on all topics. It may show
sensibility and imagination and reason in due order
and proportion, but it lacks vitality. Its main support is the truism ; the chief staple of its material is
the commonplace. It is prim and respectable, and
certain people consider it admirable reading for the
young. But they are mistaken. To bore the youth-
ful mind becomes the death of all intellectual activity.

7. There is the poetical method. It comes from
the habit of seeing in objects the ideal that beautifies
them and lifts them out of the ordinary and commonplace. The poet need not write every line glittering

with bright thoughts ; it is only the purely clever man who can achieve this feat, and the purely clever man never becomes more than a second rate poet. Emerson has truly said—and we can accept the saying as a sound canon of criticism—that a single line suffices to embalm a poem for all time. Sometimes there may not be a single line worth remembering, still less a line that burns itself into the memory as so many of Browning's do, and yet, as in the case of several of Wordsworth's poems, in spite of bald expression, the reader finds himself, by the time he has finished the poem, lifted into an atmosphere of poesy. A new sense—a second sight —has been added to his intellectual vision. This is the function of true poetry.

8. Finally, there is the method of a mind accustomed to look at subjects in all their aspects. Such a mind conceals from itself none of the difficulties surrounding a subject ; it meets them face to face ; it grapples with them ; in the light of the main issue it seeks their solution ; it employs no useless words ; it makes use of the simplest terms to express the highest truths ; there is in its expression a fullness and a completeness that grasp the whole truth in all its bearings ; reason, imagination and sensibility are there, but reason is uppermost, and holds the others in check, even while they are imparting life and color to the sentences, and a poetic glow is giving them warmth. The nearest approach to this order of mind is Cardinal Newman.

These various orders of minds will naturally leave their impress in as many different styles, each corre-

sponding to the cast of mind, and the form of method.
Here enters the third element of criticism. It is the
duty of the critic to probe the style, determine the
working-method employed, and measure the extent of
the mind-equipment which the author brings to his
subject. Does the language fit the subject? Is the
method employed, that best calculated to exhaust the
subject and ascertain the whole truth? What preparation does the author bring to the treatment of his subject? Wherein does he differ from 'hose who have
preceded him in the same field? Has he added any
new idea? Has he discovered any new fact throwing
additional light upon the topic? Is there an evident
reason for the existence of the new book? Here are
leading questions the conscientious critic puts to himself and seeks an answer for in the book before him.
Other questions that follow are these : What has the
author said? What has he left unsaid? How far
does the book lack completeness from the omissions?
It is a frequent practice for the critic to quarrel, not
with the book that the author has written but with the
book that he has not written. The critic apprehends
the subject from one point of view , the author from
another. Now it is the critic's duty first to take the
author's point of view, enter into his intentions
and determine how far he has carried out his
projected plan. Afterwards, the critic may return
to his own view and with profit to the author and his
readers, give another aspect of the subject.

This leads us to consider the legitimate function of
criticism. It is to regulate the methods of work, to
lay out the limitations within which to work, and to

establish the laws of good taste according to the
nature of the work.   It is to awaken and cultivate the
literary conscience, by virtue of which the writer
scruples to insert a word or phrase not in accord with
the strictest propriety, dreads to deviate by the least
shade of meaning from what he knows to be the
precise truth, and does justice to his authorities by not
garbling or tampering with their works, and by quoting them only in the full sense of their meaning and
known intention.   It is also the function of criticism
to cultivate deference to the ideal in art-work.   No
matter how profound and fruitful one's ideas may be,
they lose all value and permanent efficacy by being
put into slovenly, rude, or uncouth form.   It is part
of the critic's duty to call attention to the form best
suited, and even direct as to the easiest and most
efficient manner of so moulding the idea.   Criticism
wages incessant warfare against rudeness, vulgarity,
and in season and out of season seeks to develop intellectual delicacy and urbanity.   Men may differ;
they may carry on a fierce and uncompromising controversy ; but for all that, they need never cease to
be courteous and urbane, and their home-thrusts
will be all the more telling.   Men may speak their
minds out without calling their adversa .es by nick-
names.   Your opponent may possibly be a fool ; why
not point out wherein lies the foolishness of his actions
or assertions, without applying to him the opprobrious
epithet?
    Another and an important function of literary criti-
cism is to break down the barriers of prejudice, let in
the light and extend the sphere of knowledge.   With

this view, it raises itself above party; it even seeks to overcome national predilections, and recognize merit the world over. Therefore, does it develop a strong resentment against these most pernicious barriers to all intellectual growth—Chauvinism and provincialism in every shape and form. One's country may be very beautiful and fertile, one's people may be endowed with many noble traits of character, one's national literature may possess great worth in **many** departments of thought; but to think that outside of one's country there is nothing to be learned, that one's people is supreme in everything, that one's literature is lacking in no excellence—this were at once to bar the road to all progress. One sets up household gods —idols of one's own making—and worships them happy and self-satisfied. Now, it is a chief function of criticism to break the idols and destroy the illusory peace. It brings one to see how little has been done, how imperfectly that little has been done, and how much still remains to be done. It defines one's limitations. And this is the secret of success in every walk of life, **that a man should know his limitations.** He who confines himself strictly to that which is within his capacity to do, and who does that work well, be the work what it may, is the man who is heard from. His work is lasting. He who has never determined the limitations of his own capacity, who deems himself equal to all things, who has never got beyond a vague desire to achieve something in the world of letters, and who now seeks success on this line of thought, now on that other, is simply beating the air and wasting energy to no purpose.

Criticism performing these functions brings with it instruction as. well as judgment. It opens up new vistas of thought. It is healthful and hopeful. It is in the highest sense educative. The law of criticism, as we have conceived it in these pages, is this: *To know what is best in thought and in style, and to make thereof a criterion whereby to judge literary work according to the degree of its approach to the ideal standard. The basis of criticism is knowledge, its object is truth.*

CHAPTER IV.

SUMMARY AND CONCLUSION.

LITERATURE is the expression of man's affections as influenced by society, the material world, and his Creator. It expresses individual feelings, as in the lyric; national feelings, as in the epic; and appeals to our common humanity, as in the drama.

2. Its fundamental principle is that a common humanity underlies our individual personalities.

3. Its legitimate function is to interpret the fainter emotions of our nature.

4. Its origin dates from the fall, and man's consequent degeneracy.

5. Climate influences language and language reacts in the moulding of thought. There are "plastic moments" of language, when it throws off the chrysalis of an old speech and puts on the garb of a new one, and at such moments appear geniuses who give it a

significance it retains afterwards.   Such geniuses are
Homer, Dante, the author of the *Nibelungen-lied*, and
Shakespeare.

6. The architecture of a people, as a rule, is inspired by a spirit akin to that which inspires its literature.   It is therefore an excellent counter-check in
determining the predominant spirit of a people or an
age, and should not be overlooked in criticism.   He
has but a partial acquaintance with Mediæval Europe
who shuts his eyes upon the Gothic cathedrals.

7. There are epochs when the expression of a people is mature, rounded, fully developed.   Society has
an external polish.   Language reflects the refinement which society affects.   It also is polished, and
becomes the standard for after-times.   Such epochs
develop the drama.   Given a people with an initial
literature, engaged in a long period of struggle, and
triumphantly issuing from that struggle, a golden era
of literature may be predicted for such a people
immediately after the first flush of victory.   A Pericles
will beautify his Athens.   An Augustus will find his
Rome of brick, and will leave it of marble.   And then
can we look for the decline of that nation ; for with
refinement in manners, in letters, in art and architecture, there invariably appears corruption.   Labor is
the law of life.   When men cease to fulfil that law—
when, instead, they abandon themselves to a life of
ease and indolence, they already begin to hatch the
germs of degeneracy.   Such is the lesson to be learned
from the law of literary epochs.

8. Literature is the varied expression of thought,
laboring under emotions produced by different in-
18

fluences.   Religion and philosophy are among the most potential.   They shape the same thought in many ways.   They underlie the whole history of literature.

9. The sum of thought is a constant quantity. Time may develop and apply in different directions the same thought, so that it appears a new idea. Strip it of its accidentals of time and place, and it will be seen to be an old acquaintance.   And this suggests a good rule in reading.   Deduct all the negations, all the side views, all the merely illustrative matter, all the digressions of a book, and it will be found that the absolutely positive in it—the main idea —can be condensed in the space of a paragraph.

10. The spirit of rationalism, fostered by the Renaissance, and fanned into a great religious flame by Martin Luther, is, in its nature, tendency, and results, destructive of sound thought, inasmuch as it doubts, denies, and grows inconsistent, without adding or developing any positive idea, and thus begets illogical habits of mind.   The instinct of faith is necessary for man.   Those loudest in its abuse are in a thousand ways it creatures.   All great intellectual discoveries and achievements are based on this instinct.

11. The spirit of rationalism undid the work of centuries by widening the breach between the secular and religious elements of society.   To reconcile these two elements is the great problem of modern thinkers, and the most earnest efforts to solve it seem to have no other effect than to widen the breach. Witness the theories of Positivism, Evolutionism, Hegelism, and Pessimism.   The great social charac-

teristic of ancient times was, that the religious and secular elements were harmoniously blended. This harmony is reflected in their literature. Its absence is felt in ours. A completely developed modern literature will only result from this harmonious development.

12. Modern subjectivism is a literary disease. It arises from the spirit of rationalism. In breaking from the moorings of the past, men found in themselves only self for a criterion ; they adopted it, and made it enter into all their views.

13. We must go beyond self for the source of truth, which is also the source of beauty. In God is found both. But, beginning with the denial of revelation, men have ended with the denial of God. Hence there is no science in modern times beyond the science of the material. The science of beauty is not explicable in the light of materialistic principles. The beautiful is the expression of the ideal—the created ideal placed in man by the creative act, and recognized more or less clearly when the sense of the beautiful is awakened in the soul.

14. Literature is classical in proportion as it expresses the beautiful. Eliminate that, no matter how broken its reflection may be, and there is destroyed the conservative element that constitutes the essence of a classic. Unbelief, in destroying the religious basis of literature, weakens its power.

15. Literature requires art. Art in its highest expression is the product of genius. Genius is talent intensified. As art is imitative of the creative act of God, and as whatever God creates is symbolical of

Himself inasmuch as it symbolizes some one or other of His attributes, so the product of art is expressive of the ideal in the artist's mind, and the more faithful the expression is, the more the creative intellect resembles the Divine Mind ; and as that Mind has but one idea—His own essence—if that may be called an idea which is essentially subject and object—Himself—so the more elevated the intelligence is, the less is the number of ideas in which it comprehends all things.

16. As literature reflects the Divinity in its most essential characteristics, the higher, the holier, the more ennobling it is, the more clearly it reflects these characteristics. It fulfils its true mission, then, according as it ennobles man's nature, and makes it like to Him who said : "Be ye holy, for I, the Lord your God, am holy ;" and it is ennobling to man's nature in proportion as it is in strict accordance with the immutable laws of morality. The morality of life is not one thing, and the morality of art another. They are both one. This is a canon of criticism the critic should hold to under all circumstances.

CONCLUSION.

In reading the history of a particular country, the student sees a people rise from comparative barbarism to civilization ; he is very apt to generalize the fact, and say that such has been the order of things from the beginning ; and he has but one more step to take in asserting that man is a development of the lower order of life. Rousseau prepared the way for

Darwin and Herbert Spencer. But when all literature is taken into account ; when we see nation instruct nation ; when we realize the fact that society
is a creature of education, that men may invent a
new mechanical power, but that they cannot create
an idea ; we are led to seek a beginning for this in-
fusion of knowledge, and we find it when God created
everything good and perfect in its kind, and gave
man dominion over the earth and all it contains ; *
when he brought "all the beasts of the earth and all
the fowls of the air . . . . to Adam to see what he
would call them ; " † when, to use the beautiful words
of a voice that is stilled for time, " He plants an
Eden for His new-made creatures, and there comes
to them Himself ; and the evenings of the young
world are consecrated by familiar colloquies between
the creatures and their Creator."‡ When God walked
with Adam "in Paradise at the afternoon air,"§
what profound secrets His presence must have revealed to this child of earth ! What grand thoughts he
must have suggested ! What mysteries unravelled !
What revelations made known ! The knowledge
that men boast of to-day is, in its totality, but a
broken fragment of that grand whole possessed, in
germ and principle, by the primeval man.

* *Genesis*, i., 26.
† Ibid., ii. 19.
‡ Father Faber, *The Creator and The Creature*, p. 132.
§ *Genesis*, iii. 8.

INDEX.